"Fire in the hole!"

David McCarter loped down the line of vehicles, a lighter in his hand, wicks blazing as they dangled from the gas tanks of two trunks behind him.

Bolan threw himself behind the last jeep's steering wheel, and as the vehicle responded to his touch, he shifted into first and released the parking brake. He felt McCarter pile into the back, glimpsed Manning as he gained the shotgun seat, and they were rolling, the headlights off. Their sudden charge startled several gunners, leaving them standing there, frozen, unsure of what was going on.

Almost on cue the motor pool went up in fire and thunder, trucks and four-wheelers detonating like a string of giant firecrackers. Bolan concentrated on his driving, heard the others firing back at snipers in the dark. Beyond the camp's perimeter, the desert waited for them, dark, hostile, menacing.

And on their track, three sets of headlights locked in.

DON PENDLETON's
MACK BOLAN®
TERROR
SPIN

A GOLD EAGLE BOOK FROM
WORLDWIDE®

TORONTO • NEW YORK • LONDON
AMSTERDAM • PARIS • SYDNEY • HAMBURG
STOCKHOLM • ATHENS • TOKYO • MILAN
MADRID • WARSAW • BUDAPEST • AUCKLAND

First edition October 1997

ISBN 0-373-61456-X

Special thanks and acknowledgment to
Mike Newton for his contribution to this work.

TERROR SPIN

Printed in U.S.A.

Against naked force the only possible defense is naked force. The aggressor makes the rules for such a war; the defenders have no alternative but matching destruction with more destruction, slaughter with greater slaughter.

—Franklin D. Roosevelt

Our enemies start the game and make the rules up as they go along, but they have no monopoly on seizing the initiative. They want to play for blood, let's max out all the bets. That's just my game.

—Mack Bolan

To victims of domestic terrorism

PROLOGUE

Patrolman Jeff O'Malley was a rookie, thirteen months in uniform, which meant he caught the unpleasant jobs more often than the veterans. That was SOP with most any job, not just the cops, and he wasn't complaining. Well, no more than anybody else, at least. The bitching was a part of it, as well. It was another step toward camaraderie, the Brotherhood of Blue, where you could trust a total stranger with your life because you knew he wore a badge and understood the code.

O'Malley was fourth-generation NYPD. His old man was on disability now, and two uncles were still on the job. It was a standing joke around the house: you puncture an O'Malley, and the blood you got was blue, just like their uniforms.

Some joke.

It wasn't blue the day his old man got it, two rounds from a sawed-off 12-gauge when he tried to stop a junkie holding up a liquor store in Flatbush, Queens. He lived, but they could never really fix his leg, and he was only fit for desk work after that. He tried it for a year or so, then pulled the pin and took his disability. Game over, man.

You live and learn.

What Jeff O'Malley learned from his old man was that you never let your guard down for a second, and you capped any bastard with a piece before he had a chance to think if he should fight or fold. Screw the review board.

It was better to be judged by twelve than carried by six.

So Jeff O'Malley walked his beat in Central Park, from 8:00 a.m. to 4:00 p.m., and kept his eyes peeled. Rotation came around in six more weeks, and he could wind up riding shotgun on the graveyard shift in Bedford-Stuyvesant for all he knew. It wouldn't stop him bitching over beers and pizza, but he understood some gigs were worse than others.

O'Malley had the east side of the park, from Eightieth to Eighty-fifth Street. His beat included the Metropolitan Museum of Art, facing Fifth Avenue, plus sundry bicycle and jogging paths, a children's playground north of the museum and Cleopatra's needle on the west.

It was the best part of a city block to the museum from where he was. O'Malley took his time. If a beef went down, he had a walkie-talkie on his belt, and the dispatcher wasn't shy about inviting him to move his ass to field a call.

Until that happened, though, O'Malley saw no reason why he ought to rush. A few more minutes, and he saw the bulk of the museum ahead of him, due south. It could have been a castle full of knights and squires, the way it looked. Sometimes he could imagine men in armor, riding chargers, jousting lances heavy in their hands.

But that was all a fairy tale.

They had a fair amount of crime at the museum, some vandalism, petty theft around the bookshop, drunks or junkies dropping in to check out how the other half amused themselves. O'Malley could recall a stabbing on the second floor six or seven weeks earlier. High-schoolers on a field trip, with a couple of them carrying a grudge against each other.

Mostly, though—

The shock of the explosion froze O'Malley in his tracks. It wasn't all that loud, in truth—his instinct told him it was muffled, coming from inside the building— but it startled him all the same.

The sound of automatic weapons broke his spell and sent the policeman sprinting south toward the museum, his service pistol drawn and cocked almost before he knew it, left hand fumbling with the walkie-talkie.

"Two-sixteen! Shots fired, Museum of Modern Art on Fifth! Send backup now!"

IT HAD COME DOWN to the museum or the United Nations Building after two days of debating targets in the greater New York City area. The problem was that there were too many targets begging for attention, what the Americans described as an embarrassment of riches.

Rani Ayoub had cast his vote for the UN, but all in vain. It was a question of security versus publicity, as always, and the other four men on his team preferred a target where they had at least some chance to live and read about themselves the following day in the *New York Times*. Security was brutal at the UN, since the World Trade Center bombing and the blast in Oklahoma City, with all manner of devices, dogs and watchmen, guns and barricades.

They would face no such difficulties when they raided the Museum of Modern Art.

It was decided that the action should commence at 12:15 p.m., allowing strollers on their lunch hour to swell the ranks of tourists who had come from out of town. School buses in the parking lot told Ayoub there had to be at least one field trip going down. Americans went crazy when their children were attacked, as if they mattered more than Third World babies and should somehow be immune to suffering.

Rani Ayoub was about to provide his enemies with what they liked to call a reality check. He would remind them that no one was safe, anywhere on earth, as long as *his* people were at risk.

It was a warm day, early spring, but no one gave a second glance to Ayoub's overcoat. New Yorkers were accustomed to eccentric garb and madmen babbling to themselves on street corners. A knee-length coat was nothing, even when the temperature outside was pushing seventy degrees.

But it concealed the weapons he was carrying: a Norinco SKS rifle with a folding stock and a 40-round magazine, slung beneath his right arm; a 9 mm Maadi Cadet pistol tucked inside his waistband at the back;

spare magazines and hand grenades that made his pockets sag.

Tools of the trade.

They had perused maps of the museum in a Michelin guide to Manhattan and agreed to stage their action on the ground floor of the massive building, thus avoiding stairs and elevators, which would hamper swift retreat. Three men would do the job inside, and one would wait in the van, and while they hoped to live to fight again another day, the mission took priority over survival. If he had to sacrifice himself, Ayoub took satisfaction from the knowledge that there would be others waiting to continue the struggle after he was gone.

From the entryway Ayoub drifted toward the wing reserved for Egyptian art. He started counting heads, but quickly gave it up as fruitless. There were ample targets, male and female, representing every race and age bracket he could imagine. A blind man could take them, the way they wandered aimlessly about and massed before particular exhibits.

Pulsing with adrenaline, he forced himself to make a show of staring at the artwork, really watching out for the others. It took him a moment to spot Kaliq, browsing near the entrance of the Gold Room, where ancient jewelry was displayed, but there was still no sign of Malik. Glancing back toward the entryway, he was startled to see the third member of their team walking away from him, headed in the wrong direction, toward the Greek and Roman art exhibits.

There was no time to go chasing after him, and it

would be too risky, anyway. They would proceed without him and hope Malik was smart enough to recognize his error when they started shooting. He could double back and join them then, or raise hell on his own, among the tourists in the other wing.

It was the body count that mattered, after all, not where they fell.

A wall clock told Ayoub it was almost time. His right hand slipped inside the pocket of his coat, where he had cut the lining out, and found the rifle's pistol grip. He had a live round in the chamber, with the safety off, and the Norinco had been modified illegally for automatic fire. The weapons had been tested at a sanitary landfill in New Jersey, cleaned and oiled in preparation for this day. Ayoub had no fear that his weapons would fail him.

All he needed was the nerve to kill—and die, if necessary—for the cause.

He turned toward a display of model boats and buildings, carved in wood and taken from the plundered tombs of pharaohs. People stood close against the glass, oblivious to death approaching on their blind side. No one saw him swing the SKS from beneath his jacket, bracing it against his hip. He didn't see Kaliq palm the fragmentation grenade, release its pin and lob it through the entrance to the Gold Room, but he knew exactly what was happening before he opened fire.

The shock of the explosion rocked him, people screaming as his bullets cut them down. Too late to save themselves, they tried to scatter, as if there were anywhere to hide.

He had to shout for them to hear him over all the racket, screams and gunfire, making sure he spoke in English.

"Glory to God!"

O'MALLEY KNEW about a side door that the public didn't use, and he ignored the alarm that went off automatically when it was opened from outside. Another bell was clamoring somewhere ahead of him and to the left. It sounded like a fire alarm, and that was all he needed now, some extra panic when he had heard shots fired already and had no clue to what was going down.

He came in through the arms-and-armor exhibit, behind the auditorium. The people he encountered looked confused, as if their instinct to evacuate when fire alarms went off had been shorted out somehow by sounds of gunfire echoing from the adjacent wing. Some of them crouched or lay prone on the floor, unmoving, even though the shots were clearly being fired in an entirely different wing.

O'Malley didn't have the floor plan memorized, but he was smart enough to follow sounds. Another moment brought him to an entrance on the hall that held Egyptian art, his nostrils flaring at the odor that reminded him of weekends at the pistol range—the only place where he had ever fired the weapon he now carried in his hand.

He risked a glance around the corner, edging forward far enough to see a skinny dark-skinned man unloading on some panicky civilians with an automatic rifle. O'Malley saw a man go down, blood spurting from a chest wound, while a woman running for her life slipped on more blood, lost her balance and went down screaming.

O'Malley knew that if he gave the skinny guy fair warning, he was dead. His pistol was no match for an assault rifle any way you looked at it.

He shot the gunman twice without a call. If someone on the review board didn't like it, he could damn well take his place the next time something crazy like this went down. O'Malley saw the gunman stagger, with a dazed expression on his face as he half turned to face the man who had already killed him.

Jesus!

Bullets spraying from the autorifle brought plate glass down in sheets and knocked divots in the marble walls. O'Malley gave his target two more rounds and saw one of them snap his head back, ending it. The shooter folded like a rag doll, sprawling, and his weapon spun away from lifeless fingers as he fell.

O'Malley stepped into the slaughterhouse, still covering the fallen shooter with his pistol. A hasty scan showed him twelve or thirteen people down, besides the shooter. They were lucky, even so. It could have been a whole lot worse. But there was something nagging at him, urgently demanding his attention. What about—?

The first explosion he had heard!

O'Malley smelled the cordite, was aware of drifting

smoke, but saw no evidence of any blast from where he stood. He kept his pistol trained on Mr. X, and started to scan to his left. He got all the way to ten o'clock before he saw the second shooter glaring at him, leveling some kind of short submachine gun from the waist.

The patrolman spun to face him, cursing silently, his next round wasted, high and wide. He didn't hear the SMG cut loose as much as he felt it, bullets streaking toward him faster than the speed of sound.

Explosive impact punched O'Malley backward off his feet. The hard, cold floor rushed up to meet him, and the final breath was driven from his lungs. O'Malley felt like he was drowning and tried to catch his breath before a white-hot pain lanced through his body, turning arms and legs to useless rubber. Overhead the vaulted ceiling seemed to come apart and reassemble while he watched, a huge kaleidoscope installed to keep his faculties engaged while life ran out of him through half a dozen holes.

What about the light and tunnel he had heard so much about from people who survived near-death experiences? Maybe, Jeff O'Malley thought, that was a part of coming *back* when things went wrong, and you were called before your time. Suppose the rest of it was nothing, just like that?

O'Malley thought about Denise and Amy, waiting for him, thinking he was safe and sound.

He closed his eyes and waited, praying for the light.

CHAPTER ONE

What's in a name?

This part of New Jersey, north of Warren Grove in Ocean County, had been called the Pine Barrens as long as anyone could remember. The "pine" part was easy to explain—just look around at the trees that crowded close on either side of Highway 539. As for the "barren" tag, it conjured images of desert wastelands, nothing like the woods where darkness settled in at least an hour short of sundown.

Barren was the feeling of the place, Mack Bolan thought as he removed his street clothes and began to dress for battle. Standing in the darkness, listening to night sounds and depending on the stars for light, he knew how skittish hunters had to have felt three hundred years ago, when they went out in search of meat and prayed their hunt wouldn't be terminated by a war whoop and a flashing tomahawk. He knew why legends of the hulking Jersey Devil still hung on in those parts, less than thirty miles from the Atlantic City boardwalk.

Never mind. He had no time for superstition, and the only hostiles remaining in the neighborhood were half a mile due west of where he stood. They weren't expecting company.

With any luck at all, his visit would be a complete surprise.

Beneath the jeans and long-sleeved denim shirt, he wore a combat blacksuit that fit him like a second skin, its several pockets cleverly concealed. The military webbing, also black, supported ammo pouches and a Ka-bar fighting knife. On Bolan's right hip, a .44 Magnum Desert Eagle nestled in its fast-draw holster, while a shoulder rig contained the sleek Beretta 93-R, with its custom sound suppressor attached. His front piece for the mission was a CAR-15, a stubby carbine version of the M-16 A-1 that shaved five inches and nearly two pounds off the original weapon, while sacrificing none of its firepower.

Bolan left his car, concealed by trees and scrub brush in the darkness, satisfied that it wouldn't be found unless someone was looking for it. Hiking overland, he took his time to keep from stumbling in the dark and injuring himself. The topographic maps were fairly detailed, but they wouldn't show him gopher holes or clutching tree roots that could drop him in his tracks or maybe snap an ankle.

He had time.

His targets had been waiting seven days, and they weren't going anywhere tonight.

Except, perhaps, to hell.

In normal circumstances, it would be the FBI's job to go in and root them out, secure the area and collect evidence for trial. But this wasn't a normal case, and there would be no trial in the accepted sense. This time, the verdict had been handed down before the suspects were identified, expanded to include the men behind them. Judge and jury had already spoken.

Now it came down to the Executioner.

Ten minutes brought him to the target, and he spent another five examining the layout, counting windows, doors and vehicles. There was an outhouse in the back, a kind of minibarn off to the left. It was too dark inside to make out any details through the grimy windows, but it seemed to be unoccupied. Lights burned in the front room of the house; the bedrooms were dark in back.

He was approaching through the darkness, drawing closer to the house, when lights flared in the kitchen and the screen door slammed behind a slender dark-skinned man with bushy hair. The stalker froze and watched his prey move toward the outhouse, walking with his head down, as if studying the ground. He had a flashlight, and he played the beam in front of him, relaxed enough to ignore the night around him.

Seven days, and he believed he was home free. So much the better. Bolan hoped the others shared his view and let their guard down. It would make things easier.

How many men were inside the house? He couldn't tell from counting vehicles, but even if the cars were packed when they arrived, he wouldn't expect more than eight or nine guns. The house was too small to sleep a dozen comfortably, and hit teams on a job like this were traditionally compact units, self-contained and limited in size for security's sake.

His quarry of the moment reached the outhouse, swept the flashlight beam around inside, then entered, leaving the door ajar for ventilation. Bolan drew the 93-R and closed the gap with long, deliberate strides.

He eased the door back with his left hand, aiming the Beretta with his right. An errant moonbeam lit the young man's startled face before the automatic whispered, and a keyhole opened up between his eyes. The Arab slumped backward on the wooden seat, until the rough pine snagged his shirt and held him fast.

One down.

Bolan turned back in the direction of the house.

MALIK KHALED WAS STARTING to relax. It was a week since the hit on the Museum of Modern Art in New York City, and no one yet had chastised him for his foolish error. Could it be that no one knew he was disoriented when he entered the museum and wandered in the wrong direction?

Ayoub knew, of course, but he'd been killed by a policeman at the scene, his body left behind. Kaliq had either failed to notice Malik's blunder or else he had forgotten it in the excitement of the moment—shooting, tossing hand grenades, the pale-skinned devils screaming, dying everywhere he looked.

The final body count had been a disappointment: only thirteen dead, not counting Rani, with another twenty-seven wounded. The police and FBI had so far been unable to identify Rani, as far as he knew, since his fingerprints weren't on file with any agency. None of their team had ever been arrested, and none had been recruited into normal military service or held any government position that would call for background checks. They carried no ID that bore true names—indeed, there was a standing joke among the jealous pigs who didn't qualify to share their company that some of them couldn't remember who they really were.

Khaled had no such problem. Time would never wipe away his memories of blighted childhood in the teeming camps maintained by the Israelis for his people in their stolen homeland. He wouldn't forget his older brother, killed by soldiers for the "crime" of tossing pebbles at an armored vehicle, or his mother, blinded in one eye when she was beaten by police. His father disappeared when Khaled was eleven years of age, arrested by Israelis in a sweep that bagged two thousand "terrorists" in Gaza. Six weeks later, when he died in custody, it was reported as an accident.

He knew otherwise. The Jews had killed his father, doubtless tortured him to death on the erroneous assumption that he was a warrior of the Palestinian resistance. They were wrong, of course, but now Khaled was doing everything within his power to make their nightmare fantasy come true.

It was embarrassing, his first great mission bungled out of nervousness. The art museum had been so huge, once he was standing on the steps outside, that he had felt himself begin to tremble—fear and excitement all rolled into one. It was a natural enough mistake that he had turned left in the crowded lobby, rather than proceeding to his right. He had the floor plan memorized, but they had only worked out the mission on paper, never on the site, with crowds of people to distract him from his purpose.

It had all come together, though, even if they hadn't killed as many pigs as hoped for. Losing Ayoub came as no surprise; all three of them were told before the raid that it could be their last. From Khaled's first day in the movement, he had pledged himself to sacrifice his life, if necessary, for the cause. A soldier who wasn't prepared to spill his own blood went to war with one hand tied behind his back.

He was prepared to die…but it was good to be alive.

The irony of that didn't escape him. He knew some warriors for the cause who were embarrassed, even angry, when a mission didn't offer them the chance to die a glorious, flamboyant death. They were fanatics, in his opinion. Willingness to die was one thing, but a morbid urge to die was something else.

Khaled was quite prepared to kill pigs for another twenty-five or thirty years, if necessary, then retire and find a scribe to write his memoirs, publish them as inspiration to the freedom fighters who would follow him. Somehow the prospect of a victory that would eliminate the hated state of Israel never really entered his mind. Without an enemy, his life—the cause itself—would have no meaning. Preachers never seriously tried to do away with Satan, after all, and the resistance needed something to resist.

Next time, the terrorist assured himself, there would

be no mistakes on his part. He would watch his step, proceed according to the numbers and achieve a higher body count. He wouldn't be like Ayoub, taken by surprise and killed before he had a chance to do his job.

His stomach growled, reminding him that he hadn't eaten in close to seven hours. Rising from his hard cot in the room he shared with three more soldiers, he padded toward the kitchen, barefoot, wondering what might be left in the refrigerator. He was carrying a pistol, tucked inside his belt, forbidden by Amal al-Qadi to go anywhere without a weapon.

He stepped into the kitchen, flicked on the lights, saw a black-clad stranger standing on the threshold of the door that led outside and froze.

Khaled was grabbing for his pistol when the stranger raised a weapon of his own. The terrorist had time to recognize a sound suppressor before a bullet drilled his larynx, staggered him, prevented him from crying out as blood filled up his throat.

He felt life going and clutched the pistol, squeezing off one shot inside his pants. He barely felt the powder flash, as the bullet snapped his femur. It amazed him that his own death could be so miraculously free of pain.

The stranger loomed above Khaled, then passed by him, moving on. The Palestinian was ready for another shot, which never came. Instead, the darkness settled over him and carried him away.

THE KITCHEN WAS A GAMBLE, granted, but it beat the notion of attacking through the front door, where he could expect to find an unknown number of his adversaries waiting for him, probably with weapons close at hand. This way, if he was lucky, he would have a margin of surprise.

The lock was nothing, requiring only six or seven seconds with the Ka-bar, never mind the work of picking it. A bit of leverage, gouging at the weathered wood and cheap pot metal of the latching mechanism, and the way was clear. He entered with the 93-R in his left hand, carbine braced against his hip and steady in his right, giving him the choice between a silent execution or full-auto rock and roll.

The lights were off in the kitchen, but darkness didn't mask the smell of fried meat in the room; if anything, he thought, the odor was intensified. No matter. He had work to do: pursue the light that shone through a connecting doorway, trail the sound of voices to a kill.

The thought had barely taken shape, translated into action, when a shadow fell across the doorway. Fingers brushed wallpaper, found the light switch, then flicked it on. The sudden brightness made him wince, but he was ready for it, sizing up his opposition in a heartbeat, squeezing off a silenced round from the Beretta as the man in the doorway started to reach for his gun.

It was a clean shot to the throat, blood spouting, producing almost instant death. Not quick enough, though, as the young man's trigger finger spasmed, squeezing off a shot.

So much for the surprise.

Bolan holstered the Beretta, rushing past the body of his second kill to reach the living room. It was apparent that his quarry—some of them, at least—went armed around the house, and every second counted now.

A door swung open on his left, and light spilled into the hallway as he passed. Another Arab gaped at him from a smallish bedroom, one hand holding up his jeans, the other wrapped around a stainless-steel revolver. Bolan hit him with a 3-round burst, chest high, and slammed the small man over backward, bare feet tangled in a ratty-looking throw rug as he fell.

Three down. How many left to go?

He reached the living room, found three men waiting for him, weapons in their hands. One knelt behind a sway-backed sofa, while another crouched beside an easy chair. Number three stood off to Bolan's left, apparently unable to decide where he should go.

The hardmen opened up in unison, two of them with handguns, while the guy behind the sofa had an SMG. You couldn't fault their willingness to fight, Bolan thought, but it was apparent that they hadn't practiced what to do if someone caught them checking out the late show and they had to do or die.

He dropped into a combat crouch and hit the standing gunner with a rising burst that stitched him from his groin to his sternum, 5.56 mm tumblers slamming him against the nearest wall and ending any threat he might have posed.

The other two terrorists had missed him when he ducked, but they were already correcting. Bolan pushed off to his left and went prone, the carbine tracking on another target, pointed at the easy chair. Thick padding lined a heavy wooden frame, but it was still no match for modern military firepower.

If he could only make it two for two, before the sofa gunner found his mark and made the next burst count... It would be all for nothing if they nailed him. The pursuit would have to start from scratch, with someone else.

He snarled and held down the carbine's trigger.

AMAL AL-QADI HAD BEEN dozing, fully dressed except for shoes, when he was wakened by a gunshot. He was on his feet and reaching for his weapon seconds later, when a short burst from an automatic weapon told him it wasn't a dream.

Somehow the enemy had found them.

They were under siege.

His shoes were slip-ons waiting at his bedside. With the H&K MP-5 submachine gun in his hands, al-Qadi moved to stand beside the bedroom door. Behind him, Ibrahim Salim was also on his feet, still groggy, groping for a weapon on the floor beside his cot.

Amal al-Qadi was the leader of their team, selected for his expertise in striking at the enemy's home turf, conducting raids that left an adversary reeling. Since he arrived in the United States from France eight weeks ago, he had been scouting targets, planning for a series of attacks that would have stunned America and left the superpower feeling vulnerable as it never had before. He'd started out with eight men, the number now reduced by one with Ayoub's death at the Museum of Modern Art. One loss was no great problem, and al-Qadi was prepared to carry on, the next strike scheduled only three days hence...but that was changing now.

He cracked the bedroom door, saw no one in the corridor outside and was about to poke his head out for a better look when automatic-weapons fire exploded in the living room. The Palestinian recoiled, his hands white knuckled on the submachine gun, muttering a curse as Salim came up behind him, almost breathing down his neck.

"Is it the FBI?"

"How would I know? Be silent!"

Even as he snapped at Salim, al-Qadi told himself it couldn't be the FBI. If they had found his team, there would be floodlights, tear gas, helicopters circling overhead—but none of that was evident. Someone was in the house—that much was clear—but there was none of the expected shouting, men in body armor racing up and down the hall.

Who, then?

It hardly mattered at the moment. He was more concerned with getting out alive, if possible, than in determining the names and government affiliation of his enemies. He closed the bedroom door again, as softly as he could, and dragged a folding metal chair across the floor to wedge it underneath the doorknob. Racing to the window, he flicked back a corner of the curtain, peered outside at darkness and saw no evidence of squad cars, armored vehicles, no sign of anyone at all.

He hesitated for another heartbeat, whipped the curtain back and ducked below the windowsill, prepared to fight if he was wrong and someone started to shoot at him from outside. When nothing happened, he stood and beckoned Salim to join him.

"Come! We're getting out of here," he said.

"The others—"

"Buy us time," al-Qadi told him. "Would you rather die?"

Salim thought about it for perhaps three seconds, then shook his head in an emphatic negative. It went against his training to desert the others when he had been prepared to stand and die if challenged by the enemy, but he adjusted fairly well.

Al-Qadi unlatched the window and raised the sash as far as it would go. He was forced to crouch before he poked his head and shoulders out into the night. The sill was sharp against his stomach as he started to wriggle through, off balance, one hand clinging to the submachine gun while the other tried to brace his weight against the outer wall.

"Help me!" he grated at his companion.

The soldier did as he was told. He grabbed al-Qadi by the ankles and upended him, administering a strong shove that propelled the man through the window in a kind of awkward somersault. He crashed down on his side, dirt in his face, wind driven from his lungs.

Before he could recover fully, Salim was scrambling through the window.

"What now, Amal?"

"The cars. Hurry!"

Al-Qadi thanked the instinct that had made him leave the keys in the ignitions of their vehicles. It was a system that couldn't be used in urban areas, where thieves abounded, but their safehouse in Pine Barrens was secure from prowlers.

Or at least it had been until now.

Suppose the cars were guarded? Never mind. He ran around the east side of the house, with Salim close on his heels. No one was near the vehicles. He chose the nearest one, a Nissan Maxima in navy blue, shoved Salim in the direction of the driver's door and ran around the other side.

They had a chance, however slim. Once they were on the road, unless the enemy had spotters in the air, it should be relatively easy to elude pursuit and find another place to hide.

If they survived that long.

The engine growled to life, and Salim released the parking brake. A moment later, they were rolling, and Amal al-Qadi suddenly remembered how to breathe.

THE SECOND BURST of 5.56 mm rounds ripped through the easy chair and found Bolan's target, spinning the young man and dropping him facedown, the shiny automatic pistol spinning from his grasp, across the hardwood floor. His body shivered for an instant, then lay still.

And that left one. The gunner crouched behind the sofa had to have known the odds had shifted from his favor to the enemy, but he would no more let himself be taken than he would have eaten pork or worshiped in a synagogue. Resistance was a virtue in itself for men like these, and paradise was waiting for the faithful soldier who gave up his life for God's benefit.

The gunner came out shooting, shouting some kind of high-pitched battle cry in Arabic. The words were meaningless to Bolan, but he grasped the man's intent and met him with a short burst from his CAR-15.

The Palestinian went down as if an unseen rope had jerked his legs from underneath him, crashing to the floor and bouncing once before he came to rest. Blood pooled beneath him, spreading out in crimson tributaries to create the image of a large, four-fingered hand.

The Executioner was on his feet before the echo of his rifle shots had died away. He had to search the house, find out if there were any other gunmen on the premises.

He was distracted by the sound of someone starting up a car out front. The driver had a fair lead, taillights dwindling, by the time he cleared the porch and brought the carbine to his shoulder.

There was one man in the speeding car, at least, and maybe more. His mission would be incomplete while any of the terrorists was still alive and running free, but how could he pursue?

On impulse, Bolan checked the nearest cars—a Ford Escort LX—and found a key in the ignition. Logic told him there had been no time for the escaping terrorists to booby-trap the vehicles they left behind. In any case, he had to take the chance.

He slid behind the Escort's steering wheel and bit

his lip as he gave the ignition key a twist. The engine started instantly, and in another moment he was rolling, following the twin sparks of the lead car's taillights, running with his own lights off the first two hundred yards or so, until the road began to curve and he was forced to sacrifice the slim advantage of surprise.

It all came down to speed and brute force now, and he would have to get it right the first time.

There would be no second chance.

CHAPTER TWO

"Someone is coming after us," Ibrahim Salim stated.

Amal al-Qadi swiveled in his seat and stared out through the Maxima's rear window. He saw headlights in the distance, flashing into high beams now, as if the driver who pursued them had abandoned any thought of stealth. There were no flashing colored lights or siren, though, which puzzled him and made him frown.

If it was the police, they should have pulled out all the stops by now. Even their unmarked cars had sirens, and red lights that could be mounted on the roof or dashboard in the case of an emergency. This silent chase, with nothing but a pair of headlights glaring back at him like dragon's eyes, unnerved the Palestinian, made him wonder who it was that they were dealing with.

Salim seemed to read his thoughts. "Police?" the driver asked, his voice stretched taut by apprehension.

"I don't think so."

"But who else would—?"

"Just drive, and let me think!"

Salim shut his mouth, but he kept shooting furtive

glances at the rearview mirror, where the second pair of headlights was reflected, growing larger by the moment.

"Faster!" al-Qadi snapped.

"It's all the speed we have. This road was not designed for racing."

As he spoke, Salim jerked the steering wheel to dodge a crater in the pavement, almost losing it as the Maxima began to drift across the faded double line and toward the trees that lined the far side of the road. It took a moment for him to control the skid, and he was sweating as he brought the Nissan back into its proper lane.

"Watch out, you fool! You'll kill us!"

"It's all right," the driver said, but he couldn't disguise the tremor in his voice.

Al-Qadi couldn't tear his eyes away from the pursuing headlights. For a moment, he considered that some other members of his team might have escaped the trap, as he had. What if there were comrades in the vehicle behind him, trying to catch up? The doubt came close to paralyzing him, but he recovered swiftly, knowing that decisive action was required to save himself and Salim.

If those were friends in the second car, then they already knew about the rendezvous arranged for just such an occasion. It would make no difference if he ditched them on the highway; they would simply make their way to Philadelphia and meet him there. However, if the man or men behind him turned out to be enemies...

His memory was excellent, unhampered by the present stress. He summoned up a local highway map, imagined their position and began to select routes for their escape.

"Stay on this road until we cross the bridge and come to Highway 563. Turn north from there and stay on that road."

They had rehearsed evacuation from the safehouse, ran it down on paper time and time again, until his soldiers knew what they had to do in the event of a surprise by enemies. If those were friendly faces in the car behind him, they would automatically turn south on Highway 563, a ploy to split their forces if they were pursued, and thus confound their adversaries. If the other vehicle turned north and followed his, al-Qadi would assume hostile intent and act accordingly.

He faced forward, staring at the road illuminated by their headlights. It took a conscious effort for him to release the submachine gun he held cradled in his lap, and wipe his sweaty palms against the seat.

They hadn't trapped him in the house, though he'd been fast asleep when the attack began, and it would be more difficult for enemies to stop him on the highway. If the second car turned north when he did, then al-Qadi would be forced to kill its occupants. A tricky bit of business, that, but he could manage it.

His enemies were fools to think that they could take him out so easily. They had a rude surprise in store for them.

Picturing the carnage made him smile.

THE POINT CAR HAD a lead, but Bolan was shortening the gap between them, yard by yard, the Escort LX straining as he mashed the pedal to the floor. A glance told him that the tank was nearly full, so there was no risk of running low before he overtook the other vehicle and made his move. The CAR-15 was in the seat beside him, cocked, a live round in the chamber, the fire selector set for automatic.

But he had to catch his quarry before the gun would do him any good.

He had already cut the target's lead by half, reducing it to something like a hundred yards. He left the high beams on intentionally, hoping it would spook the other driver, since he had no chance to sneak up on him by surprise. If necessary, he would ram the other car, attempt to force it off the road.

The motorcycle cop came out of nowhere, riding up on Bolan's tail before he switched on the red lights and gave a short blast on his siren. The soldier hadn't seen him coming and wondered why in hell he was patrolling that deserted stretch of country road at half-past midnight.

It complicated matters, since the officer could radio ahead for backup if his lights and siren were ignored. And when the shooting started, he would be without a clue to what was happening, his first instinct to fire on Bolan from behind.

What, then?

He was working on the problem when the siren came back, wailing long and loud behind him when he didn't brake in answer to the flashing lights. He had no clear view of the policeman in any of his mirrors, but he knew that his pursuer had to be on the verge of calling out for reinforcements, if he hadn't broadcast the alert already.

Up ahead, the point car's headlights lit the rusty girders of a narrow bridge. Some kind of stream or culvert was coming up, and in their wisdom, the department charged with building highways had decided that a one-lane bridge would do the trick. If there was two-way traffic on the highway, someone would be forced to wait. No problem at the moment, but the motorcycle cop would have no chance to pull abreast of Bolan before they cleared the bridge.

A pothole jarred the Escort, snapping Bolan's teeth together, and he bit off a curse. The light show in his rearview mirror wobbled, swerved and came back into line behind him as the cycle jockey dodged another trap.

Bolan saw the pothole coming this time and drifted slightly to his left, so that the Escort straddled it and made a beeline for the narrow bridge. The cop on the soldier's tail was concentrating on his quarry, scoping out the license tag and reaching for his microphone to call in the cavalry. He failed to see the pothole rushing at him and struck the jagged lip with force that nearly bucked him from the Harley's saddle. Bolan never understood exactly how he saved it, kept from going down right then and there, but it was only a reprieve. The bike was wobbling badly, something jarred or twisted out of line, still clocking speed but weaving dangerously on the highway.

The Executioner saw his quarry clear the bridge. He goosed the Escort, trying to get another mile or two per hour from it as he held the wheel rock-steady, going into his approach. The Harley-Davidson was airborne for a heartbeat, then touched down again with yelping tires, the rider losing it, arms crossed before his face in self-defense.

The Harley went down on its side, spilling man and various accessories, and sparks flew from the point where steel kissed asphalt. Bolan raced across the one-lane bridge and saw the sliding motorcycle meet the left abutment with a crash. He couldn't spot the driver, as a ball of fire engulfed the west end of the bridge, but there was nothing he could do for him in any case.

The car ahead of him was something else, a target still attainable, if Bolan stood on the accelerator.

AMAL AL-QADI WATCHED the motorcycle cop go down in flames as suddenly and unexpectedly as he had joined the chase. The traffic officer had seemingly been after their pursuer, one more indication that the car behind them wasn't an official vehicle.

Salim saw the splash of flame beyond the narrow bridge and barked a startling laugh. "Take that!" he said. "Pig bastard!"

"Watch the road," al-Qadi commanded.

"I *am* watching."

"And be quiet!"

Salim kept any further comment locked behind his teeth and concentrated on his driving, while his companion turned back to watch the chase car gaining on them steadily, devouring the blacktop one yard at a time.

Another two, three hundred yards to Highway 563, and he would make the final test. Would it be north or south? A choice of life or death?

His mind was racing, and he clutched his submachine gun tightly, wondering if he would have to use it. Were those his men in the second car? If so, he would congratulate them on disposing of the motorcycle officer. If not...

A tension headache had begun to throb behind his eyes, imperiling his concentration. There was nothing he could do about it except ignore the pain.

It would serve just as well, he knew from prior experience, to shoot and kill the men pursuing him. But first, before he found that sweet relief, he had to satisfy himself that they were enemies. A few more moments at their present speed, and he would know beyond the whisper of a doubt.

Al-Qadi cranked down his window and felt the night air whipping at his face, the open collar flaring on his shirt. He saw the sharp turn coming and braced himself with one hand on the dashboard while his other clutched the SMG. Salim barely touched the brakes, and they were sliding through the turn, tires screeching as they fought for traction. He could feel the Nissan fishtail, but it held and stopped short of the shoulder, gaining speed again as the driver maintained control and proceeded north along the highway that was barely wider than the one they left behind.

The terrorist leader swiveled in his seat again and

watched the chase car, unconsciously holding his breath as he waited to see which way the driver would turn.

The headlights cut a blazing arc behind them, swinging into line and barreling along in hot pursuit. He cursed softly, knowing what had to be done.

"Slow down," he ordered.

"Slow down?"

"That's what I said." Amal al-Qadi's voice was as cold as death. "We have to let the bastard catch us."

BOLAN FELT a moment's hesitation as he saw the point car slowing. The brake lights didn't flare—nothing as obvious as that—but it was clear the driver had removed some of his weight from the accelerator. They were definitely losing speed, dropping back from almost ninety miles per hour, through the eighties, stabilizing once more around seventy-five.

There was no way they could outrun the Escort at that speed, which had to mean they were no longer running.

The soldier saw the trap, knew that the only way he could avoid it would mean giving up the chase. By definition, he could only overtake his enemies if he reduced the gap between them—which, in turn, meant giving them a chance to gun him off the road.

So be it.

Bolan drew the Desert Eagle semiauto pistol, switched it from his right hand to the left and stuck it out the window, with his elbow braced against the door. If he could make the shooters nervous, maybe spoil their aim, he had a chance. He would be pushing it to hope for any mortal wounds at that range, when he couldn't really aim, but scoring hits on something the size of a car was no great challenge.

He braced himself for the big pistol's recoil, squeezing off a round to find his mark. His first shot hit the Nissan's trunk and chipped off a paint blister the size of a silver dollar. He corrected for the second shot and gouged a two-foot scar across the trunk lid, smiling as the driver swerved.

He saw the muzzle-flash in time to cut his own wheel to the left, then hastily accelerated as the Nissan's wide rear window shattered, spraying pebbled safety glass across the trunk. It was an automatic weapon, something light but lethal. Bolan heard a couple of the bullets ping away from impact on the starboard fender.

Close, but no cigar.

To hell with it, he thought, and dropped the Desert Eagle on the shotgun seat beside him, picking up the CAR-15. He braced its stubby muzzle on the dashboard, closed his eyes and cleared the Escort's windshield with a raking burst, from right to left. Some of the glass shards blew back in his face, and the vehicle was drifting slightly by the time he opened his eyes again.

The Nissan was accelerating. The shadows visible inside were moving, but he couldn't tell exactly what was going on. A moment later, it was clear to him, as the muzzle of a compact submachine gun was thrust out through the shattered window, braced against the seat and window ledge.

The shooter had been crawling back to gain a better field of fire.

Their guns went off together, Bolan steering with his left hand, shooting with his right. He smelled cordite and heard the spent brass pattering around him, on the seat, the dash, the floorboard. Muzzle-flashes from his CAR-15 almost eclipsed the flashes from his adversary's SMG.

Almost.

It would have helped if they were firing tracers, but he didn't need a visual display to know his enemy was scoring hits. He heard and felt those bullets ripping through the Escort's radiator, sparking off the hood, a couple of them sizzling close enough to scorch him. Bolan held down the trigger until his rifle's slide locked open on an empty chamber, but the Arab gunner kept on firing, ten or twelve more rounds, most of them plunking through the Escort's grille, the headlights, glancing off the bumper.

Steam was spouting from beneath the hood when Bolan's left front tire exploded, rubber slapping at the road. He tried to keep on driving, but had to settle for a sharp drift toward the shoulder on his left or risk a flip that could have left him upside down, unconscious, maybe dead.

The Nissan's brake lights flashed as Bolan's Escort drifted to a smoking halt. For half a moment, he thought—hoped—that his enemies were coming back to finish him. Instead, the gunner in the Nissan fired a parting burst that missed by yards, then the driver powered out of there, his taillights dwindling, winking out in seconds flat.

Bolan sat there for another moment, staring at the darkness, listening to water dripping from the Escort's punctured radiator. Even now, the engine hadn't died, but there was an erratic knocking underneath the hood, and Bolan knew it could give out at any time.

His rental car was five or six miles distant, now, a long walk through the dark, when more police were almost surely on the way.

He nursed the wounded Escort through a limping U-turn, then started back in the direction he had come from. Any distance he could cover was a bonus now, and when the car died on him, he would finish it on foot.

There were no sirens yet, but there was still no time to waste. Each passing moment gave his enemies a greater lead, and he had no idea where they were going.

He would have to start from scratch and pray for luck.

CHAPTER THREE

The telephone rang twice before the sleeper found it, fumbling the receiver from its cradle, speaking with a tongue that felt like it was wrapped in cotton. Fragments of a dream clung to his drowsy thoughts like cobwebs, and he blinked his eyes to make them go away.

The bedside clock told Hal Brognola it was 2:15 a.m.

"Hello?"

"It's me. You want to scramble this?"

The cobwebs vanished in a flash as the familiar voice hit home. "Hang on," the big Fed said. "I'm hanging up to take it in the other room."

"Okay."

He didn't ask if Bolan was secure enough to hold while he changed telephones. The soldier knew what he was doing; they wouldn't be talking if he hadn't found a phone secure enough to let him speak. That didn't mean the line was clear, of course. No matter how Brognola checked his end, despite the fact he swept the lines twice weekly, you could never be too careful.

He got out of bed without disturbing Helen. All those years of phone calls coming in at crazy hours, and she could sleep through anything—or keep from asking what the problem was, at least.

The den was downstairs and around the corner, sixty seconds in the dark. He only switched the lights on when he got there, lifting the receiver, thumbing down a button that would activate the automatic scrambler.

"Go," he said.

"I've got a problem."

"Which is?"

"A couple of the mice got by me. Two at least."

Brognola frowned, more at the tone of Bolan's voice than at the content of his message. Even partial failure in the face of killer odds galled a perfectionist.

"It happens," Brognola replied, knowing there was no cliché available to help his longtime friend relax. "We got the others, though?"

"Six down. You should hear about it over breakfast."

"Well—"

"The trouble is, that was our only address, but it may not be the only team. If they've got reinforcements, chances are that all I've done is slap a hornet's nest."

Brognola's frown became a scowl. He didn't want to think in terms of escalating payback, not this early in the morning.

"Yeah," he said, "but if they don't…"

"Then they'll be running," Bolan finished for him, "and I don't know where they'll go. New Jersey's hot, but that leaves forty-seven states to pick from, maybe Canada or Mexico.''

"If they're hurt bad enough," Brognola said, "they may go home.''

"I thought of that. Same problem, though. They could leave out of Philly, New York, Washington—you name it. They've got paperwork to spare. We know that much. No shortage in the cash department, either. Hell, for all I know, they could be flying first-class down to Acapulco or Jamaica as we speak."

"Sounds like we need a travel agent.''

"It couldn't hurt. You have someone in mind?''

"I might," Brognola said. "I'll have to run a check through Stony Man and see what we've got. Could take a while.''

"I'm not exactly overbooked right now.''

"You're where, again?''

"Whitesbog, New Jersey. Ever hear of it?''

"Can't say it rings a bell," Brognola said.

"It's spitting distance from Fort Dix. McGuire's just down the road.''

"The Air Force base. Okay.'' Brognola had a mental fix on the vicinity. "Hang in there if you can. It could be handy for some transport if we hit a winner. Maybe save some time.''

"Sounds fair. I passed an all-night diner down the road a bit.''

"I should have something in an hour," the big Fed informed him, "if there's anything to find.''

"I'll keep my fingers crossed.''

"You have a call-back number there?''

He wrote digits down as Bolan read them off, then repeated them for confirmation.

"That's affirmative," the soldier said. "I'll drop back in an hour, then. And if a stranger answers—"

"Right," Brognola said. "I'll do my Dizzy Dean impression."

"Dizzy who?"

"Don't bust my chops, all right? I need some coffee first."

"One hour."

"Right."

He severed the connection, reengaged the scrambler that had cut off automatically and tapped out the number for Stony Man. Brognola knew what he was looking for, but names were something else. For that, he needed the computer data banks to guide him.

And a ton of luck.

He had to figure there would be a list of "travel agents" specializing in the kind of "package tours" preferred by fugitives and terrorists, the kind of travelers who maxed on risk and stress. Illicit people-movers were a whole subspecies of their own, but finding one who held the secrets he required could be like searching for a roundworm in a truckload of spaghetti. Even if you didn't find the wriggly little bastard, you could count on getting slimed.

Still, it was worth a shot.

In fact, Brognola told himself while he was waiting for an answer at the Farm, it was the only game in town.

THE WHITE LINE DINER WAS a magnet for the kind of people who had to drive all night on darkened highways, keeping schedules of their own: some long-haul truckers, a bland young man with wiry hair who could have been a transient Bible salesman or a homicidal maniac, a frowsy working girl who sized up the truckers and thought to hell with it, too tired by two-thirty to care if she scored any tricks or not, and Bolan.

He fit right in, considering his mood. It could have been a damn sight worse, he realized, but missing two of eight commandos was a lousy average, in his opinion. Self-recriminations weren't the warrior's game, but he had already determined to do anything within his power to retrieve the play, pick up that spare.

He ordered ham and scrambled eggs from the waitress and didn't chase her off when she came back for small talk, something that would kill the time. He lied about his business, told her he was driving through the predawn hours to surprise a nonexistent family. She grinned and told him that would be some sweet surprise.

She left him when his breakfast came, retreating to the kitchen, and his mind switched back to Hal Brognola's manhunt for the travel agent. Time was of the essence, Bolan realized. Ideally he would hope to trace the pair who got away and head them off before they had a chance to escape from the United States or start raising bloody hell and trashing countless lives. In fact, he knew he would be lucky to get anything at all, much less a timely and specific tip that put him on the trail of those he sought.

Still, there was always hope.

The ham was overdone, the scrambled eggs a little runny for his taste, but Bolan wolfed down the breakfast and finished off the toast, as well. He had to keep up his strength, store the energy he needed for pursuit of those who had slipped through his fingers back in Ocean County.

There was nothing on commercial radio about his strike so far, and Bolan had no scanner for police calls. It was fairly certain that the motorcycle cop had been relieved by now—assuming he was still alive—but it was still a long jump from investigating a highway accident to running down the safehouse, miles from nowhere, with its five dead occupants and one corpse in the outhouse. He had left the house intact, and with no neighbors to report the gunfire, it could well go undiscovered for a week or more, unless he dropped a coin and tipped off the law.

Why bother?

It could help with his surviving adversaries if the runners thought some of their comrades had survived. The team had to have some kind of fallback option, but he knew the way things worked in covert operations. Even planning for the unexpected, you were never really ready when it hit you in the face. Sometimes the wires got crossed, and Plan B went to hell in spite of all your best intentions.

Maybe it would slow the rabbits a little, give him just a bit more time to find their trail and get a start on cleaning up his mess.

He checked his watch as he finished his breakfast.

Twenty minutes remained before the call-back from Brognola, whether the big Fed had something to report or not. He checked the tab and left a tip that would make the waitress smile without planting his face too deeply in her consciousness. She waved as he was leaving, and he nodded to her, pushing through the glass door to reach the parking lot.

Bolan gave his car a superficial walk-around, since it hadn't been visible from his position in the diner, but the vehicle was nearly tamper proof. It had a shrill alarm, cranked up to wake the dead if anyone tried opening the doors, hood or trunk. The steering column had a dead lock on it, which prevented driving if the engine somehow started without Bolan's key. If all else failed, there was a nifty hidden C-4 plastic charge beneath the driver's seat—deactivated at the moment—that could turn the four-door into smoking, twisted wreckage if anyone jostled its sensors.

It was everything he needed for a night drive through the killing grounds.

Out on the highway, the soldier checked the time again and gave the vehicle a bit more gas. He wasn't late by any means, but you could never tell with public phones. Find a booth out in the middle of nowhere, and the first time you really needed it, some hitchhiker from out of state would get there first and hog the line.

The phone booth occupied one corner of a half-acre lot, the rest of it sprouting gasoline pumps, a drive-through car wash and a small convenience store erected out of cinder blocks. It was still closed at

3:14 a.m., and Bolan had the telephone all to himself, no place for eavesdroppers to hide.

He waited, trying not to focus his attention on the silent telephone. Instead, he thought about his enemies—the ones who got away, and those who didn't. Brognola's intelligence had been correct in terms of nationality, and Bolan didn't have to ask about the motive. Palestinians attacking U.S. citizens on U.S. soil could only mean one thing in Bolan's book: Jihad.

The motives varied slightly, while the groups changed names and leaders every time he turned around, but there were certain basic givens any time you dealt with Middle Eastern terrorists. They hated Israel with a passion, likewise any country that supported Israel economically or militarily, and so allowed it to survive. They also feared Israeli payback and preferred attacking other targets, often in the West, since it reaped free publicity, with the retaliation factor pared down to a minimum, and it gave the shooters an excuse to see the world on someone else's dime. Since the collapse of Russia and the East bloc, the money came primarily from states like Libya, Iraq, Iran, Algeria, Syria and Sudan, oil money, most of it, invested by the likes of Moammar Khaddafi and Saddam Hussein, in their megalomaniacal desire to see the world dance while they called the tune.

This time around, the heavy seemed to be—

His train of thought was interrupted by the telephone, the kind of harsh metallic shrilling rarely heard from the designer models. He picked up halfway through the second ring.

"Hello?"

"It's me," Brognola said. "Are you secure?"

"For now."

"Okay. I ran our problem past the Farm, and they kicked back a shortlist of potential travel agents on the Eastern Seaboard. Guy in Boston, mostly handles Irishmen—or did, until the cease-fire came along. Semiretired, they tell me now, and probably too racist to accept our kind of clientele."

"Go on," Bolan prompted, waiting for the punch line.

"Got a second-generation people-mover in Miami. His old man spent some time in one of Castro's lock-ups, following the Bay of Pigs. The jailers worked him over pretty good. His family has been smuggling refugees from Cuba ever since he was released in '63."

"No Arabs?"

"Not unless they come disguised and call themselves José," Brognola said.

"How many left?" he asked.

"Two in New York, and one in Jersey. One of the New Yorkers is a made man in the Ricoletti Family, in case you want to scratch him off the list.

"The other two, you've got a guy in New York's Chinatown who handles mainly Far East types, with possible connections to the Triads, or a fellow in New Jersey. Newark, if you want particulars."

"So, what's his story?"

"Not much on the books," Brognola replied. "The INS crowd popped him twice for selling bogus ID to illegal immigrants. First time, it was a bunch of Haitians, then a colonel in the Stasi, from the former GDR.''

"No ethnic prejudice, I take it."

"Hey," Brognola said, "the only colors this guy sees are green and gold."

"And that's the list? Five names?"

"Five known professionals. You want the whole list, I can try to get you names of every Asian, Haitian, Mexican and African in the United States who might have friends or family outside. Some other pros are mobbed up with the Yakuza, the Russian Mafia, the Triads, the Jamaican posses, but they mostly help their own get past the border."

"Arabs?" Bolan asked.

"Hell, yes, we've got 'em. Students, doctors, refugees, cab drivers, soda jerks at the convenience store. They show up under Other Races on the immigration spreadsheets. Legally we take in several thousand every year. Illegally...who knows?"

He got the message. For a search to fly, he had to start on known professionals, exhaust that field before he started any kind of random checks on groups or individuals of Middle Eastern ancestry.

"Where in Jersey?" Bolan asked.

"Newark. I've got an address and description for you, if you're ready."

"Shoot."

He listened carefully and memorized the information even as Brognola spoke. It was an address fronting the Passaic River, nothing flashy. Even so, the guy made money at his trade, and some of his connections—the East Germans, for example—could have bled into a link with Mideast terrorists.

It would be worth a shot, certainly better than twiddling his thumbs and waiting for the one who got away to surface somewhere else.

"What about the French end?" Bolan asked.

"Still working on it," the big Fed replied. "You'll know as soon as I do, guy."

"All right. I'd better move on this before it gets cold."

"Need anything from Dix?" Brognola asked. "Some extra hardware?"

"Not this time. Thanks for asking, though."

"We aim to please."

"That's what I've heard. Go get some sleep."

"Too late," Brognola said. "You chased my dream away."

Bolan severed the connection, walked back to his waiting car and started to calculate distance. Call it forty-five or fifty miles to Newark, mostly turnpike. He could make it in an hour easily, and have his target spotted prior to sunrise.

It had been a long night, and it wasn't over yet.

Tough luck if he had ruined Hal Brognola's dream. He was about to do the same for someone he had never met. The "travel agent" didn't know it yet, but he had one grim nightmare coming, C.O.D.

And if he didn't have the necessary information, he could always pay in blood.

THE TRANSATLANTIC LINE was scratchy, with a hollow sound about it, reminiscent of those children's "telephones" concocted out of strings and old tin cans. Amal al-Qadi fought against the urge to shout, aware that it would make no difference if he raised his voice.

"What kind of trouble?" asked the gruff voice on the other end, so far away.

"It's critical," al-Qadi replied.

"Your mission has been compromised?"

"I'm coming back." Al-Qadi couldn't prevent a note of bitterness from entering his voice.

"As you think best." If he was disappointed or angry, the other hid it well. Al-Qadi didn't like to think about how he would be received when he returned.

"There will be other chances," he began, "and I—"

"Of course," the other person interrupted him before he had a chance to brag. "When are you leaving?"

"Soon. About six hours, from LaGuardia."

In fact, his flight was taking off from JFK in just four hours' time. The lie was automatic, bred from years of guarded language over open lines, now buttressed by suspicion that his friend's calm voice might hide a plan for devious revenge. When they were face-to-face, had time to talk it out, al-Qadi would feel safe, but until then...

"I'll see you later, then," the gruff voice said. "Be careful."

"Yes, of course."

They never said goodbye, a kind of superstitious quirk making them both avoid finalities. It was a childish game, he realized, but each profession had its little eccentricities. The men who dealt in death for ideological reasons were frequently ready to die for some cause, but suicide missions aside, they were subject to all the same emotions shared by other men.

It was the hate that made them special.

Amal al-Qadi had grown up hating the Israelis, the United Nations, any Western country that supported Jewish occupation of his Palestinian homeland, finally the members of his own race who had turned their coats and now spoke out for "peace and harmony." The hate grew numbing after thirty-seven years, but it would never go away. If every Jew on earth was vaporized at dawn tomorrow, he would have to find another cause to kill and die for.

After all this time, it was the only life he knew.

In years gone by, he knew from reading history, some nations had trained war dogs, starved and tortured them to the point where they feared one master and hated the rest of mankind, attacking blindly, viciously, whenever they were finally unleashed and pointed at an enemy. When peace descended on the realm for any length of time, the war dogs were a liability. And since they couldn't be reprogrammed into household pets, they were destroyed.

So it had to be one day with him, al-Qadi thought. If he survived the plotting of his enemies and the occasional incompetence of fellow soldiers, he would have to be eliminated by the peacemakers before their work was done.

Or maybe he would simply disappear and find himself another war.

The concourse of John F. Kennedy International Airport was crowded, as always, with travelers on business or pleasure, some no doubt pursuing desperate errands that eclipsed all other questions from their minds. Amal al-Qadi sometimes wondered, in great airports, whether some of those who passed him by were toting death and guilty secrets in their luggage, paying their air fare with blood money, accepting their tickets with dirty hands.

Why should he be the only one?

His overseas connection was secure for now. He wasn't going home, but Europe was the next-best thing. If it lacked sand and broiling sun, the difference was more than compensated for by its mountains, open spaces, unrestricted travel.

And the women.

He wasn't a monk or eunuch, even though the nature of his work sometimes required him to forsake the pleasures of the flesh for weeks or months on end. It was another sacrifice al-Qadi made without complaint, to help his Palestinian brothers win their freedom from the demon's yoke of bondage.

He spotted Ibrahim Salim emerging from the men's room.

"You got through?" Salim inquired when he joined his companion.

"Of course."

"We're not in trouble?"

"It is understood that we have done our best,"

Amal al-Qadi said. Not quite an answer, but it was the best he had to offer, and he shied away from making empty promises. Hassan Jubayl hadn't seemed angry on the telephone, but you could seldom tell what he was thinking from his tone of voice. Al-Qadi would need to see his eyes, and even then, the truth might be obscure.

Until the trap was sprung.

They reached the gate and found a pair of seats, well back from the flow of foot traffic through the concourse. Now it all came down to waiting—for their boarding call, the takeoff, hours in the air before their feet were back on solid ground.

But they were still alive, still free.

Amal al-Qadi would be back to fight another day.

CHAPTER FOUR

The travel agent's name was Hershel Weaver, "Hershie" to his friends. It was a nickname seldom used, since he had only half a dozen friends on earth, and three of them were doing time. It made no difference to his business, since he dealt primarily with strangers, on referral from old customers. He kept them satisfied, and thereby kept himself alive, with ample cash and travel documents on hand in case he had to make a hasty trip to parts unknown.

His normal stock-in-trade was paper goods, with a sideline in plastic—passports and birth certificates, diplomas and drivers' licenses, green cards and gun permits, military discharge documents and credit cards. You name it, and Weaver could forge it...for a price. He specialized in package tours, and while the actual accommodations were the customers' responsibility, he smoothed the way with documents from fifty states and every English-speaking nation on the globe.

Considering his skill, plus the variety and number of his clients, Weaver had been lucky. Three arrests in twenty years, and only one of those had sent him down for any time: a three-year jolt for counterfeiting in the early 1970s. It was the first and last time he played around with funny money. Having once been burned, he left the game to more-adventurous competitors and concentrated on producing fake ID.

The travel agent's combination home and office was a spacious loft on Fourth Street, fronting the Passaic River, a mile and a half north of Newark International Airport. Bolan came in on the turnpike, passed the sprawling airport on his left and got off on Wilson Avenue to make the last leg of his trip on surface streets.

There is a smell to Newark, something tangible that waits to catch you at the city limits, crossing over Newark Bay from Jersey City or approaching from Elizabeth, from Irvington, from Belleville. Bolan couldn't give the smell a name, precisely. There were elements of car exhaust and smoke from factories, the river's contribution and the reek of any ghetto you could name.

It smelled like desperation and defeat.

He thought about Brognola's sketchy information, wondering if Weaver was his man. Proximity was on his side, the likelihood that foreigners who planned on terrorizing New York and New Jersey would obtain the necessary paperwork to help them pass inspection. One member of the team had died at the Museum of Modern Art, and while the FBI hadn't been able to identify him yet, the bogus passport in his pocket had been good enough to pass inspection anywhere. It took a scan of State Department files to prove the document was fake, and that meant they were dealing with a pro.

As with the rest of Newark, Weaver's neighborhood had gone to hell. Graffiti scarred the warehouses and tenements. The skeletons of junk cars rusted out in vacant lots, some of them occupied by homeless people. Weeds grew rampant in the lots and clung defiantly to life in sidewalk cracks. The few shops that were still in business wore steel shutters after nightfall to protect their stock from thieves and vandals.

It was late enough—or early enough—that most of the street people had made themselves scarce. He guessed that it would be a downscale market for the pimps and pushers anyway, well off the beaten track for their illicit customers. His car might not be safe by any normal definition of the term, but he would park it out of sight as best he could and keep his fingers crossed.

He pulled into an alley far enough to keep from being spotted by a simple passerby, and flashed his headlights to confirm that he hadn't invaded someone's sleeping quarters. He appeared to be alone, the alley's single garbage container heaped to overflowing with the kind of refuse that would make it anyone's last choice for an impromptu crash pad.

Hershel Weaver's pad was three doors down and two floors up, a short walk from the alley. Bolan locked the car and switched on the alarm, but left the C-4 package disengaged. Whatever happened next, his visit with the travel agent should be fairly brief. If Weaver made the wise decision to cooperate, it would be easy to discover what he knew. If not...

The Executioner couldn't be sure his mark knew

anything of consequence, but it was definitely worth a shot.

He had the sidewalk to himself, and it was nothing to defeat the lock on Weaver's outside door. Inside, the building smelled like age and rotting plaster.

Bolan palmed his silenced automatic and started up the stairs.

AT FIRST he thought it was a dream. They happened like that sometimes, when sounds or smells or anything at all from the surrounding room invaded a sleeper's consciousness and wove themselves into a dream. He was familiar with the process, so it didn't frighten Hershel Weaver right away, the subtle noise that woke him, lying in his bed, the covers up around his neck.

And then he heard the sound again.

The man's eyes snapped open. He was wide-awake now, thinking of the neighborhood he lived in and what could go wrong when you were least expecting it. He had been ripped off only once before, and that three years ago, so Weaver figured maybe he was overdue.

It was the reason why he kept a .38-caliber pistol under his pillow when he went to sleep at night. One reason, anyway. The other had to do with his clients, most of whom were cool as long as he provided first-class service, but you never really knew for sure. Some guys in Weaver's business had come in for grief because a client got too paranoid and started thinking he'd be better off if no one on God's earth knew all the different handles he was using. When a client started to think that way, you were in for major trouble. It had never happened yet to Weaver, but he knew enough to watch his back and be prepared for any kind of shit that came his way.

He had to sleep, though. He hardly even felt the pistol after all this time, but he never once forgot that it was there.

Right now it felt good in his hand as Weaver lay still and listened for a repetition of the noise that had awakened him. Was it the door? A footstep on the concrete floor? He kept no pets around the loft, so that eliminated any casual explanation. He knew all the sounds that his old building made by day or night, and this wasn't part of the repertoire.

He didn't throw the covers back, no sudden moves to let the prowler know he was awake. Instead, he made a point of turning over like he would if he were still asleep, a little grumbling noise thrown in for realism's sake, his right foot poking out from underneath the sheet and blankets as it might do, accidental like. A few more seconds, and the other foot was out there, goose bumps rising on his skin as he shifted, inching off the mattress.

There was no cool way to do the next part. Rolling out of bed and landing in a crouch was simple when you thought about it, but he wound up tangled in the sheets and dragged them after him, his .38 aimed straight across the loft at nothing. Weaver scanned the loft, all shadows, with reflections from the streetlights beaming through the higher windows that he hadn't painted over when he took the place.

So much for privacy. It worked against you when you least expected it, but he would take his chances on a prowler any day, rather than the prying eyes of cops and would-be burglars.

What to do?

He couldn't call the cops and have them blundering around the place with the equipment he had there. Too many questions would be sure to follow, and he didn't have the kind of answers that would get him off the hook.

So, take a chance.

"Who's there?" he asked the silent loft, and thumbed the pistol's hammer back to punctuate the question.

Nothing.

Weaver got untangled from the bedding, straightened and took his first few cautious steps into the darkness.

"I can hear you, man," he told the darkness, trying not to whine. "I got a gun if you want to try your luck."

"I might as well," a graveyard voice said. A yellow flash winked in the darkness barely registering on Weaver's retinas before the .38 was ripped out of his hand and flung across the room. His fingers burned, and there was something warm dripping from his palm. He didn't need a light to know that it was blood.

A man-shaped shadow detached itself from the

greater darkness and moved closer to Weaver. A click, and the fluorescent lights came on.

The prowler was a tall man, at least five inches better than Weaver's five-seven. He was dressed in ordinary street clothes, more or less, clean shaved, with the kind of face that specialized in delivering bad news. The automatic in his right hand had some kind of sound suppressor attached, and that told Weaver he was in deep trouble. Few burglars carried guns, and none he'd ever heard of would take time to buy a sound suppressor, assuming they knew how to use one. They were used by professionals.

Weaver was considering who might be angry enough or paranoid enough to want him dead. Before he had a chance to put a list together, though, the prowler spoke again.

"You're Weaver." It wasn't a question.

"That's right." Too late he thought about denying it, and knew it wouldn't make a difference if he did. "Who sent you?"

"What I need," the stranger said as if he hadn't spoken, "is some information."

"Yeah?"

"About your work."

Gears meshed in his head. The guy wasn't a cop. That much was obvious, considering the sound suppressor, his mode of entry and the fact that he hadn't produced a warrant. Good news and bad news, Weaver thought. The stranger couldn't bust him, but he didn't have all kinds of rules to follow, either. There was nothing to prevent his breaking Weaver's arms—or killing him, dear Jesus—if it struck him as the thing to do.

"What kind of information?"

"You do work for out-of-towners now and then," the stranger said. "I mean, *way* out of town."

"It's possible. I knew a guy from Philly once."

The pistol shifted slightly, muzzle pointed in the general direction of his groin.

"You want to play it cute," the stranger said, "it's no skin off me. Are you a singer, Hershie?"

"Huh?"

"I'm thinking, maybe you could try soprano."

Pop!

He heard the gun this time, just barely, and the bullet passed between his chubby thighs. He glanced down, saw the tidy rip in his pajama bottoms and the damn loft seemed to tilt, like he was on a sailing ship at sea, in a monsoon.

No blood. No pain.

The stranger missed on purpose, showing Weaver he could hit exactly what he aimed at, anytime he wanted to.

"Hey, man, come on…"

"The out-of-towners, Hershie?"

"Foreigners, okay? I do all kinds. You got me. What's the beef?"

The stranger was approaching him, his left hand disappearing in a pocket of his sport coat, coming out with a photograph. He stopped at arm's length from the travel agent, showing him the picture—two men talking on a street that looked like somewhere in the Middle East.

"You recognize the fellow on the left?"

"He looks familiar."

"It would have been within the past three weeks or so," the stranger said. "He brought some friends along. They needed paper in a hurry."

"Friends is right. I hardly ever done nine guys at once, you know? In this line of work, it's mostly one guy who wants to get away somewhere, and maybe take his girlfriend with him, if you get my drift."

"These guys," the stranger said to bring him back on track.

"Yeah, right."

"They had to come from somewhere, Hershie. And they have to go somewhere, when they get finished with their business, right?"

"I guess."

"You might have fixed them up with plastic."

"That's a possibility."

"And you're the kind of man that keeps his records straight, I bet. A little something for a rainy day."

"I ain't no slouch."

"I need the names you gave them, and the numbers for their plastic."

"Hey, that's—"

"What?"

The sound suppressor was touching Weaver now, the metal warm against his chin.

"I was about to say that's easy."

"Excellent."

"I keep my files in there." He nodded toward the far end of the loft. "On the computer."

"So boot it up," the stranger said. "The quicker I get what I need, the sooner you'll be back in dreamland."

"I can dig it, man."

It took five minutes, booting up the file, selecting what he needed, routing all the information to his printer, waiting while the paper filled with names and numbers. Weaver had to work one-handed, with his left, which slowed things a bit. He didn't know if he should pray for extra time or be relieved when it was done.

"That's it," he said at last, and watched the stranger tuck the printout in his pocket.

"Are you sure?"

"Hey, I'm no hero, man, you know? I'll never see those guys again, whatever happens. You can have them, man, just don't take *me*, okay?"

The stranger seemed to think about it for a moment, then he put his gun away. A trick? Dear Jesus, let him leave. Just get him out of here right now!

"You need a bandage, Hershie. Maybe let a doctor take a look at that."

He raised the wounded hand and looked at it. "It's just a scratch," he said, surprised to find that it was true. No fingers missing, just a bloody crease across his knuckles where the round had grazed him.

"Suit yourself. If those boys left a contact number—"

"No! I mean, that's not how I do business. Once

they get the merchandise, they're gone. Some call me back for seconds, but these guys, I'd say I've seen the last of them.''

"You'd better hope so, Hershie. Turn around.''

He did as he was told, imagining the worst, unable to resist. Instead of being slugged or shot, though, Weaver heard the front door close behind his uninvited visitor. He spun and found himself alone. He sprinted to the door, where he secured the triple locks.

Sometimes a man caught a break, he thought, and started to run toward the bathroom, hoping he would make it there in time.

THE BANK CARDS WERE BOGUS, but they left a trail like any other, through assorted airline-ticketing and billing agencies. Once he had patched the numbers through to Stony Man, all Bolan had to do was to wait for the computers to disgorge their data on command. The men he sought had booked two first-class airline tickets out of JFK, for Orly. They were airborne, on their way to Paris, by the time he got the word.

The hard part, Bolan realized, was catching up.

He let the Stony Man computers swing his reservation out of Newark International and left his hardware for a pickup when they sent someone around to fetch the car. He could have grabbed a military flight from Dix and taken weapons with him, but it would have been an extra risk he didn't need. This way, with a connection waiting for him on the ground and money in his pocket, Bolan could rearm himself with no chance of a stop at customs that would end his game before it started.

All he had to do was catch his flight and spend the next few hours resting, thinking through the moves that would be necessary when he got to Paris and beyond.

The Palestinians had operated out of France for decades, even after Carlos the Jackal brought the heat down on their heads by killing French policemen, touching off a lethal bomb at Le Café in Paris. It was like some kind of open secret—a clandestine love affair of sorts between a people who had forged their nation out of revolution—and had no great fondness for the Jews, as witnessed by events from Dreyfus to the Vichy deportations—and a group of rebels viewed by many Europeans as courageous underdogs. Since Carlos, pains were taken not to rile their hosts, the Palestinians preferring sanctuary to another killing ground. They had the whole world to fight in, as it was, and all they had to do for shelter was make sure they kept their noses clean in France.

So cozy had the guests and hosts become, in fact, that rumor made the Palestinians responsible for ratting out French radicals and stickup men to the police. It was by way of paying "rent," the stories ran, and helped them curry favor with authorities who looked the other way while they—the Palestinians—were running guns across the border, resting up from desert training in Algeria or raids in Israel.

Of course, some French authorities still tried to buck the trend. They kept an eye both on terrorists in transit, as it were, and on those who tried to set up shop. In recent years, more energy had been expended tracking groups devoted to the Muslim revolution brewing in Algeria, which still maintained emotional and diplomatic ties to France. It rarely helped prevent atrocities in other nations, but at least there was normally some kind of documentation on the groups and individuals residing in France.

Bolan entered the Newark International departures terminal, pausing long enough to read the signs above his head before he turned hard left and moved in the direction of the airline-reservations desk. There was no line to speak of at that early hour of the morning. Sleepy-looking ticket agents stood behind the counter, shuffling paperwork and waiting for the next rush to begin. He drew a twenty-something blonde who wore her hair tied back and smiled through the fatigue that readily identifies a member of the graveyard shift.

"Yes, sir?"

"I have a ticket waiting for the next flight out to Paris," Bolan told her. "It was booked in by computer, from my corporate headquarters in Washington."

"Your name, sir?"

"Mike Belasko."

"Just a moment, please."

The "corporate headquarters" was Stony Man Farm, operating by fax and various long-distance telephone cutouts from the Blue Ridge Mountains of Virginia, via Washington, D.C. This month, the cover logo was Laconia, Inc.—vague enough to stand for almost anything, backstopped by an answering service that would confirm any current cover stories being used by soldiers in the field. At any given time, that covered Bolan, Jack Grimaldi or Phoenix Force and Able Team.

"Ah, here we are." The young blonde favored Bolan with another smile. "You're traveling first-class with us today, I see."

"The only way to fly," he told her, paying back the smile with one of his.

"And no return flight?"

"I don't know my schedule yet," he told her honestly. "It could get complicated."

"Just one moment while I print your ticket, sir."

He stood and listened to the printer rattling underneath the counter. Sixty seconds later, Bolan had his ticket, printed out in duplicate on flimsy sheets.

"Your flight departs in ninety minutes, sir. Did you have any bags to check this morning?"

"Just the carryon," he told her, lifting the valise that held spare clothing, toiletries, the combat black suit. His private war chest—fifty thousand dollars, give or take, had been distributed between his pockets and a money belt that left no telltale bulge beneath his clothes.

"You travel light," she said.

"I do my best."

"You'll need to turn left at the bottom of the escalator, over there," she told him, pointing, "and proceed to international departures. There are markers all the way, and you've got time to spare. We should be boarding thirty minutes prior to takeoff.''

Bolan thanked her with another smile and started toward the escalators with his leather bag. He had some time to kill and contemplated breakfast, but there would be breakfast on the flight, and he could use the time ahead to plan the moves he had to make when he arrived in Paris.

Picking up new hardware.

Picking up the trail.

He had been hoping he could wrap up the mission in Jersey, but the opportunity to finish it had slipped through Bolan's fingers. He would have to play the cards as they were dealt to him, and that meant shifting to another table, all the way across the broad Atlantic.

One point in his favor, Bolan knew, was that his enemies wouldn't anticipate a tail. Their near miss in the States might leave them shaken, but he couldn't count on anything. His one true edge was the advantage of surprise.

And how much would that edge be countered by the enemy's home-court advantage? Did they have enough security in place to block his second move—or even take him out—before he had a chance to close in for the kill?

Too many questions, and he couldn't answer any of them until he was on the ground in Paris, armed and in pursuit of those who got away.

And he wouldn't be backing off the trail until he brought them down.

And he wouldn't be facing them alone.

CHAPTER FIVE

The worst thing about flying transatlantic, David McCarter thought, was waking up stiff when you dozed in your seat. Even in first class, with its larger, more-comfortable seats and twice the leg room allotted for the sardines flying coach, there was still no such thing as a normal-sized pillow or seats that reclined beyond a forty-five-degree angle. You were neither sitting up nor lying down, inevitably slumping to one side or the other, head cocked in a manner that guaranteed muscle spasms on awakening.

McCarter cursed and cupped a palm beneath his chin, giving his head a sharp twist, first in one direction, then the other. His vertebrae popped twice, a sound like muffled gunshots in his ears, but there was still a nagging stiffness in his neck and shoulders that would take a drink or dose of aspirin to finish it off.

The Briton glanced to his left and found Gary Manning, in the window seat, perusing an in-flight magazine. He checked his watch and saw that they were forty minutes out of Paris, still too early for the 747 to begin its slow descent.

McCarter unbuckled his seat belt, rose and walked

forward to the rest room that was barely larger than a phone booth. Once inside, he locked the door and spent a moment staring at his own reflection in the mirror. There were smudgy shadows underneath his eyes, and scrubbing with cold water left them there, untouched.

"You look like shit," he told himself, and scowled in answer to the insult.

Still, he thought, it could be worse. They had been getting ready for a flight from L.A. to New Zealand when the hurry call came in from Hal Brognola, changing everything. The shift in destinations saved them six or seven hours' flying time, but he couldn't help thinking of the others—Calvin James, Rafael Encizo and Hawkins—who were going on with half their normal strength to face the Rasta posses that were terrorizing Christchurch and environs with a drug war that had racial and political overtones. Stiff neck aside, a part of him still wished that he were with them, ready to support their play however it went down.

But there was work to do in France, as well.

McCarter had the basics down. They would be linking up with Bolan when they got to Paris, backing any play he made against a team of Palestinian guerrillas who had made the grave mistake of broadening their battleground to take in the United States.

It sometimes struck McCarter as ironic, after all the time that he had spent pursuing terrorists with Britain's SAS, that he should wind up doing much the same for Phoenix Force and the Americans when he "retired" from active duty. It was part of who he was, the burning need to get involved, instead of standing on the sidelines while somebody else went in to fight his battles for him.

McCarter didn't know the details yet, but Bolan would fill in the blanks once they were reunited on French soil. He tore his eyes away from the reflection in the mirror, almost smiled as he retraced his steps to the reclining seat and Gary Manning.

"Come out all right?" the Canadian asked as McCarter settled into his chair.

"You need some new material, old son. That's bloody sophomoric."

"So I'm tired."

"Your *jokes* are tired," McCarter said. "Of course—"

A shock of turbulence surprised him, making the 747 lurch as if it had just run over a speed bump. Overhead the seat-belt sign came on, accompanied by soft, almost melodic chimes. A disembodied voice told them that everything was fine, but everyone should remain in his or her seat for the duration, seat belts snugly fastened.

"Lots of clouds down there," Manning commented, peering out his window as the minicrisis momentarily distracted him from talk and reading.

"Should be," McCarter said gruffly. They were cruising at an altitude of thirty thousand feet. It would have been a miracle to see the ocean or the land from that high up.

They would be back in action soon enough.

McCarter thought of Yakov Katzenelenbogen, wondered how he *really* liked his desk job at the Farm. It had to be a drastic change from fighting in the field, but everybody—Katz included—had agreed that it was time.

It could have been much worse.

McCarter wondered, sometimes, whether there would be a desk reserved for him, when he attained the age where eyesight dims and muscles fail.

Sometimes he wondered whether he would live that long.

Forget it!

There was work to do right now, and he was ready to begin, as soon as they met Bolan and the warrior told them what was going on.

In the meantime, a little turbulence never hurt anyone. He would pretend it was a roller-coaster ride, as in his youth. He couldn't see the end of it, but knew instinctively that there were more steep climbs and plummeting descents waiting before he reached the end of the line.

McCarter pushed his stiff neck out of mind, leaned back again and closed his eyes.

ELISE DUBOIS WAS running late. It was the story of her life: too little time and too much work. She never quite caught up, and just about the time she thought she might, the men upstairs were sure to dump another pile of cases in her lap.

She was the only woman working on the antiterrorism beat for Interpol in France. It hadn't been a problem once she let her colleagues know that she was more than just another pretty face. Of course, she had looks, too—Dubois hadn't been blinded to her image in the mirror by false modesty—but sex wasn't the same issue in France that it would have been in England or America. Of course, she knew some of her colleagues took a chance with on-the-job liaisons, but she didn't play that game. For now, the job was all she needed in her life. The quest for a relationship could wait.

She thought about the scheduled meeting as she drove her battered Citroën eastward, along the Boulevard Haussmann. Behind her, she could barely see the Arc de Triomphe in her rearview mirror, sunlight glinting off chrome and shiny paint jobs in the middle distance. She was used to Paris driving, having grown up in the city, and she didn't let the rush of steel or bleating horns distract her from the job at hand.

She had been tracking down a cache of weapons from Algeria when she was summoned to the office of her supervisor and ordered to a meeting with a stranger from America. She had a vague description of the man—six feet plus, two hundred pounds or so, dark hair—and knew his name was Mike Belasko.

Dubois had worked with federal agents from America before. They had no jurisdiction on French soil, but agents of the FBI and DEA were present all the same. They operated from their embassy and made no effort to disguise themselves. As for the CIA, its agents—while presumably unknown in countries where they did their spying—frequently collaborated with the team at Interpol to gather information on their common adversaries. In the past, Dubois had worked with all three groups, and they had always come to see her at the office or received her in their own.

Which meant this had to be something different.

When she had pressed her supervisor for an explanation, he had given her two names: Amal al-Qadi and Hassan Jubayl. It was a start—two Arab terrorists with links to France, al-Qadi known to operate sporadically from Paris and Marseilles—but there was still too much she didn't know and couldn't guess.

There were the rumors, granted, that Amal al-Qadi had gone hunting in America, that he might be responsible for an attack on the Museum of Modern Art in New York City. Nothing solid, but it seemed the sort of thing that he would do. All terrorists desired publicity, and most were fairly indiscriminate in choosing targets, quick to note that everyone was fair game in the modern world. But there was something in al-Qadi that set him apart from the rest. Or maybe, Dubois thought, it was something *missing* from his makeup. Rumor had it that he enjoyed his bloody work, beyond the arguments of racial or political "necessity" she had come to know so well.

If there had been no cause to fight for, said the rumors, then Amal al-Qadi would have killed for sport.

Hassan Jubayl was something else, at least in her opinion. A tactician, scholar of guerrilla war from Mao to Vietnam and Belfast, he was a fanatic Palestinian who shunned the "weakness" of men like Arafat, who found a way to make their peace with the Israelis after years of killing. It wouldn't be over for Jubayl until he died or drove his enemies into the sea. And yet, for all his hatred and fanaticism, he wasn't a madman. Rather, he was cunning, well above the average in intelligence, a master of his game. When it became too hot for him in Jordan, when the Libyans began to quibble over picking up his tab, Jubayl had found himself another patron, and his war went on.

Dubois could only wonder if the Americans had now organized a special unit to respond, once terrorism reached their shores. She was accustomed to procedures, going by the numbers in her job with Interpol. If this Belasko and the men behind him now had something else in mind...

What then?

She didn't want to think about it yet. A part of her abhorred the notion, but there was another part that almost hoped it would be true. How novel and refreshing it would be to see some action for a change, instead of simply trailing terrorists around the city, taking notes and snapping surreptitious photographs that wound up in some ever growing file.

She spotted Rue Charras ahead and flashed her left-hand signal once to warn the drivers close behind her, then swung sharply through a gap in traffic, leaning on her horn as she went through the turn. Ahead and on her right, she spotted the Café Montagne, where Belasko was supposed to meet her. It was early yet, but not by much. She still had time to park the car and walk back to the small café, pick out her table and be waiting for him when the man arrived.

She wondered if he would be young or old, plain or attractive, dour or charming. In her experience, Americans involved in law enforcement overseas were almost equally divided between flirtatious James Bond types and sour-faced men who acted as if they carried the weight of the world on their shoulders. Neither was particularly pleasant to work with, and she always hoped that she would find one someday who would break the mold.

She would listen, see what the American had on his mind and go from there. Her boss had asked her to cooperate if possible, but otherwise he had been vague, refusing to elaborate. Dubois interpreted his silence to suggest the choice was hers, and she was on her own.

The American would have to win her trust—no easy proposition on the best of days, but it wasn't impossible.

Elise Dubois decided she would have to wait and see.

MACK BOLAN STOOD across the street from the Café Montagne and waited for his contact to arrive. She stood out from the average passerby: tall and trim, with her auburn hair square cut at shoulder length. She wore a two-piece suit in navy blue, its tailored cut designed to emphasize without exploiting her athletic body. She had long legs, sleek in neutral-colored nylon hose, and her shoes, with two-inch heels, combined sensibility and style.

So far, so good.

He gave her time to enter the café and take a seat, then walked back to the corner, crossing with the light. The locals seemed to take a special pleasure in jay-walking, daring the swarm of erratic drivers to mow them down, but Bolan had time to spare. The lady from Interpol was several minutes early, checking out the set. There was no point in rushing her right off the top.

Brognola had arranged the meet through Interpol, pulling strings and nudging a couple of acquaintances to bring it off. While he was fixing it, Bolan had kept his rendezvous with Manning and McCarter, glad to have the pair of them along as backup for what could become a rather dicey situation. Together they had gone to shop for hardware straightaway, a place on Boulevard Jean Jaures, where sporting goods were sold out front, with military hardware in the back. They had enough to see them through a week or so, at any rate, and Bolan knew the Paris action wouldn't last that long, whichever way it went.

There was no way. No way at all.

He hesitated on the sidewalk fronting the café and peered through the window casually, but long enough to spot his contact seated near the back, a corner booth. She faced the door, as any cop would learn to do within a few days on the job. He wondered whether she was armed, a front-line soldier in the cause, or someone drafted from the clerical department.

Either way, it hardly mattered. Bolan didn't need another gun for his campaign. He needed information that would help him find Amal al-Qadi and his comrades with a minimal amount of wasted time. He was prepared to carry it from there, with Manning and McCarter at his back. A native "helper" would confuse things, multiply the risks, and more particularly if a woman was involved.

He didn't question the ability of women on the firing line, but there was something in himself—a weakness, he supposed—that kicked in with protective instincts any time he had to share tough duty with a female. And the last thing Bolan needed at the moment was distraction from his enemy, his goal.

The café had a seat-yourself arrangement, and Bolan moved toward the booth his contact had selected. She had green eyes, Bolan saw when he was close enough, and they were studying his face as he approached.

"I'm Mike Belasko," he informed her, waiting for the woman to extend her hand before he raised his own.

"Elise Dubois," she said. "Please, sit."

He slid into the booth across from her, untroubled by the door behind him, since he knew that Manning and McCarter had the street. If anyone suspicious happened by and tried to enter the café, he would be covered—long enough, at least, to reach the sleek Beretta holstered underneath his arm.

An anorexic-looking waitress took their order. Bolan settled for a cup of coffee, while Dubois requested salad and a glass of wine.

"It's lunchtime," she remarked. "You don't mind talking while I eat?"

"No problem," Bolan said. "Were you advised of what I'm looking for?"

Her shrug was interesting, provocative. "The Spear of Allah," she replied. "Amal al-Qadi."

"And the man or men behind him."

"That would be Hassan Jubayl," she said. "But he doesn't reside in France."

"Okay. I'll take what I can get," he told her.

"You require no more from me than information?"

"That's the deal."

"May I inquire as to your plans? Some might consider me responsible if anything goes wrong."

"I won't," Bolan said. "Neither will your boss."

"You know him, then?" One lifted eyebrow showed her skepticism, loud and clear.

He shook his head. There was no point in lying to the woman when a lie would be so easy to disprove. "I've got connections from the States," he said. "It all works out."

"Amal al-Qadi is suspected of attacks in the United States, I understand."

"It goes beyond suspicion," Bolan said. "He's on the hook, no doubt about it."

"And you plan to take him back for trial?"

He thought about the question for a moment, wondering how much the woman ought to know, what kind of difficulty he could stir up with an honest answer. She was cool—he gave her that much—never flinching from his gaze, her green eyes holding Bolan's.

"Not quite," he said at last.

She frowned at that. "It's vengeance, then?"

"You're not involved," Bolan said. "All I need are certain names, addresses, and we never have to meet again. You eat your salad, go back to the office and forget we ever had this talk."

"I'm not inclined to do that."

"Oh?" He heard alarm bells going off, still faint, but recognizable.

"Amal al-Qadi and his kind have used my country as their base of operations now for over twenty years. Except with the Algerians and Carlos when he got out of control, the government prefers to look the other way. It's easier, you see? Less trouble, paperwork, expense."

"You disapprove?"

"I hate it," she replied. "It makes us all seem weak, or worse. We are accomplices to everything these bastards do, as long as they find shelter here."

"You don't make policy," he said.

"It's all the same." Her green eyes flashed with glints of emerald fire. "I'll help you if I can."

"You mentioned that Hassan Jubayl is not in France."

"Sudan," she said. "He comes to see Amal al-Qadi now and then, but not for several months."

"Too bad."

"I have the others, though. They may have hiding places that we haven't found—they must, of course— but I can tell you where to find al-Qadi and his friends, unless they've all gone underground."

"You understand that information's *all* I want?"

"Of course." There was a hint of rancor in her tone, but nothing he could put his finger on. He hoped the woman didn't have a personal agenda waiting to surprise him when he had a battle on his hands.

"And that's okay with you?"

"'They also serve...'" she said, and left the rest of the quotation hanging. He was almost startled when her full lips broke into a smile.

"All right, then. Let's get down to cases," Bolan said.

"Where shall I start?"

He thought about it, shrugged and told her, "How about the top?"

"A TASTY BIT of pastry, that," McCarter observed.

"With that kind of attitude," Manning said, "it's no wonder why the ladies love you so."

"You've heard the stories, then?"

"Who hasn't?" Manning dropped the banter for a moment, glancing once again toward the Café Montagne. "You think she has it?"

"Oh, I'd say."

"I mean the information," Manning said.

"Hope springs eternal," McCarter replied, with a crooked grin.

Manning didn't have to ask the Briton what was troubling him. By now, their comrades would have joined the battle in New Zealand, and it felt strange, being on the wrong side of the world when he was needed elsewhere. At the same time, Manning knew that he was needed here, and from the brief description

Bolan had provided at their meeting, it was no less urgent than the mission that was dealt to Phoenix Force before their plans began to change.

At least, Manning thought, they were ready for the enemy in terms of hardware. Bolan's Paris contact had provided them with rifles, submachine guns, side arms, ammunition and grenades, plastique, incendiaries—everything, in short, that they should need to stage an all-out war against the Spear of Allah, if it came to that.

Not *if,* the big Canadian corrected, *when.*

It always came to killing when Brognola passed the orders down from Stony Man. The men of Phoenix Force weren't negotiators. The very fact of their employment meant that other means had failed to solve a problem where the stakes were high enough to justify the use of deadly force.

Like now.

The Spear of Allah had been raising hell in Europe and the Middle East since Arafat and company negotiated peace with Israel. It was one of several die-hard factions that would never bargain with its chosen enemies or recognize their right to live, much less to live in peace. He didn't carry details of the group's grim record in his head, but Manning could recall the highlights well enough: car bombs outside the Israeli embassy in London with multiple deaths in each blast; grenade attacks in Rome and Bonn; drive-by assassinations in Amsterdam and Maracaibo; the massacre in the Museum of Modern Art, in New York City.

Right.

The soldiers of the Spear had pushed their luck too far with that attack. He knew that Bolan had already scrubbed the New York hit team—most of it, at any rate—and they had been dispatched to help him finish off the wounded octopus. With any luck, they might be able to complete the job in France. If not, then they would chase the trail wherever it might lead, of course. He knew that going in, came to the game prepared for anything.

And he was ready, watching, when the woman left the café, with Bolan following some thirty seconds later, turning in the opposite direction, crossing at the corner to walk back and join them in the car.

"How was the quiche?" McCarter asked.

"Informative," Bolan said. "I've got names, addresses, everything we need to wrap the French end of the pipeline."

"Meaning there's another end," Manning said.

"Right. Hassan Jubayl is in Sudan. Has been since they kicked him out of Jordan some time back."

"We going after him?" McCarter asked.

The Executioner was smiling as he answered, but the smile wouldn't have comforted a living soul.

"Could be. Unless the bastard comes to us."

CHAPTER SIX

The Spear of Allah, as a covert body, had no public headquarters. Instead, it operated from a network of locations—homes, shops, offices—where members or committed sympathizers lived and carried out their normal daily tasks. A warehouse on the Seine, at Port de la Tournelle, was said to be a staging depot for munitions and supplies.

All things considered, Bolan had to give them credit for selection of a scenic spot. The warehouse district was as drab as any other he had seen, but there was Notre-Dame, a thousand yards to the northeast, and a museum almost directly opposite, across the Quai de la Tournelle. You couldn't spit in Paris without striking some historic monument, and that fact only emphasized the urgency of Bolan's mission.

When the savages were left unchecked, allowed to run amok, the risk went far beyond the cost in human lives and suffering inflicted by sporadic violence. In fact, the stakes were nothing less than civilization itself, a struggle to determine whether men of reason and goodwill would rule the day or yield control to predators with no regard for human sensibilities.

The Executioner had made his choice long years ago, and there could be no turning back.

It was approaching five o'clock as Bolan locked the driver's door of his rented Fiat and began to walk back toward his target. In concession to the time and place, he wore civilian street clothes, with a lightweight raincoat to conceal his weapons. The Beretta 92-F in a fast-draw shoulder rig was backup to the Uzi submachine gun Bolan carried underneath his right arm, on a custom swivel sling. A sound suppressor increased the Uzi's length by some twelve inches, tacking on another two pounds to the weapon's total weight, but he had deemed it necessary for the strike. The outside pockets of his raincoat sagged, weighed down with thermite canisters on either side.

In 1944, the story went, Hitler had demanded that the capital of France be destroyed before it fell to Allied hands. His general in charge of Paris had ignored the order, cringing when Hitler called to ask, "Is Paris burning?"

If that question was repeated, later on tonight, the Executioner would answer with a grim affirmative.

Two cars were parked nose-in against the warehouse loading dock, the driver's window down on one, no keys in the ignition. Bolan didn't need a car, and he moved past them, mounted concrete steps and walked across the loading dock to try a door with Privé stenciled on it, white on rusty brown.

He tried the knob and felt it turn, stepped across the threshold, reaching underneath his raincoat for the SMG. He held it ready as he followed voices and the smell of cigarette smoke past a smallish office cubicle, around a corner to the warehouse proper.

There were four of them, three huddled for a conversation, while the fourth was piloting a forklift on the far side of the warehouse, shuttling heaps of cardboard boxes into line. All were Arabs, Bolan saw, which helped confirm his information from Elise Dubois, but he would take no chances with the possibility that one or more of them were innocent.

"Bonjour," he said, and watched the three men jump, responding to an unfamiliar voice. At sight of Bolan's gun, they scattered, reaching for the pistols they wore hidden under coats and shirttails.

Fair enough.

He started on the left, a target slightly closer than the others, and his index finger stroked the Uzi's trigger, squeezing off a 5- or 6-round burst. His parabellum manglers caught the running target in the back, high up between his shoulder blades, and pitched him over forward on his face. The concrete offered no resistance, and the dead man slid for several feet, facedown, before he came to rest and stirred no more.

The other two were taking off in opposite directions, one man sprinting toward the forklift, while his friend broke toward the nearest exit, off to Bolan's right. So far, the second of the two survivors posed a greater threat, since his escape would certainly be followed by the raising of alarms, reports back to the Spear of Allah's leadership. It wasn't part of the Executioner's plan to keep the warehouse raid a secret, but on the other hand, he didn't care to hand the enemy a clear description of himself.

He pivoted and dropped the runner with a rising burst that stitched him diagonally, from his left hip to his right shoulder blade. Momentum kept the man moving for a few more paces, then his feet got tangled up on nothing and he went down in an awkward belly flop. His pistol spun across the concrete, still unfired.

The third man was a good deal quicker, squeezing off two quick shots on the run. Both bullets missed, the first one by a yard or so, but the reports of gunfire were enough to tip the forklift operator to some heavy action going down.

The Executioner took first things first. He tracked the frantic runner with his Uzi, pressed the trigger and unleashed a burst that rolled the man up as if he had no bones.

The forklift operator had him spotted now, and spun his vehicle around, accelerating as he charged. The stack of cardboard boxes balanced on the twin forks made an effective shield, absorbing half a dozen Uzi rounds with no apparent damage to the driver or machine.

One thing about the cartons: if they shielded Bolan's target, they obscured his vision, too. He had no warning, then, when Bolan darted to his left, a dozen paces off the mark, to find another angle of attack. Before the driver recognized his danger, Bolan had him spotted, stitched a tidy line of holes across his chest and left him slumped across the steering wheel. The bulky vehicle kept going and collided with a wall, its progress arrested while the engine kept on burning fuel.

It took another moment to convince him that the place was clear, then Bolan primed his thermite canisters and left them among the stacks of boxes, one on each side of the warehouse. He was on the loading dock before they blew and scattered white-hot coals of phosphorus around the warehouse, starting countless fires that water wouldn't quell.

Round one against the home team, Bolan thought as he walked back to fetch his car, but he wasn't done yet.

Not even close.

McCARTER STOOD across the Rue Séguier and watched the office staff begin to straggle out at closing time. He counted heads, scanned faces, making sure he didn't miss the boss. As for the small fry, they were mostly innocent and unconnected to the Spear of Allah, putting in their time from nine to five as if the travel agency they worked for were completely normal—which, as far as any of them knew, it was.

The Briton wanted the proprietor, a Palestinian named Akhmed Salah, who had arrived in Paris fifteen years ago and set up shop, bankrolled by ''friends and relatives.'' The travel agency he operated from a corner lot on Rue Séguier was known to specialize in tours of the Holy Land and Eastern Europe, which provided cover for his operations with the Spear of Allah.

Salah was an accomplished people-mover. He had

shuttled terrorists and fugitives around the map for years without a hitch, and while authorities suspected his involvement with the Spear of Allah, they could never make a case against him that would stand in court. It was believed that Salah provided bogus travel documents to Palestinian guerrillas and booked them onto tours that offered excellent mobility when they were reaching out for targets. Conservative estimates named him as an accessory before the fact to some three hundred murders in the past ten years, with many times that number wounded when his clients ran amok in airports, shopping malls, hotels and other public places.

Akhmed Salah would have to go.

McCarter watched the last two clerks emerging from the travel agency and noted that they didn't stop to lock the door behind them. Perfect. He wouldn't be forced to crash it, drawing that attention to himself before he found his mark.

He crossed the street, moved briskly toward the door of Salah's agency. There was a moment, just before he reached the door, when he was worried that it might lock automatically, but then it opened at his touch. He stepped inside, taking time to turn the hanging plastic sign around to tell latecomers the office was closed.

He walked through the deserted outer office, homing on a male voice that was muffled by the intervening walls. McCarter wondered for a moment whether Salah had company—a secretary working late, perhaps—or if the man was talking to himself. A few more steps, and he was in position for a peek around the doorjamb, into Salah's office. He solved the riddle when he found his target talking on the telephone.

The Arab leaned back in his chair, feet propped up on a corner of the desk, gesticulating with his left hand while he spoke, as if the person on the other end could see him. He was animated, rocking in his high-backed chair and jabbing at the ceiling with the index finger of his free hand, speaking up to make his point. A smile indicated victory, before McCarter cleared his throat and watched it vanish in a flash. Salah's round eyes focused on the gun McCarter pointed at his face.

The Browning double-action automatic didn't have a sound suppressor, but it wouldn't be necessary. They were well back from the street, and it was rush hour, with heavy traffic flowing past.

Akhmed Salah dropped the telephone receiver, bolted upright in his chair and raised both hands, reaching for the sky.

"Who are you?" he blurted in French. "What do you want?"

McCarter saw no point in talking. There was no way Salah could make amends, and he had other work ahead, still waiting for him. He was deadpan as he raised the pistol, aiming at the Arab's torso.

"No! Wait!"

Two rounds at point-blank range punched Salah backward, his chair rolling until it hit the wall. Bright crimson blossomed on his shirtfront, and his body sagged, began its slow ooze to the floor.

McCarter checked the street outside, found no one

showing any interest as he left the travel agency. His car was parked two blocks away, but there was time. He had all night to run his list.

The targets weren't going anywhere.

SADIQ HASHIM WAS TIRED of Paris. He had spent the past six months among strange-smelling Frenchmen, trying to stay clear of the police, although Amal al-Qadi told him there should be no problems. Still, he kept expecting the police to come for him and his companions, drag them off in chains to wait while hostile countries argued over who should try them first.

Hashim was wanted for acts of terrorism in Israel and Belgium. German authorities hadn't identified him yet, but there would be the question of a bombing once they got around to checking out his fingerprints against the files maintained by Interpol and the Mossad.

Meanwhile, he sat in France and waited for his next assignment, waited for the other shoe to drop. Hashim didn't believe that he would die in prison. It had always seemed to him that he was meant to fall in God's service, waging a relentless war against the infidels. In that case, said the mullahs, he would be assured of Paradise.

Still, it was getting on his nerves, this time he had to spend in France. They could have slipped across the Mediterranean Sea, to hide out in Algeria, and he would have felt himself at home—or nearly so. As it was, he was stuck in a small apartment off Rue Brillat, sharing the crowded space with six other men, all of whom were less concerned with bathing than with watching television, waiting for a glimpse of Western women taking off their clothes.

Sometimes Sadiq Hashim believed he was the only pure soul in the lot.

The blast knocked Hashim sprawling, facedown on the rug. Gunfire ripped through the apartment, hammering from the direction of the living room. Whatever notion he had harbored of an accident—the boiler blowing up, for instance—was immediately driven from his befuddled mind. Someone had found them, and a desperate assault was under way.

Hashim wasted no time wondering if it was the Mossad, the French police or someone else. A bullet didn't care who sent it on its way or whom it killed. He scrambled for the closet, where they kept the AK-47s lined up, locked and loaded, ready for emergencies.

Someone was screaming in the living room as Hashim got the closet open, leaned inside and snatched out a rifle, flicked off the safety and went to find the enemy. His instinct told him he should run and hide, but he was trained to fight.

Three strides brought Hashim to the bedroom door. No sooner had he reached it than the sounds of combat faded on the other side. He hesitated, listening for a familiar voice or anything that would allow him to discover who had emerged victorious. They would be forced to leave, of course, regardless of the outcome. Someone in the block of flats had doubtless called for the police already, but it would be better, safer, if they left dead enemies behind. That way it would be certain no one followed them.

He was about to crack the door and peer outside when someone gave the door a solid kick and slammed it back into his face. Hashim lurched backward, blind in one eye where the door had struck him, lost his balance and dropped to one knee. He kept his grip on the Kalashnikov, refraining from firing for a moment as he shook his head and tried to recognize the figure standing in the bedroom doorway.

By the time he realized it was a tall stranger, with a submachine gun in his hands, it was too late. Hashim squeezed off a burst from the Kalashnikov, but it was low and wide. The submachine gun hammered at him, bullets ripping through his shirt, his flesh, and he toppled backward in a boneless sprawl.

Incredibly he felt no pain. There was a warm, wet numbness that enveloped him. He knew his legs were twisted at an awkward angle beneath him, but they didn't hurt. He tried to lift the AK-47 to defend himself, but there was no more feeling in his arms.

A shadow fell across his face, and Hashim stared up into the grim eyes of the stranger who had shot him. There was no excitement in the stranger's face, no pleasure or relief. He simply studied the terrorist for a moment, then stepped back and turned away.

Hashim tried to call out to him, but found that he could make no sound. His vocal cords felt parched and paralyzed, despite the fact that he could taste blood in his mouth.

He wondered if the fight that he had made would

be enough to count and win him entry to the gates of Paradise. If not, he wondered whether he would go to Hell.

The darkness settled over him a moment later, answered all his silent questions as it carried him away.

THERE WAS NO OVERTIME in Interpol. You worked until a job was done, and thanked your lucky stars if there was time to catch up on your beauty sleep. The paperwork was typical of any law-enforcement agency, compounded by the fact that international crimes and criminals were involved. It was a rare day indeed when any member of the Paris team could be found in the office with nothing to do.

The hours and routine meant nothing to Elise Dubois. She had understood the job before she took it, came to Interpol expecting drudgery to overshadow danger. What discouraged her the most, in recent days, was meeting with informants, men and women she would cheerfully have sent to jail if they didn't possess some bit of gossip, rumor or information that she could use to fatten up her files.

How much of what they told her was the truth? It would be anybody's guess. Dubois passed information on to her superiors, who made a record of it, sometimes passed the information on, in turn, to other agencies and nations. Interpol was a clearinghouse for data, its men and women rarely called upon to make arrests, much less to race their cars in hot pursuit of fugitives, guns blazing as they let their fantasies unwind.

Tonight she was supposed to meet a girl whose

lover was a member of the Spear of Allah. Chance had thrown them into contact—a referral from a friend of a friend—while a combination of greed and anxiety kept the girl coming back to Dubois with new stories, more names and addresses. She was paid for the information, of course, but she also professed concern that her lover would find himself in prison if he kept running with the rebel set. She seemed to love the man, though it didn't prevent her taking money to betray his friends.

So far, the girl had managed to provide a list of contacts and locations where Amal al-Qadi and his warriors of the Spear were known to gather, eat their meals, discuss their plans or simply spend the night. She had obtained the names of several other women who were seeing members of the group, but it was slow work turning more of them into informants. One or two were prostitutes, deliberately indifferent to the business of their clients, while the rest were good-time party girls, enamored of their Middle Eastern lovers at the moment, loath to jeopardize their own fun—or their lives—on Interpol's behalf.

Dubois was waiting in the parking lot behind a strip club on Rue Saussier Leroy, her fingers drumming on the Citroën's steering wheel. Brigitte was late, as usual, an irritating habit that bothered Dubois more than usual this evening, after her talk with Mike Belasko. Now, when it appeared that something was about to happen for a change, each moment wasted struck her as a personal affront. She lit a cigarette, took two quick drags and tossed it out the window, cursing fluently.

A flash of headlights made Dubois squint briefly, then she recognized the blue Renault, watched Brigitte park and cross the lot to join her. The interpol agent had switched off the Citroën's dome light, so there was no flash to illuminate their faces as Brigitte climbed in to occupy the shotgun seat.

"What's so important?" Brigitte asked her as she lit a cigarette.

"It's nothing special. We haven't spoken for some time."

"A week, is all."

"Ten days," Dubois corrected her. "Of course, if you don't need the money—"

"Don't be hasty now. There must be something on your mind to call me out like this."

Dubois wasn't about to speak of the American or what he had in mind. Instead, she told Brigitte, "I've heard there might be trouble coming with another group of Palestinians, some kind of argument that could turn physical. We need to keep a fix on members of the Spear, in case there's trouble on the street. You understand?"

"Whatever," Brigitte said. "I haven't heard of any trouble, and the only other groups they talk about are Jihad and Hamas. They disagree on certain things, of course, but if it's getting ugly on the street, I've heard nothing about it."

"What about Amal?" Elise could only hope she sounded casual. "You've seen him lately?"

"Yesterday, in fact," Brigitte replied. "He was away for several weeks. I told you that. Some business in Algeria, I think it was, but now he's back. Is this about Amal? What has he done?"

"You're in a better place to answer that than I am. What has he told you?"

"Nothing!" Brigitte's sudden laughter sounded forced. "He hardly speaks to me at all. You know the way he feels about Western women."

"So you've said."

Brigitte was working on her second cigarette. "There's nothing more to say right now. It's been a quiet time, without Amal around to stir them up. If I had anything at all..."

"I understand."

"If you can spare a hundred francs..."

Dubois considered refusing payment for the meager information she had shared, but there was nothing to be gained by angering her best informant on the Spear of Allah. There was no good reason to believe her own excitement, after listening to Mike Belasko, would be shared by this young woman who attached herself to criminals for pleasure's sake. Dubois relaxed, or tried to, reaching in her purse to get the money, passing it across.

"Two hundred?" Brigitte said, surprised.

"I'm feeling generous tonight. If it's too much..."

"No, no." Brigitte was quick to make the money disappear.

"You'll keep in touch?"

"Of course."

It had been a waste of time, Dubois considered as she watched Brigitte walk back to the Renault. She had been hoping for some kind of bombshell, something she could share with Belasko that would make her feel as if she were a part of his plan to uproot the Spear of Allah, rather than a mere observer on the sidelines, marking time.

Oh, well.

She wouldn't give up trying. There were other sources she could tap, and while the American had urged her to do nothing, take no extraordinary action whatsoever, she wouldn't be relegated to the status of a mere informant, like Brigitte, who could be trundled out and questioned on a whim, then put back on the shelf as if she had no brain and no initiative.

She felt a flush of angry color in her cheeks and wondered what it was about Belasko that provoked her so.

She had work to do, the American aside. She didn't work for him, and she wasn't about to let him tell her what to do or when to step aside. *He* was the stranger here, despite his "in" with her superiors, and she wouldn't let him forget it.

She would prove herself to spite him, and he would have to notice her.

Dubois was giving him no choice.

THE SMALL REPAIR SHOP two blocks east of Rue d'Amsterdam wasn't exactly what it seemed to be. The owner was Iranian, presumably an exile who had found the climate too oppressive in his homeland and

who chose to stay in France, where he was troubled
neither by a shah nor by an ayatollah. Few among his
customers knew the truth of his beliefs. They would
have been surprised to learn that Hashemi Pahlavi was
an ardent Muslim fundamentalist who had remained
in Paris on instructions from the ruling government in
Baghdad, ordered to cooperate with certain groups in
Western Europe who made war against Israel and the
United States. His little shop was thus a conduit for
information and supplies, and his skill at fixing clocks
and kitchen gadgets periodically applied to building
bombs. One group Pahlavi served, from time to time,
was the fanatic Spear of Allah.

Gary Manning knew that much from listening to
Bolan, after his discussion with the slim brunette from
Interpol. It was enough to put Pahlavi and his shop on
Manning's hit list and the Canadian was relieved to
see a light still burning in the shop as he approached
it, dusk already lengthening his shadow in the street
outside.

He stood across the way and watched a short dark
man approach the shop. He rang the bell and waited
for Pahlavi to admit him, both men moving out of
sight, behind the counter, toward another room in
back.

Still, Manning waited, wondering if he should burst
in through the front or sneak around in back. He had
decided on the rear approach when yet another Arab
wandered into view, his destination clearly the repair
shop in the middle of the block.

There would be no time like the present, Manning

told himself. He crossed the street in long, swift strides, the silenced black Beretta already in his hand. He came up on the Arab's blind side, made no sound to warn him as he rang the bell. When it was done, he let the muzzle of his weapon touch the man's neck and said, "Don't speak. Don't move."

The man did as he was told.

Another moment brought Pahlavi bustling from the back room of his shop. The big Canadian stood back, beyond Pahlavi's line of sight, his pistol pressed against the Arab's skull. Pahlavi turned the dead bolt, stepped back to admit his visitor and gaped in horror at the sight of yet another man, unknown to him, who followed close behind the newcomer, with a pistol in his hand.

Pahlavi panicked, turned and ran, already shouting to his comrade in the back room. Manning shot the new arrival first—no point in giving him a chance to turn and fight—before he lifted the Beretta, sighting down the slide, and put his second round between Pahlavi's shoulders. Momentum carried the Iranian a few more steps until he crashed face first through the plate glass of a long display case, hanging there with jagged shards of glass wedged underneath his chin.

So much for stealth.

The sound of voices from the back room warned Manning that he had at least two enemies to deal with, still alive and ready to resist. The shops were back-to-back on this street, no rear exit for a hasty getaway, which meant the others had to come past him...or he would have to root them out.

He stepped across Pahlavi's outstretched legs, was moving toward the curtained back-room entrance, when a slender man in denim shirt and jeans burst through the portal, brandishing an automatic pistol in his hand. One glimpse of Manning, and he tried to find his mark, the first round fired before he had a target, whispering past the Phoenix Force commando's face, a good foot to the left.

The Arab never got a second chance.

Two rounds from Manning's weapon ripped into the man's chest and rocked him on his heels. He staggered forward, dropped his pistol, arms out-flung as if to catch himself, but he was dead before he took the final lurching step, legs folding under him.

Manning caught him, held the dead man upright with one arm looped around his chest. He walked the life-size puppet back in the direction of the storeroom. It required coordination, but he managed. He shoved the dead man through the curtain, letting him absorb the first rounds from another autoloading pistol.

The sole survivor of their little clique was standing to Manning's left in a corner of the room. He gaped at the remains of what had been his friend, had time to recognize his fatal error and react with something like a cry of panic before the Canadian shot him in the face. One round was all it took, and he slumped backward, sliding down the plaster wall and leaving crimson smears behind to mark his passing.

Done.

The Phoenix Force commando dropped an incendiary on the cluttered desk that stood against one wall and left it sputtering. He was already on the sidewalk, stepping out into the street, before the first dark curl of smoke was visible inside the shop. If there were automatic fire alarms inside, he would be well clear of the area before firefighters could respond.

He checked the street for witnesses, kept moving with determined strides.

The Paris blitz had barely started, and he still had work to do.

CHAPTER SEVEN

All terrorists needed money, and they seldom had the luxury of trusting banks. If they were forced to flee at midnight, running for their lives, there was no time to make withdrawals or clean out a safe-deposit box. The wise guerrilla dealt in cash exclusively and kept it close at hand.

Amal al-Qadi was no fool in that regard, but he wasn't entirely covered, either. Someone knew the secret of his monetary stash, and he or she had spilled the information to Elise Dubois, from whom the information passed to Bolan's hands. He stood outside the block of flats on Rue Danton and counted windows, up and over from the entrance, checking for a light.

There, on the sixth floor, three flats over to his left. Someone was home, unless they left the lights on in their absence to deter potential burglars. Either way, he meant to have a look inside and see what he could do to hit the Spear of Allah where it counted, in the pocketbook.

He knew the way Amal al-Qadi's mind worked, without ever having met the man. His soldiers were expendable, their deaths anticipated as a normal cost of prosecuting a guerrilla war, and new recruits were always waiting in the wings to sacrifice themselves for this or that exalted cause. It was a different thing with money—critical for keeping up supplies of arms and ammunition, buying friends in hostile lands, securing hideouts and the like. Financial donors came and went, depending on tomorrow's headlines, the perceived success or failure of a given group. A major source of income for the Palestinians had disappeared when Russia and the East Bloc began to fall apart, each nation suddenly concerned with its domestic problems, rather than supporting terrorists around the world. Even Khaddafi and the leaders of Iran had grown more thrifty in the past few years, as oil embargoes and assorted problems in their own backyards cut back on funding for the "liberation armies" they had once supported without a second thought.

Some nations, such as Sudan, still came up with cash for Palestinian guerrillas, but the flow wasn't unlimited, and leaders like Amal al-Qadi or Hassan Jubayl were asked more often to account for what they spent, to show results before investments were renewed. A major loss hurt more these days than at any other time within the past ten years. It was the kind of pain that Bolan could appreciate, and he wasn't about to miss a chance to gouge his adversaries where it hurt the most.

The front door was unlocked, despite a sign outside restricting access to the building's tenants. Bolan checked out the lobby, bypassed the elevator and began to climb the stairs. Twelve flights, and he could feel it in his thighs before he reached his destination, peering down the dingy corridor on six.

The flat he wanted was positioned three doors down on the right. He stood outside the door and listened for a moment, picking up the sounds of a television from inside. Another glance to left and right confirmed he was alone, and Bolan brought the Uzi from underneath his jacket, muzzle heavy with the sound suppressor, a live round in the chamber as he thumbed off the safety.

There was no peephole in the door, and Bolan took a chance by knocking. Someone on the other side inquired as to what he wanted. The soldier muttered something in French, stepped back a pace and raised his submachine gun. As the question was repeated somewhat louder, he unleashed a burst that ripped the upper panel of the flimsy door to tatters, followed with a kick that slammed it back against the wall and bulled his way inside.

A dead man sprawled before him, leaking crimson on the threadbare carpet, his companion scrambling off the sofa, lunging for a handgun on the coffee table. Bolan almost let him reach it, squeezing off another burst when he was nearly there, the parabellum manglers chewing up his arm and shoulder, spinning him and dropping him across the low-slung table, crushing it beneath his weight.

Three steps put Bolan at his side. The Executioner reached down and turned the young man over, careful to avoid the blood still pumping from his shattered arm and shoulder.

"Where's the money?" Bolan asked, repeating it in French and Arabic to cover all the bases.

The young man's eyes were fading in and out of focus, glazed with pain, but he retained sufficient understanding to reply.

"*Fi hi-nehk,*" he said weakly, pointing with his good arm toward the bedroom.

Bolan found the young man's pistol and took it with him as he went to check the sleeping quarters. It was but a moment's work to turn out the dresser drawers, dumping laundry on the floor and little else before he tried the closet. Two suitcases stood packed and ready underneath a rack of hanging clothes. He opened both, found guns in one and bundled stacks of franc notes in the others.

The solidier left the hardware scattered, took the money with him and retreated through the living room. A glance in passing told him the young terrorist would be dead from loss of blood before an ambulance arrived, and he left the guy where he lay and headed out.

No one attempted to detain him as he walked back to the stairs and made his way down to the street. Someone had doubtless summoned the police, but the squad cars would be several minutes getting there, at least. By that time, Bolan would be well clear of the action, carrying at least a portion of Amal al-Qadi's war chest.

Bolan would have loved to see al-Qadi's face when

he received that news. In fact, the Executioner decided, he might call and break the news himself.

It was another way of turning up the heat, and Paris was about to sizzle.

Amal al-Qadi didn't know it yet, but he was on the verge of getting burned.

GARY MANNING PARKED the Audi four-door sedan in a narrow alley behind Rue de la Glacière. Two blocks west, the giant bulk of Ste. Anne's hospital dominated the Parisian skyline, many of its windows brightly lit now that purple dusk had fallen over the City of Lights.

Manning didn't regard the hospital's proximity as an omen. Rather, he considered it a simple fact of life. Those who survived the next few moments would have no great distance to travel in search of medical aid.

He double-checked his little Heckler & Koch MP-5 K submachine gun from force of habit rather than necessity. He was a bit of a perfectionist, particularly when his life was riding on the line, and Manning left nothing to chance. He wouldn't let himself become obsessive, though, and refused to check the Beretta 92-F in his shoulder holster, knowing that it had a live round in the chamber, with the safety off, the sound suppressor in place.

For all the good that it would do, he thought, frowning.

The job at hand didn't require much subtlety, once

he was past the first defensive cordon, and close enough to recognize his enemies and act accordingly.

The target was a combination nightclub and restaurant, C'est Magnifique, where Spear of Allah members and associates were known to pass their leisure time. As Muslim fundamentalists, most of them shied away from alcoholic beverages, though it wasn't a rule Amal al-Qadi rigidly enforced, except where clarity of mind was called for on a mission. Otherwise, the Palestinian guerrillas and their cronies ate, drank coffee by the gallon and spent time with any one of twenty-seven dancers working at the club. It was an open secret that the dancers—most of them, at least—were B-girls who would also make a run upstairs with any customer who showed the proper generosity and spirit of adventure.

As for ownership, Elise Dubois of Interpol had claimed al-Qadi was a silent partner in C'est Magnifique. He seldom visited the premises himself, but used his portion of the weekly profits for expenses such as payrolls, rent on other properties, the cost of weapons, ammunition and explosives in a seller's market. Any well-planned strike against the club would cost him dearly, both in cash and men.

The crucial phrase in that scenario would have to be well-planned, and Manning was intensely conscious of the short time he had to plot the strike before he made his move. No matter, it was in and out, the floor plan memorized from blueprints, no chance whatsoever of a careful search for hidden cash or evidence.

So what? he asked himself. The case wouldn't be

tried in court, regardless of the evidence available. Al-Qadi had been selected for indictment by the team at Stony Man, convicted in absentia by his own recorded words and deeds, the sentence affirmed on appeal by Hal Brognola and the Oval Office. Now all Manning had to do was carry out the judgment of the court.

He crossed the street and made his way along an alley on the east side of the club. A back door served the kitchen, and fire codes and common sense dictated that the door remain unlocked through business hours.

Manning stepped inside, the MP-5 K ready in his hand. He wasn't challenged on the threshold; racket emanating from the kitchen told him that the workers had their hands full, taking care of orders from the dining room. He passed them by and started for the main room of the club, where music and the rumble of conversation told him he would find his quarry.

Glancing through a door that opened on the left side of a well-appointed bar, he understood that there would be a problem separating members of the Spear from the civilians in the audience. It wasn't Manning's plan to spray the dining room at random, but he realized that innocents would be at risk once he had put the ball in play and his adversaries rose to respond.

Okay.

The best way to get everyone's attention was a short burst from the MP-5 K, shattering at least a dozen wine and liquor bottles shelved behind the bar. The jukebox kept on playing, deaf and blind to danger, but a pair of shapely dancers got the message, breaking for the wings with no thought for the bits of lacy costuming they left behind.

Some of the patrons broke and ran immediately, others dropping to the floor and flipping tables over as a shield, their drinks and dinners splashing on the floor. A few—it looked like four or five, all swarthy younger men—were drawing weapons, standing fast or seeking cover while they tried to find a target in the screaming chaos of the nightclub.

One of those who grabbed a weapon was the bartender, a few steps off to Manning's right. He pulled a sawed-off shotgun from somewhere beneath the bar, a sleek pump-action model holding six or seven rounds. Not that he needed them at that range. One squeeze of the trigger ought to do it, if he wasn't blind or stoned.

The scattergun was swinging into target acquisition when a burst from Manning's SMG ripped through the would-be shooter's chest and torso, dumping him a few yards backward from his starting place. The 12-gauge bellowed once, aimed at the ceiling, and unleashed a rain of buckshot-riddled acoustic tiles.

A Palestinian on Manning's left cut loose with a pistol as the Canadian swiveled back to face the room at large. One bullet whispered past his face and gouged a divot in the wall behind him, while another tugged at his sleeve. He caught the shooter with a rising burst of automatic fire that staggered him and spun him like a rag doll in the wind, his pistol glinting under the fluorescent lights as it was flung aside.

At least three other gunmen were unloading now,

forcing Manning back through the doorway to the dining room. He closed his eyes against a spray of plaster dust as bullets pocked the wall mere inches from his head, and suddenly he heard a sound of rushing footsteps from the direction of the kitchen.

As he spun in that direction, opening his eyes, the big Canadian spotted an Arab charging from his blind side. This one had no gun, but he was brandishing a heavy cleaver large enough to cancel Manning's ticket with a single blow. He held the cleaver poised to strike, and started to shout threats in Arabic.

The MP-5 K stuttered, cut the blade man's legs from under him and dropped him squirming on his face. The cleaver spun away from dying fingers, slid across the polished floor and came to rest against the wall, where Manning could have scooped it up with ease. No other ambush from the kitchen threatened immediate jeopardy, and he faced back toward the dining room, fishing in the outer pocket of his trench coat for a stun grenade.

The SAS and other hostage-rescue units called them "flash-bangs," built to blind, stun and deafen human targets in the kind of situation where a stand-up firefight maximized the lethal risk to innocent civilians. This one, in addition to the primary explosive charge, was packed with "stingers"—solid rubber balls the size of buckshot that provided extra knock-down power, bruising without risk of mortal injury.

Flash-bangs could kill, of course, if they went off directly in a subject's face, safer than a burst of automatic fire, no matter how well it was controlled.

Without a moment's hesitation, Manning yanked the flash-bang's safety pin and lobbed the grenade toward the spot where three young Arabs stood or crouched, unloading on him with a deadly rain of pistol fire.

He was prepared for the explosion, ducking back to put a wall between ground zero and himself, already moving as echoes died away. He found one member of the Spear still on his feet, but weaving like a drunkard, hands clasped to his ears, the gun discarded at his feet.

No matter. Manning nailed him with a short burst to the chest and spun to face the others, who were writhing on the floor. He finished them with two more bursts and left them there, no room for mercy in his mind or heart when he was caught up in the heat of battle.

Manning scanned the room in search of other enemies and came up empty. He stood his ground and shouted to the remaining patrons in French and English, warning them to leave at once. Retreating from the slaughterhouse, he dropped a small incendiary stick behind the bar, where pools of alcohol would give it ample fuel.

Outside, the night smelled fresh and clean, in spite of sidewalk urinals, industrial pollution, car exhaust and all the other smells that made Paris unique. A cool breeze helped remove the stench of gun smoke from his clothes.

But it wouldn't be long before he smelled the battle reek again, Manning thought. He was on a roll, the night was young and there were other targets waiting to be killed. Some who had started out that night with simple pleasure on their minds were in for a surprise.

And some of them, he knew, would never see another dawn.

AMAL AL-QADI SAT and listened as Hakim Rashad related details of the hearsay conversation, filling in the crucial gaps in information that had haunted him since earlier that afternoon, when unexpected violence had begun to chip away at his brigade in Paris. He had soldiers dead, the river warehouse and C'est Magnifique in smoking ruins and several hundred thousand francs deducted from the Spear of Allah's war chest by an unknown gunman.

He hadn't lived this long by trusting in coincidence. The slaughter in New Jersey, not two days earlier, had been the first suggestion of disaster, breathing down his neck with breath like fire. It had been close for him in the United States, almost the end, but by fleeing back to France, al-Qadi had believed that he was safe.

He had been wrong.

Rashad was one of those who liked Western women, taking full advantage of the Paris nightlife anytime he had a chance. One woman in particular had fascinated him for several months. Her name was Brigitte something, an exotic dancer who did most of her contortions in a supine posture if the price was right. Al-Qadi didn't approve, but he had more-important matters on his mind than whom his soldiers took to bed, as long as they were suitably discreet.

It was a fluke that he had learned of Brigitte's link

to the authorities. In fact, the girl herself had told Rashad, perhaps attempting to ingratiate herself and guarantee a stronger place in his affections. She was barking up the wrong tree, that one, but al-Qadi had encouraged her to maintain her position as a paid informant, dutifully reporting to her lover, imparting false material from time to time, when something critical was planned. Along the way, the terrorist leader had no doubts that the bitch had spilled much honest information to her contact—this Elise Dubois, from Interpol—but there was little he could do about it once the data had been filed. In his experience, Western women didn't have the sense to curb their tongues. Long years of too much freedom had led them to believe they were men's equals, prompting them to act accordingly.

No matter. She continued to report, and Rashad passed the word along. This very evening, Brigitte had been surprised by an emergency summons to meet her control, questioned about al-Qadi's recent movements and rumors of a feud between the Spear and other groups of Palestinian resistance fighters. By that time, the death toll was already mounting, members of his cadre being killed on sight by someone he couldn't identify.

"You say she asked specifically about Hamas and Jihad?" al-Qadi pressed Rashad.

"That's right. It seemed as if she were expecting trouble, as for one of them to challenge us."

"Perhaps."

Al-Qadi wondered. It could just as easily have been

a plant, subliminal suggestion of an explanation for the mayhem then already under way in Paris. What if the Americans had somehow traced him back to France and sought to punish him for his activities in the United States? Would they be bold and swift enough to mount a paramilitary strike this soon in Paris? Could the suggestive inquiry from Interpol be meant to throw him off his guard, prevent him from running down his assailants, perhaps induce him to retaliate against his fellow Palestinians instead?

It was a paranoid idea, but that didn't mean it was wrong. A lifetime in the trenches of his people's war with Israel and the West had taught al-Qadi to respect and cultivate a fair degree of paranoia.

It was better to be frightened of a shadow than to let the shadow creep up on your blind side, maybe kill you in your sleep.

Of course, those bastards from Hamas were capable of anything. It *could* be a coincidence, the raids in Paris coming close upon the heels of his debacle in America. If someone from Hamas or Jihad found out that he was in the States, it could have set them thinking, plotting to destroy his cadre, undermine al-Qadi's leadership while he was busy somewhere else. The cause of Palestine had been beset by rifts and private feuds from the beginning, hampered by persistent animosity between groups that competed for support and members in a hostile world. Sometimes he thought the Jewish tyrants would have been destroyed by now, if only Palestinians could manage to unite themselves behind a single leader who would not betray them, in the sniveling mode of Yasser Arafat, and lead them on to victory.

It hadn't happened yet, of course, and there were days when he believed it never would. At other times...

He caught his thoughts before they started drifting into abstract theory, brought his full attention back to what Hakim Rashad was saying. Whether Interpol had something solid on Hamas or was running interference for a vanguard of Americans, the only way to know for certain was to ask the source. Al-Qadi couldn't visit Interpol himself, couldn't browse through Dubois's files, but he could reach out for the woman who expressed such interest in his travels.

He could reach out for Elise Dubois.

It would be risky, granted. Any confrontation with authority was always perilous, but he would have to take the chance. If they could manage some discretion, nothing obvious, he reckoned they could pull it off without incurring too much damage in the process.

And it would be worth the risk if he learned something that would help him snare his enemies before they struck again.

"This woman, Brigitte, she can call for meetings, too, instead of waiting for a summons?"

He already knew the answer to that question, but he wanted confirmation from Rashad.

"She can."

"Then have her do so. She will tell her contact that she has new information. Something urgent, it should be. She does not trust the telephone, and she wants extra money. Yes?"

"I understand."

"Once she has made the call and fixed the meeting, you will terminate her," he instructed.

Rashad blinked, surprise and consternation showing on his face, but he didn't object. He knew the penalty for bucking orders in the Spear of Allah. He had seen such judgments executed at first hand, while standing close enough to smell and taste the end result.

"It shall be done," Rashad replied.

"Have soldiers waiting at the rendezvous when she arrives. Remember that we need her fit to talk, Hakim. No 'accidental' deaths, you understand?"

"Of course, Amal."

Al-Qadi could have reprimanded him for the familiarity, but in his flush of generosity he let it go. There was no point antagonizing the man at the moment, when his full attention should be focused on the task at hand. If there was any problem with the lift, some negligence on Rashad's part, al-Qadi would take the opportunity to punish him accordingly.

Meanwhile, eliminating Brigitte would prevent the proof of any link between Elise Dubois's abduction and the Spear of Allah. She wouldn't be left alive, and there would be no evidence for Interpol to use in tracking down her killers. Let the mystery remain unsolved, and if her bosses should suspect al-Qadi, why, so much the better, just as long as they couldn't prove their case in court.

The perfect crime, he knew, wasn't a total secret.

Rather, it was an event where the authorities knew those responsible but couldn't make the case. Such incidents were those that built a hard man's reputation, elevating him above the crowd of mundane killers, stickup men and terrorists who could be had for pocket change in any Third World country.

Either way—secure or known to men who couldn't prove it—the abduction and elimination of Elise Dubois was less important than finding out what information she possessed. With her assistance, he would identify his enemies and track them down, annihilate them while they were busy congratulating themselves for their early victories.

His turn was coming.

He could hardly wait.

CHAPTER EIGHT

The Walther WA2000 is a sniper's weapon par excellence. It measures 25.59 inches overall, from butt to muzzle, and weighs eighteen pounds with its ten-power Schmid & Bender telescopic sight attached, fully loaded with six rounds of .300 Winchester Magnum ammunition. Constructed in the classic bullpup design, with its detachable box magazine and gas-operated bolt mechanism behind the trigger group, the WA2000 features a free-floating barrel clamped at front and rear, fluted longitudinally for cooling purposes and to reduce vibrations when the piece is fired. A certified killer at five hundred yards, this night the Walther would be serving Bolan's needs at something like one-fifth of that range.

He crouched atop the flat roof of an old apartment building on Rue Cauchy. Across the street and half a block to the southwest, another block of flats showed lights at half the windows.

Bolan needed only one.

His target was the corner flat, fourth floor. Positioned three floors higher, as he was, he would be firing downward at an angle of some twenty-five degrees, over a range of barely one hundred yards. The flat was brightly lit, its curtains open wide. It was beyond the hardmen gathered there to think that anyone could find them, much less reach out from a distance to destroy them in their safehouse.

Live and learn.

He counted heads, came up with five men, one slightly older than the rest, who seemed to be in charge. There might be others Bolan couldn't see— somebody in the kitchen or the bathroom—but it made no difference for his purposes. If there was a survivor, he would only help to spread the word, the terror, through the Spear of Allah's ranks.

Their argument was heating up across the way, and Bolan had a fair idea of what they were discussing. All of them were wearing pistols, automatic weapons strewed around the small apartment in plain sight. It was the Palestinian equivalent of ''going to the mattresses,'' and Bolan reckoned each of them was vocalizing some theory as to the identity and motive of the gunmen who had lately killed their comrades.

Bolan wedged the rifle's stock against his shoulder, cheek against the rubber pad, and sighted through the scope. The profile of a shouting man sprang into sharp relief, appearing close enough that the Executioner could have counted pimples on his cheek. Adjusting for the bullet's drop across one hundred yards, he also thought about the window glass that the projectile would have to penetrate. It wouldn't be plate glass, as in an office window, but some measure of deflection was still possible. How much? It was impossible to say until he took his shot and witnessed the result.

His finger curled around the rifle's trigger, taking up the slack. Much of its recoil was absorbed by the gas-operated bolt, the first spent cartridge landing on the roof beside him even as the bullet struck downrange. He saw the window shatter, caught a crimson blur within the big scope's field of vision, and his target wobbled out of view. A short swing to the right found number two, before the Palestinians could grasp the near-decapitation of their comrade.

Two away, and Bolan saw his second round strike home, the skull of yet another Palestinian fighter bursting like a melon with a cherry bomb inside. The others had recovered somewhat, two men diving toward the floor, one lurching to his feet and fumbling with the pistol that he wore beneath his arm.

The shooter next.

A hot Winchester round punched through the standing Arab's chest and slammed him over backward, shoulders touching down before his buttocks, feet up in the air. It seemed to Bolan that his dying target got one shot off, angled toward the ceiling, but his gun's report was lost to Bolan, covered by the louder, closer sound of his own rifle.

There were at least two men still alive inside the flat, but Bolan could see neither one from where he was. He guessed that they were crawling out of range, too frightened to risk standing up within his line of sight, and that was fine. He had four bullets left before the sniper piece was empty, and he meant to use them well.

His next shot struck a smallish television on the far side of the room, its picture tube imploding with a crash. Round five took out a can of soda on the coffee table, spraying foam and liquid on the couch, the floor, one of his kills. Round six brought down a reproduction watercolor from the wall. His last shot found the telephone and scattered its component parts across the room.

All done.

He packed up swiftly, breaking down the Walther, stowing it beneath the top tray of a heavy toolbox for concealment. In his faded denim jumpsuit, Bolan guessed that he could pass for a repairman working late, but only if he cleared the roof before excited tenants came to check the source of gunfire.

Three more dead, and while he doubted whether any of them had been ranking members of the Spear, their loss would still be felt. More to the point, the desecration of their safehouse would be one more nagging problem for Amal al-Qadi to contend with as his time ran out.

The terrorist was as good as dead already.

It would simply take some time for him to get the word.

THE PHONE CALL from Brigitte, so soon after their last meeting, came as a complete surprise to Elise Dubois. She listened to the young woman, noted the undertone of anxiety in her voice and agreed to the clandestine meeting when the woman insisted that she couldn't trust her "new, important" information to the telephone.

Before she left her flat on Rue Lacroix, Dubois went to her closet and retrieved the Model D MAB semiautomatic pistol that she kept there on a shelf. Her job with Interpol permitted her to carry firearms, but she rarely took the pistol out unless she was convinced some threat to life and limb was imminent. Tonight the tone of Brigitte's voice, the violence sputtering throughout the city, made Dubois decide she would be better safe than sorry.

Part of her uneasiness, she realized, stemmed from her own involvement in the violence that had shaken Paris in the past few hours. She thought of Mike Belasko, teamed with other men she hadn't met, attacking Palestinian guerrillas on the streets and in their hangouts, even in their homes. She had supplied the names and addresses for many of those targets, and the paranoia that resulted from participation in such mayhem, even once removed, had gotten her nerves on edge.

Brigitte desired to meet her near the Louison Bobet Stadium, three and a half miles due west of the apartment. She drove the Citroën north on Avenue de Clichy, picked up Boulevard Berthier north of the railroad tracks and followed it back south and west, until she reached the Avenue de la Porte d'Asnières. From there, it was a short drive to the stadium, a left turn on Rue d'Alsace, and she began to watch out for the nightclub Brigitte had selected for their rendezvous.

Dubois wouldn't be going in. These meetings were a risk to all concerned, best carried out in darkness, where she had at least some chance to know if they were being shadowed. Public places, not too crowded, with restricted avenues of access. All her training went to one objective: minimizing contact with the enemy unless she could control a given situation from the start.

Brigitte had no car of her own, relying on the subway or on taxicabs to carry her around the city. Sometimes she caught rides with friends, or with her lover from the Spear of Allah, but she wouldn't call on anyone she knew this night. If this new information was so critical and so explosive that it couldn't wait, Brigitte was wise enough to watch her back and guard against discovery.

Or was she?

It would take only one slip, one careless word to let her lover and his fellow "freedom fighters" know she had betrayed them. There was no doubt what the penalty would be. Dubois had known it from the start, took pains to warn Brigitte about the risk while trying not to scare her off. It was a wicked game, but the job required a constant flow of information, and the Interpol agent obtained it where she could.

Brigitte was several minutes late—the usual pattern—when Dubois saw two men walking toward her Citroën from the far side of the parking lot. She couldn't see their faces in the shadows, but she recognized their type—tough guys, intent on trouble.

She withdrew the pistol from her handbag, flicked

off the safety and thumbed back the hammer. It might
be nothing, two young men intent on finding liquor
and some willing women, but in that case, why were
they approaching *her* instead of moving toward the
club?

She reached for the ignition key, the pistol in her
left hand. As the Citroën's engine came to life, the
two men started running toward her, one of them grappling with an obstinate zipper, trying to reach inside
his jacket.

For a gun?

She wasted no time finding out, but rather put the
car in motion, aiming through her open window as she
fired a shot, deliberately aiming high. Twin muzzle-
flashes marked the answer from her enemies, and now
she could see more men unloading from a car across
the street, already sprinting toward the parking lot in
hopes of trapping her.

An image of Brigitte flashed in her mind, and she
couldn't decide if she should offer up a silent prayer
or curse the girl for tricking her. There was no time,
as shadow figures hurried to surround her car and cut
her off from access to the street.

As if mere flesh and bone could stop a car with a
determined driver at the wheel.

Dubois pressed down on the accelerator, fired another shot at her original pursuers as the Citroën began
to move. She was rewarded with a cry of pain, the
sight of one man stumbling, going down. His partner
ducked and dodged behind the nearest car for cover,

while the others hesitated in the midst of their advance.

The time was now or never. She could run or stand and fight, but hesitation was the surest way to lose her life.

She switched on the headlights, saw one of her male assailants raise an arm to shield his eyes. The moment's hesitation cost him dearly, as she stood on the accelerator, clipping him at speed and rolling him across the hood. His skull smacked hard against the windshield, leaving cracks, a brilliant smear of blood, before he rolled away and vanished off the starboard side.

Another heartbeat saw her through the cordon, bouncing roughly over sidewalk, curb, into the street. She turned hard left, glanced back in time to see bright headlights flaring in her rearview mirror.

She had cleared one hurdle, but she wasn't safe. Not yet.

Elise Dubois was running for her life.

HAKIM RASHAD CURSED bitterly and slapped his driver's shoulder as the Citroën burst from the parking lot, two bodies sprawling in its wake, the other members of his team disoriented, running aimlessly around the parking lot. Two of them fired shots at the speeding car, but they were both too late. The woman had a lead, and she was on the run.

"Get after her, you idiot!"

The driver muttered something unintelligible, revving up his engine, smoking rubber as he pulled out from the curb. The Citroën had a full block's lead on Rue d'Alsace, northbound toward Rue Victor Hugo, where the woman could turn either left or right, thereby avoiding a dead end. A right-hand turn would bring her into more-congested traffic, with a greater likelihood of meeting a police car on the way.

Rashad couldn't permit that. He was pledged to bring the woman in for questioning, and he was worried that the price of failure might be more than he could bear. Amal al-Qadi had been adamant about his need to grill the woman, find out what she knew of the various attacks upon the Spear of Allah. It appeared to be the only way they could effectively defend themselves. If Rashad failed in his assignment...

No! He wouldn't fail. He had already killed Brigitte, as ordered by al-Qadi, delivered her remains to a disposal team for dumping in the Seine. The bitch from Interpol was almost in his hands, dumb luck permitting her to break the cordon he had thrown up to contain her. Still, she wouldn't get away.

She was a woman, after all. How could she hope to best so many men?

Rashad reached backward, snapped his fingers and took the submachine gun Zafir handed him. It was an Uzi, loaded, with the safety off. He took care to keep his finger off the trigger as he held it in his lap.

It would require some skill to stop the Citroën without inflicting damage on its driver, but Rashad was confident that he could do the job. He had been trained extensively with automatic weapons, had completed numerous guerrilla missions and assassinations for the cause. Who better to disable the getaway car and capture the woman alive?

Besides, he was in charge. Success or failure would reflect on him, regardless of who pulled the trigger, made the snatch. He knew that his life was riding on the line. He wouldn't trust it in another's hands, when those he picked to help him had already failed in one attempt.

He saw the Citroën's brake lights winking crimson, held his breath and waited. She was turning left! The silly bitch had chosen to avoid the heart of Paris with its crowded boulevards. But why? Did she believe she could outrun him, lose him in a maze of residential streets?

Rashad was smiling for the first time since his meeting with Amal al-Qadi. He would have her soon. The prospect of success brought heat to his loins. He cranked his window down and felt the rush of wind against his face, rippling his hair. The Uzi in his hands seemed feather light.

"I need a clear shot at the back tires," he said.

Boulus Lufti, driving, grunted at him like a caveman, concentrating on the road. He gave the steering wheel a subtle tug, and Rashad felt them drifting slightly to the left, across the center line. When he leaned out the window, dark eyes squinting in the rush of wind, he had the Citroën in his sights.

Another moment...

Now!

He held down the Uzi's trigger, tried to fire low and lost it when the Audi struck a pothole in the pavement.

It only took an instant, with the Uzi spewing bullets at a cyclic rate of 750 rounds per minute, and he saw the Citroën's rear window shatter, raining pebbled safety glass.

Inside the other car, he saw the woman jerk, lurch forward, as if she were trying to kiss the dashboard. The Citroën swerved across the center line and met a truck coming from the opposite direction. Rashad bellowed, reaching for the Audi's steering wheel, but Lufti beat him to it, jerking to the right and down a side street as the Citroën and truck came together with a rending crash.

"Go back!" Rashad demanded, twisting in his seat to see the jumbled wreckage. "She may still—"

The Citroën's fuel tank detonated with a flash, the fireball towering above both car and truck, spreading to engulf them both. Rashad felt as if someone had punched him hard in the stomach, driving the air from his lungs, leaving him to choke on the foul taste of bile.

There was no living through a blast like that, he realized.

The bitch from Interpol was dead.

Rashad could only wonder whether he would soon join her.

THE NIGHT WAS COOL and damp as McCarter walked back to his car, slid in behind the wheel and reached inside the glove compartment for the radio-remote transmitter. At the far end of the block, on Rue Raspail, the self-serve storage facility was brightly lit but presently unguarded.

He had seen to that.

The single lookout had been a Palestinian. He had been leafing through a nudie magazine, appreciating some of France's natural resources, when McCarter scaled the fence and tracked him down, came up behind him with a wire garrote and finished him in seconds flat.

The man's body still reposed inside his guard shack, with the skin-zine open on his lap. McCarter hoped that he had taken pleasant thoughts along with him to Hell, since they would have to last him for a while.

But then again, he didn't really give a damn.

The guard was dead because he chose the losing side, went out to play with monsters who thought nothing of destroying helpless innocents to make a point and snag a headline. He would make the news himself tomorrow, even though he wouldn't be around to read the copy. It was more than he had any right to ask for in a world that he and his associates had terrorized and pillaged for the past three years.

Elise Dubois had fingered the facility as being owned and operated by a front man for the Spear of Allah. It was a supply dump, plain and simple, where the Palestinians stashed everything from guns and ammunition to spare vehicles, hot license plates and gear intended for their comrades killing Jews in other countries. They had access to the storage sheds at any time of day or night, while other would-be clients were politely asked to sign a waiting list, assured that they would get a call as soon as space became available.

McCarter reckoned he could help with that right now.

After disposing of the lookout, he had spent the next ten minutes planting plastique charges at strategic points around the complex, arming detonators that would go off simultaneously once he beamed the signal from the trigger mechanism in his hand. The nearby businesses would lose some window glass, perhaps some paint and plaster, but the damage would be minimal, and it couldn't be helped.

McCarter rolled down his window, although he knew it wasn't necessary. Why take chances? With a faint smile on his face, he aimed the master detonator at his target, thumbed down the single button, and watched the place go up in roiling flames. The noise and shock wave reached him half a second later, made him grimace, but at least the intervening distance spared him from the heat.

He switched on the Volvo's engine and put the car in gear, already rolling through a U-turn by the time a secondary blast tore through the rubble, ammunition going up as hungry flames took hold. He still had three more targets on his list before he met Bolan and Manning to discuss phase two, and he was running right on schedule. Three more stops, another hour at the most, and he would see his friends once more, regroup, move on.

He switched on the Volvo's radio, the last strains of a popular love song fading into news at the top of the hour. McCarter's French was fair, so he grasped enough of the commentary to know the young woman was discussing a surprise outbreak of violent incidents in Paris. Some streets and public buildings were named, with a rough casualty figure tacked on at the end: twenty dead and counting, all apparently Arabs.

The announcer segued to another story, giving details of a tragic car accident. Rue Victor Hugo was the scene, and at least two people were dead. McCarter's ears perked up when the announcer said that several witnesses reported gunmen firing at another car before it crashed head-on into a tanker hauling gasoline. His heart skipped when he heard one of the dead named as Elise Dubois.

It never crossed McCarter's mind that such a name wouldn't be rare in France. The timing and circumstances combined to make him sure it had to be Bolan's Interpol contact.

Did Bolan know? What difference would it make?

McCarter started to look for a public telephone. They each had beepers, with the numbers memorized, for linking up in the event of an emergency.

Like now.

If Bolan had already heard the news, he would be thinking of retaliation, plotting out the moves.

McCarter spied a telephone and swung his car in to the curb, fumbling coins from his pocket as he moved toward the booth.

It might not make a difference, but he had to pass the word along. The Spear of Allah had been marked for trouble from the start, but there would be no quarter now.

Amal al-Qadi and his private army had just leaped from the frying pan into the very heart of the fire. And someone, somewhere, was about to get burned.

THEY MET at an all-night café on Rue Tronchet, three men with somber faces sculpted out of stone. McCarter got there first, with Bolan close behind him. Manning had the farthest drive, and they were sipping coffee by the time he got there, pulling up a chair on Bolan's left. The waitress took his order, wondered how three foreigners would tip when none of them was having food, and left them to their low-pitched conversation.

"I checked it out through Hal's connection," Bolan said. "Her supervisor didn't feel like talking, but he shared enough. Two men, at least, were chasing her and shooting at the car. We don't know yet if she was hit or startled into swerving. Either way, the tanker came along. That's it."

His tone was leaden, nothing to suggest the white-hot rage that had engulfed him when he heard McCarter's news. That kind of anger was a suicidal form of self-indulgence, quick to get a soldier killed before he could accomplish anything. Such rage had powered Bolan's early moves against the Mafia long years ago, but he had learned to harness fury, channel it against his enemies while letting logic rule his mind and heart.

"It had to be the Spear," McCarter said.

"Who else?" Manning asked.

"There's no point guessing how they broke her cover," Bolan stated. "She had at least one pair of eyes inside the Spear. Somebody may have bagged her contact, or the contact may have sold her out. It doesn't matter now."

"Al-Qadi?" McCarter asked.

"Move him up the list," the Executioner replied. "I should have gone for him first thing instead of starting at the bottom."

"Not your fault," Manning said.

"No? Suppose you're right. It still comes out the same."

"So, we can wrap it up," McCarter said, "and catch a flight out by this time tomorrow, right?"

"I hope so," Bolan answered, "but we won't be heading for the States."

"How's that?"

"Amal al-Qadi is a field commander. Take him out, and in another week or so, Hassan Jubayl will have a new replacement on the job. Before we break the Spear, we have another stop to make."

"That wouldn't be Sudan, by any chance?" McCarter asked.

"It's where the action is," Bolan said. "Stony Man has been getting bulletins from State for the past two years or so, about Sudan's covert support for terrorism. Money and munitions, sanctuary, training bases—hell, the only thing covert about it is that the military junta in Khartoum denying what the world already knows. We have no leverage with the government to speak of. They hate Israel more than they love U.S. dollars."

"Someone needs to hit them with a wake-up call," McCarter said.

"My thought, exactly," Bolan answered. "But we have to finish cleaning up in Paris first."

"What are we waiting for?" Manning asked.

"Nothing," the Executioner said. "Nothing at all."

CHAPTER NINE

The relocation to Puteaux, across the Seine from Paris proper, was a common-sense precaution in Amal al-Qadi's view. The house off Rue Bellini had been rented months earlier, but never occupied. He was prepared to bet his life that Interpol knew nothing of his interest in the property, but even so, it was a temporary hideout. He would wait a day or two, to let some measure of the heat subside, before he made his final break.

Hakim Rashad had failed him, dared not bring the news in person after he had killed the woman he was sent to kidnap, bringing more heat down upon the Spear of Allah in the process. He was hiding at the moment, with his driver and another member of the hit team he had led to failure, cringing in the dark somewhere, afraid of what al-Qadi would do when they next met.

Rashad was right to be afraid. His weakness for Western women was the least of his problems now. Whatever happened to Amal al-Qadi and the Spear from that point on, the fault lay as much with Rashad as with their enemies. If not for him, his gross incompetence, al-Qadi might know the name and the number of their adversaries. He might be en route to kill them even now, instead of hiding like a cockroach when the kitchen lights come on.

No matter. He would leave France for a while, explain the problem to Hassan Jubayl—but cautiously; his tantrums were notorious and deadly. Later on, when Interpol and the police in Paris had grown tired of looking for the woman's killer, he could come back and rebuild his cadre on French soil.

He toyed with the idea of giving them Rashad, but first he had to find out where the bastard was. Another time, perhaps, when he had found a safer place to hide, had time to do some research on the problem, ask around among his friends. Rashad would surface— there was nowhere else for him to go—and when he did, Amal al-Qadi would be waiting for him.

But now he needed rest. The past day had exhausted him, despite the fact that he had barely stirred out of his room. Fierce concentration did that, waiting for the next blow from an unknown enemy who obviously meant to see him dead or caged. In one way, it was a relief to be in transit, even running. He was doing something for a change, instead of sitting on his hands and waiting for his enemies to strike again.

Al-Qadi wouldn't give up on learning who they were and why they stalked him. He would never truly rest until he had revenge for his humiliation—on Hakim Rashad, and on the strangers who had killed so many of his men in Paris.

Vengeance would be sweet, but he couldn't enjoy

it from a grave or from a prison cell. His first priority was safety, and he wasn't ashamed of hiding when it served his purpose.

Al-Qadi kicked off his shoes and sat on the bed. He was the only soldier in the house who had a bedroom to himself. The rest were packed in like sardines, nineteen of them with all their gear, but they would cope. This night, perhaps another day or two, and they would have more breathing room.

Algeria looked better all the time.

He wouldn't go back to Sudan just yet. It would be better if he kept some space between Jubayl and himself, at least until the man had time to understand the difficulties he had faced in Paris. Once their leader's fury had subsided, once he had a chance to think things over, calm himself a bit, there would be ample time for them to meet. Al-Qadi would apologize, because it was expected of him. He didn't mind groveling a bit, but he wasn't prepared to give his life for someone else's error.

Not this time.

He was the best of Jubayl's field commanders, and they both knew that to be a fact of life. His services were required; he was essential to the Spear of Allah.

He would survive because he had to, and if that meant al-Qadi was forced to hide, so be it. There were worse things in the world.

Like death.

THE HOUSE off Rue Bellini stood alone, its closest neighbor fifty yards away. The grounds were fenced in stone, a touch of privacy its builder would have been hard-pressed to find in Paris, even thirty years ago. It was an average dwelling, neither large nor small, with something like two acres of surrounding property, light shrubbery, scattered trees.

The tip had come from Interpol, one last communication with Elise Dubois's superior before that link was severed for all time. His voice was bitter on the telephone, at least subconsciously aware of how the information he provided would be used. He blamed the Stony Man team for what had happened to Dubois, and blamed himself for getting her involved. If he could expiate some portion of that guilt by giving up her killers to the kind of justice never seen in court, he would cooperate this one last time.

They made a drive-by, the three men crowded into Bolan's Fiat, checking out the target as they passed. The wall, trees, darkness, all conspired to hide the house from view, but they would have no trouble finding it once they were past the fence.

And past the guards.

It was a given that Amal al-Qadi would surround himself with guns, no matter what he planned to do or where he meant to go from here. Destroying him meant taking out his bodyguards, as well, and that was fine. It skewed the odds, of course, but it was nothing Bolan and his comrades hadn't faced before.

He dropped off McCarter behind the house, left Manning one block east and drove back to the starting point he had selected for himself, due west. A silent, shaded street provided all the cover he could hope for as he left the Fiat, stripped down to the blacksuit underneath his clothes and buckled on his military webbing.

Would the man at Interpol somehow ensure that the police stayed clear while Bolan and his commandos went to work? Or would he see a chance to bag them all, let the Executioner waste the Palestinians before a riot squad closed in to drop the net? It was impossible to say for sure, but Bolan guessed the man would stand aside and let the chips fall as they might. His conscience would instruct him that he owed Elise Dubois that much, at least.

Or maybe not.

He concentrated on the moment as he went over the wall and landed in a combat crouch, with shrubbery around him, lending cover in the night. His Uzi had the custom sound suppressor attached, a nod toward stealth that would be necessary in the early stages of their probe, while they were working toward the house. A premature alarm would ruin everything, tip off the guards and give Amal al-Qadi time to bolt, perhaps. They had to spot him before they took him down, and Bolan offered up a silent prayer to all the gods of war that nothing would go wrong.

He met the first guard forty seconds after he had scaled the wall. He was bored, still not convinced—despite his comrades who had died that day—that there was any danger to himself. The AK-47 slung across one shoulder, muzzle down, might just as easily have been a tennis racket or a bag of golf clubs for the way he handled it. He stood the watch because he had been ordered to, but clearly never thought he would be called upon to fight.

Not here. Not now.

The Executioner came up behind him, didn't risk his Uzi in the darkness when he had a better way. The dagger fit his hand as if designed for him alone. He stepped up close behind the man, clapped a hand across his mouth and drew his head back in a single motion, drew the six-inch blade across his throat and let him go.

If executed properly, death from a severed windpipe was the next best-thing to instantaneous. The lungs were emptied in a rush, while blood spouted from the jugular and the carotid arteries. Surprise and shock provided the anesthetic; blood loss to the brain and interruption of the target's capability to breathe or speak prevented a warning to his fellows. Bolan caught the dead man's collar, eased him gently to the ground and left him there.

One down. How many left to go?

There was but one way to find out.

He sheathed his dagger, gripped the Uzi SMG in steady hands and kept on moving toward the house.

McCARTER'S SUBMACHINE GUN was an MP-5 SD-3, the Heckler & Koch model with a factory-standard sound suppressor and telescoping stock. He wore the sling across one shoulder, but he kept a firm grip on the weapon as he made his way through darkness toward the house Amal al-Qadi and his soldiers of the Spear had occupied. His footsteps on the grass seemed loud enough to wake the dead, but that was his imagination, revved up with adrenaline. In fact, he knew that barring chance encounters or sophisticated motion sensors, he should make it to the target unobserved.

It was the chance-encounter part that almost did him in.

The sentry had been out of sight, behind a tree, then he suddenly appeared, as if from nowhere, stepping into McCarter's path. Their eyes locked for a heartbeat, and the man plainly wasn't sure if he should shout a warning to his friends or grab the AK-47 he had slung across his back.

He never had the time for either one.

McCarter's weapon stuttered, sounding like a muffled sneeze, the short burst fired at point-blank range. Three rounds punched through the Arab's skinny chest, a fourth slug opening his throat and silencing the shout that would have brought his comrades on the run. The dead man toppled over backward in a boneless sprawl, and McCarter rushed to him, dragging him back under cover in the shadow of a spreading oak.

It wasn't guaranteed security, of course, since somebody might discover him immediately. But McCarter didn't need much time, only enough to reach the house, pick out the guards and try to find a way inside.

Another ninety seconds got him there. The south side of the house included glass doors fronting a patio some fifteen feet across, redbricks laid down in tidy rows, with green grass sprouting in between. There was a kettle-drum-style barbecue on rollers, two chaise longues, and a wooden table. In other circumstances, the layout might have suggested domestic bliss, but this night, with fresh blood on his hands, all McCarter could see was flimsy cover and potential obstacles.

Pale draperies were drawn across the sliding doors, which meant McCarter couldn't see inside, but no one in the house could see him, either. Cautiously, alert to any lookouts coming at him from the rear, he crossed the patio and tried the door.

It moved an inch or so before he took his hand away.

Whoever was in charge of nailing down security needed a sound whipping for that kind of oversight. Unless, of course, it was a trap.

McCarter thought about it, crouching in the darkness, and he finally dismissed the thought. Anyone with an ounce of common sense would certainly have left the curtains open if he meant to watch the doors and patio from a position in the house. And leaving doors unlocked was simpleminded foolishness if you could spot the enemy outside and take him down before he breached your last line of defense.

It had to be an error, then, and he didn't mind taking full advantage of it—cautiously, of course. Because he couldn't see into the room beyond those doors, a possibility remained that someone could be waiting for him, even with the lights off. Not a sniper, possibly, but even someone dozing on the couch could get McCarter killed if he was fast enough or loud enough to draw the necessary reinforcements in a rush.

He turned off his thoughts and proceeded.

The Briton used one arm to slide the glass door

open, while his other gripped the silenced SMG. The door, meanwhile, was anything but silent, grating on its runners where accumulated dust and grit had built up over time. McCarter clinched his teeth and waited for a shout—or worse, a shot—to tell him he had been discovered. Stopping when the gap had opened to a decent eighteen inches, he maintained his crouch and waited sixty seconds, listening for any sounds of movement in the room beyond.

And came up empty.

Reaching out, McCarter used his free hand to draw back the curtains and peered into the darkened room. It was some kind of parlor. There was no sign of life from his position, though a light was visible some distance beyond the only door in sight, and faint voices reached his ears.

Waddling underneath the curtain, McCarter was at his most vulnerable, easy prey for any gunner who spotted him and hosed the doorway down with automatic fire. But he made it past the curtains, leaving the door ajar as a convenient exit, just in case.

There was a risk in that, as he would find in everything from that point on. A passing sentry might glance over, notice that the door was open, raise a hue and cry or come in on McCarter's blind side, shooting first and asking questions afterward. No end of dangers on a job like this, but he would have to take them as they came and leave the fruitless worrying to someone else.

A last sweep of the room with narrowed eyes, and he was moving toward the door. He was halfway there when suddenly the lights blazed on. McCarter blinked, saw two young Arabs standing in the doorway, one man with his hand still poised beside the light switch. Both were armed with pistols tucked into their waistbands, and the second shooter had an Ingram submachine gun dangling from a shoulder strap.

The Palestinians stared at McCarter for an endless moment, and he stared back.

And then they started shooting, all at once.

AMAL AL-QADI BOLTED upright on his bed, the too familiar sound of automatic weapons ringing in his hears. The noise came from downstairs, inside the house. That ruled out any feeble hope of trigger-happy guards on the perimeter.

It should have been impossible for anyone to get that far, with all the sentries he had posted. Scrambling out of bed, al-Qadi cursed his soldiers and their ancestors. He would have cheerfully exterminated them himself had there been time.

But there wasn't.

Since no one else could seem to handle it, al-Qadi would have to save himself.

A Mini-Uzi and his favorite Makarov were waiting on the nightstand, next to the alarm clock. He stood and tucked the pistol underneath his belt. The compact SMG felt good, an old, familiar friend. A spare clip for the stuttergun went in a pocket of his trousers, on the left.

What now?

They had briefly discussed evacuation of the safehouse, but al-Qadi hadn't believed his enemies could find him here, so there had been no drills or exercises. One gate, on the north side of the property, but getting out was only part of it. Success meant getting out alive, minimizing friendly casualties and leaving nothing that would help police to track them down.

If worse came to worst, al-Qadi would be satisfied to save himself. It was the prime directive for a situation such as this: protect your leader with your life.

One of his fighters barged into the bedroom while al-Qadi was putting on his shoes. The young man stared at him but said nothing; the sounds of battle echoing from downstairs conveyed the message loud and clear.

"How many?"

"Sir?" The young man stared at him blankly, as if he had forgotten how to think.

"How many?"

"I don't know. The shooting started, and I came...I..."

"Enough!" Al-Qadi crossed the room and stood before him, close enough that they were almost touching. "You will come with me. We have no time to waste."

"Yes, sir."

The young man—Amer was his name—seemed grateful that he didn't have to come up with a plan of action on his own. It was no problem taking orders, but he wasn't up to plotting at the moment. Likewise, while he was a proved killer, he wasn't accustomed to the kind of situation where his prey returned fire, much less seizing the initiative to track him down and raid his hideout in the middle of the night.

"We have to reach the cars," al-Qadi said, spelling out the obvious. "Are you prepared to fight?"

"Yes, sir!"

He didn't ask the young man if he was prepared to die. Such risks were automatic when a man joined the Spear of Allah, but reminders of that fact were detrimental to morale.

"You lead."

The young man hesitated for a heartbeat, nodded, then stepped out into the hallway, facing the stairs. The sounds of battle were intensified as they proceeded, one step at a time. It was no more than twenty feet from al-Qadi's bedroom doorway to the stairs, but it felt like a mile. One part of him wanted to rush downstairs, confront his enemies and mow them down, be done with it. Another part—the part that kept him breathing—shied away from contact with the unknown enemy, preferring stealth to make his getaway.

But how?

The layout of the house was such that he could never hope to sneak downstairs and out while men were fighting in the parlor, dining room and kitchen. They were bound to see him, one side or the other, and the fact of his desertion under fire would set a bad example for his men, even as it moved his enemies to follow him, redouble their attempts to cut him off and bring him down.

There had to be a better way.

Amer paused on the landing, turned to face his

leader, frowning in uncertainty. A stray round hit the banister and ricocheted into the wall. The hardman jumped visibly and took a firmer grip on his Kalashnikov.

"Go down and see what's happening," al-Qadi commanded.

"Down?"

"You heard me."

"Yes, sir."

Amer obeyed with obvious reluctance, taking one step at a time, almost in slow motion, moving in a semicrouch, his automatic rifle thrust in front of him. His legs would be in view of those below him when he made it halfway down the stairs. Al-Qadi stood and watched him from the landing, waiting, ready.

When the first round struck Amer, it slammed him sideways, hard against the wall, and bent him double at the waist. His AK-47 started blasting aimlessly as more rounds peppered him, his body jerking with the impact of successive bullets.

Al-Qadi had seen enough. He turned and sprinted back in the direction of his bedroom, through the open doorway, straight across the room to stand before the window. From the second floor, it was a drop of twelve or thirteen feet, he guessed. Cut that in two, if he was dangling from the windowsill with arms extended, overhead.

Six feet was nothing if he landed properly, if no one saw him bailing out. He jerked open the bedroom window and began to scramble through.

IT HIT THE FAN well before Manning reached the house. Three sentries had convened to smoke and talk directly in his path, and while he guessed that he could work his way around them, no doubt find a better way to go while they were otherwise engaged, it meant more time, and he was on a pressing schedule as it was. Conversely, if he simply stood and waited for them to disperse, he wasn't going anywhere at all.

The big Canadian had made up his mind to proceed and try to circumvent the Arabs, when he heard the muffled sound of gunfire coming from the house. It captured the sentries' attention instantly. Three cigarettes were discarded in a heartbeat, three Kalashnikovs pulled free of shoulder straps and cocked as one. They started toward the house, and Manning knew it was now or never. If he let them go, they would be coming in behind one of his friends, the shift in odds perhaps enough to finish Bolan or McCarter.

Manning broke from cover, closing from their blind side. He gave no warning, didn't spare a thought for chivalry, as he cut loose from twenty feet and raked them with a waist-high burst from left to right. They went down thrashing on the grass, one triggering a short burst from his AK-47 as he fell.

The Phoenix Force commando kept firing, giving each one of them a few more rounds to keep him down. It was a brutal business, but he saw it through, pausing long enough to pick up a Kalashnikov and add it to his arsenal before he took off sprinting toward the house.

All hell broke loose before he got there, automatic

weapons blasting from outside the house, as well as inside, sentries running aimlessly across the lawn, unloading at shadows. Manning wondered how long it would be before a neighbor called the police, but he didn't linger on the thought. The sooner they were finished with their business here, the sooner they could leave.

A burst of automatic fire from Manning's left chewed up the ground behind him, and he spun in that direction, dropping to a combat crouch. His adversary was a man dressed in denim and a turtleneck, his face twisted in a snarl as he lined up another shot.

The captured AK-47 bucked in Manning's grip, unleashing half a dozen rounds that slammed his human target over backward, sprawling on the grass. He waited long enough to guarantee the Arab wasn't rising, then turned toward the house and put his feet in motion.

They were definitely running short of time, no matter how you sliced it. Once the first shots echoed through that calm suburban neighborhood, the doomsday numbers had been running. If police arrived before they finished, Manning knew there would be hell to pay.

The house was right in front of him; the way was clear. Some lights were showing in the downstairs windows, and the sounds of combat issued from inside. He had no view of Bolan or McCarter, but it was a safe bet that the Arab gunmen weren't shooting one another.

Whatever happened to his friends, he had a job to

do, and he would know when it was finished. They had come to kill Amal al-Qadi and as many of his soldiers as they could, before their work was interrupted by policemen or an act of God. He had the mug shot of his quarry memorized and wouldn't rest until he saw that visage on a corpse, unless the walkie-talkie called him off beforehand, with the word that someone else had made the tag.

Meanwhile, the battle lay in front of him, inside the safehouse chosen by the Spear of Allah as its refuge.

FIVE BODIES ON THE GRASS marked Bolan's progress from the tree line to the southwest corner of the house. Inside, he heard all kinds of racket: weapons going off, glass breaking, bullets ripping plaster, gouging furniture, male voices cursing, shouting questions back and forth in Arabic. He didn't know which of his Phoenix Force comrades was inside, and at the moment it didn't matter. He had to help—and more importantly, he had to find Amal al-Qadi, finish it this time before the terrorist could wriggle through another trap.

Most of the noise was coming from an area he took to be the living room or parlor, on the south side of the house. It was McCarter's side, but Manning could be with him, joining in the scrap, as far as Bolan knew. It would be suicide to blunder in on that, get caught up in the cross fire, but he didn't plan to stay outside and listen to the battle from a distance, either.

Cautiously but quickly, Bolan started to circle the house, alert to any sentries who were still outside and covering the grounds. He sought a window, any means of access to the house that wouldn't make all kinds of noise and bring the heavies down on top of him before he took a step inside.

And he was at the northwest corner of the house, about to leave his cover once again, when something heavy, man-size, dropped into the shrubbery some thirty feet in front of him. He watched and waited for a moment, saw a figure scrambling to its feet, and held his submachine gun ready, finger on the trigger.

It was one of al-Qadi's men, bailing out before the ship went down. Some members of the Spear, it seemed, weren't fanatically committed to the notion of a martyr's death in God's service.

He willed the stranger to turn toward him.

Against all odds, the prowler did turn, half his face in shadow, while the other half was clearly visible by moonlight. Bolan felt as if someone had punched him in the gut.

Amal al-Qadi stood there in the flesh, about to stage another getaway.

The Executioner watched al-Qadi break in the direction of a low, detached garage. The doors were open, showing two cars parked inside, while three more generic four-doors were lined up in the driveway. Wheels for twenty men or more, if they were open to a little crowding. If the troop ran true to form, from Jersey, there were keys in the ignition, gas tanks filled and ready for a hasty flight.

Bolan left his cover, following al-Qadi toward the cars. He watched for other hostile guns, but there were none in evidence. The terrorist had reached the nearest car, was opening the driver's door, when Bolan called his name. The man turned back to face him, gaping in surprise, but he recovered swiftly, bringing up the stubby SMG he carried in one hand. The muzzle winked at Bolan, bullets whining past him as he hit a crouch and let the Uzi rip from a range of thirty feet.

Al-Qadi staggered, slumping backward, and sprawled across the front seat of the car that was supposed to carry him to safety. Bolan hit him with another six or seven rounds for safety's sake, then turned back toward the house.

The sounds of battle had abated there, as well. He raised the compact walkie-talkie to his lips and thumbed down the transmitter button.

"This is Striker. Do you read me?"

"Phoenix One, affirmative," McCarter's voice came back.

"Make that unanimous," Manning added.

Bolan felt a warm flush of relief before he pressed the button again and said, "The joker's out. Fall back. Regroup as planned, on me."

"Regrouping," McCarter said.

"On my way," Manning chimed in.

Bolan left al-Qadi where he was without a backward glance. That portion of the job was finished, but he wasn't done yet. You didn't stop a snake by breaking off one of its fangs. The Spear of Allah was alive and well, led by Hassan Jubayl. It was time to fly again, Bolan thought, all the way to the enemy's backyard.

CHAPTER TEN

Hassan Jubayl didn't enjoy his monthly visits to Khartoum. They were an exercise in forced humility, designed specifically to let him know who was in charge of military matters in Sudan. The Spear of Allah was a welcome guest, if unacknowledged to the world at large, but there were always games to play, egos to stroke along the way.

His contact in the ruling military junta was Marawi Bol, a colonel designated as liaison to the Spear by his superiors. He was an arrogant, self-righteous bastard, like most other soldiers of Hassan Jubayl's acquaintance who had risen to exalted posts in government. Libya's Moammar Khaddafi was among the worst, but Sudanese officials had learned much about pomposity since they seized power in 1989. Almost a decade of civil war had been a mixed blessing for the junta, depriving it of absolute control in the Christian south of the country, while providing an excellent excuse for the expansion of martial law, with ample profiteering on the side.

Jubayl could understand such men. He knew the way their minds worked, always looking for some personal advantage in the midst of war, exploiting their own people at every turn. They had no honor, but they *did* have money, arms and ammunition in abundance—all the things Jubayl required to prosecute his war.

And most importantly, they hated Jews.

Each month he drove to Khartoum, surrounded by his bodyguards, to meet Marawi Bol. Each time they met, he promised new attacks on Israel and its Western allies, begged for cash and hardware that would keep the Spear of Allah alive as a fighting force. Bol enjoyed the game, and the five percent he skimmed from every government donation to the Spear. Jubayl had made him wealthy in the past two years, but he was still required to come with hat in hand and play the game.

This time, he was distracted by the damage he had recently sustained in France. Amal al-Qadi was among the casualties, and while he might have brought it on himself, Jubayl would miss his daring, almost reckless attitude, which had been so successful in the field.

Now he was gone. Jubayl would have to comb the ranks for a replacement, knowing in advance that he had no one with the same dynamic qualities available. And in the meantime, he would have to ponder what al-Qadi's elimination meant, if it posed any further danger to the Spear of Allah in Sudan.

He wouldn't raise that subject with Bol just yet. There was no point disturbing him, disrupting their precarious relationship, unless some concrete need arose.

The car pulled up outside Bol's villa, on the out-skirts of Khartoum. The guards outside expected him, but they went through the motions anyway, insisting that Jubayl's protectors must remain outside the house, with men to watch them, since they carried weapons. It amused him that the soldiers seemed to think he might be planning to assassinate their master. While it would have been a pleasure to pump bullets through the colonel's sneering face, it also would have been a self-defeating gesture in the circumstances, when the Spear of Allah needed friends in uniform, with bulging pocketbooks.

Jubayl had no fear for his safety at the colonel's home. Bol wasn't above eliminating enemies—or friends, if he saw profit in it—but their common hatred of Israelis and the favors that the terrorist leader had done from time to time on Bol's behalf had kept their relationship civil. The same couldn't be said for other Palestinian commando groups, which had worn out their welcome in Sudan by putting on defiant attitudes, refusing—as the Americans would say—to kiss the junta's fat collective ass.

For sanctuary, cash and arms, Hassan Jubayl would pucker up on cue, no problem. It wasn't that he lacked pride, but rather that he understood the politics of practicality. There would be time enough to flaunt his pride when they had triumphed in their struggle. Time enough to pay back any insults he had suffered for the cause in darker days.

For now, though, he was one part soldier, one part diplomat, required to play the role of houseguest in another's country, operating under rules dictated by his host.

The cruel sun made him squint, despite his mirrored sunglasses, as he stepped from the car and followed two young men in khaki uniforms to the house. Jubayl was practicing his smile, prepared to bow and scrape if necessary, to maintain his loose alliance with the ruling junta in Khartoum.

For now, while they could help him.

Later, he assured himself, there would be time to put things right.

"Too bad we can't just walk across," McCarter said.

"Nobody's tried that for a while," the Executioner replied. "You wouldn't have an angel in your kit bag, I suppose?"

"Not bloody likely," McCarter replied.

They were fifty miles due south of Mecca, on the shore of the Red Sea. Behind them, looming in the night, the Al-Hijaz Asir mountain range resembled an immense, sleeping dragon, its bulk separating the narrow coastal plain from Saudi Arabia's vast inland desert. Opposite the point where Bolan and his Phoenix Force comrades stood, 150 miles due west, the coastline of Sudan was still invisible.

"Let's do it, if we're going," Manning said.

Bolan found a handle on the Zodiac inflatable and lifted with the others, walked it to the water's edge and floated it, the water lukewarm through his trousers as he waded several paces out to sea. They climbed aboard, one at a time, and Manning fired up the engine with one yank on the cord. It caught immediately, and he held the tiller firm as they began to buck the gentle breakers, heading out to sea.

Two days in Saudi, getting ready for the move, collecting battlefield intelligence from contract eyes across the water, gathering and testing out their gear, had Bolan's nerve on edge. He knew the stall could work to their advantage in the long run, lull Jubayl and company into believing they were safe, despite the raids in France. They had considered jumping in, a HALO—high altitude, low opening—drop in the desert, well below Khartoum, but finally opted for a boat ride, setting off at midnight, to arrive between Sawakin and Tawkar at 3:00 a.m. or thereabouts.

It was a risky move, whichever way they played it, but the U.S. military presence in Saudi helped when it came to picking up equipment, getting ready for the lift. The hardware they were carrying was mostly Russian, captured from Iraqi troops in Desert Storm, with nothing but their bodies to betray the presence of a Western strike team in Sudan if anything went wrong. In that event, they would be disavowed across the board, an understanding that prevailed on any mission overseas.

No one in Washington or at the Farm expected Bolan or the men of Phoenix Force to let themselves be caged alive.

The mission was simplicity itself, at least on paper. They would cross the water, land and make connections with a contract agent in Sudan, proceed from there to pound the Spear of Allah like the righteous wrath of God. Along the way, if they saw any opportunities to give the terrorist-supporting government a swift kick in the ass, it would be Bolan's pleasure to oblige. A simple in-and-out, four days at the outside. Beyond that, they would run short of supplies and ammunition, find themselves reduced to living off the land—a land where millions were in danger of starvation, epidemics or annihilation by the warring sides in a protracted civil war.

The way it broke down in Sudan, twelve northern provinces were dominated by the Arabs who made up some forty percent of the country's population, hardline Muslim fundamentalists who held the whip hand in the ruling military junta. The remainder of Sudan's population was black, mostly Christians or animists, heavily concentrated in three large southern provinces, which had rebelled against the Muslim government in 1988.

The fighting had continued ever since, through coups and so-called free elections in Khartoum, while famine and disease killed tens of thousands in the countryside. A massive drought in 1988 killed some three hundred thousand Sudanese, and the junta grudgingly accepted aid from the United Nations three years later, but relief was terminated when the endless civil war made distribution of supplies a hopeless, suicidal task.

Observers from Amnesty International had recently accused Sudan's government of practicing ethnic cleansing against black tribes in the south, and the UN

Human Rights Commission published a list of official abuses in 1994, without effecting any change or even drawing a reaction from the junta in Khartoum. When not engaged in killing its minorities, the military government was prone to glare at Israel from a distance, funding terrorist attacks against the Jewish state and any Western nation who supported Israel in its struggle to survive. The Spear of Allah was the latest in a series of guerrilla bands that had been welcomed in Sudan. It wouldn't be the last.

But it would be the most embarrassing if Bolan had his way.

Thus far, the junta in Khartoum had publicly denied all links to terrorism, scoffing at satellite photographs of guerrilla training camps in the desert, denouncing intelligence reports of terrorist activity in Sudan as "base lies" and "Zionist slander." Until now, no effort had been made outside of diplomatic channels to convince Khartoum that its support for terrorism was a grave mistake.

That was about to change.

The White House had approved Bolan's decision to attack the Spear of Allah in Sudan. It was an operation that couldn't be formally acknowledged, but it had the covert go-ahead, passed on from Pennsylvania Avenue to Hal Brognola and the team at Stony Man. From there, the word was beamed by satellite to Bolan and his Phoenix Force comrades in Saudi. They were on their mark and ready to proceed when they received the green light from the States. Now they were on their way, dark water foaming out behind the Zodiac, their enemies somewhere ahead of them, concealed by darkness, hopefully unconscious of grim death approaching from the east.

Whatever happened in the next few hours or days, they would be giving it their all. Nobody had to promise Bolan that; he knew it going in, from prior experience with Manning and McCarter. Even if their hearts were elsewhere, with the other members of their strike force, half a world away, they would perform as skilled professionals, because it was the only way they knew to play the game.

He checked his watch and settled back to scan the dark horizon for patrol boats, aircraft, any signs of light or life that could betray them prematurely to their enemies. If they were spotted on the water, they would fight—and doubtless die—before they let themselves be taken prisoner. There was no quarter asked or given in this war against the savages who preyed upon mankind.

By now, Hassan Jubayl should have convinced himself that Paris was an aberration, nothing to suggest a broader, more aggressive push against the Spear of Allah. He wouldn't relax, of course—real hunters never did—but he would slowly, surely, let his thoughts move on to other targets, other enemies.

It would be all the edge they needed, if they played their cards right. And if they didn't, well, there was ample room for three more shallow graves where they were going. Three men could disappear without a trace, and only those they left behind would know where they had gone.

But they wouldn't go down without a fight. The Executioner had pledged that to himself, an oath in blood.

His enemies could take that promise with them to the grave.

SIRAJ AL-MAHDI DIDN'T like the waiting. He felt terribly exposed, despite the darkness and the isolation of the point where he was scheduled to receive his visitors. His cover was intact, as far as he could tell, but it was always risky in Sudan for one who worked against the military junta, spying for the CIA.

They paid him well enough, of course. By local standards, he would be a wealthy man if he could ever dare to spend the money. Some of it was hidden at his home, in Shandi, while the rest was banked in Liechtenstein. Another year, he told himself, and if the junta still held power in Khartoum, he would desert his post, forsake his homeland and find somewhere else to spend his life in peace.

But first he had to make it through this night, the days that followed, working with the strangers who would come to kill Hassan Jubayl.

He understood that none of them were Arabs, much less Sudanese, which meant that he would have to hide them out, direct them to their targets, maybe intercede with local contacts if they needed backup weapons or supplies. He had been compensated for the risk to some extent already—a deposit to his Liechtenstein account—and there would be more money coming if he helped them pull off the mission successfully. If they should fail, al-Mahdi would have no recourse except for prayers to God, begging for his own salvation from interrogators and a military firing squad.

He checked his pocket watch: 2:45 a.m. He had another fifteen minutes if they arrived on time. Al-Mahdi had come ahead of schedule, thinking that they might be early, and he worried now that it had been the wrong decision. A patrol might come along at any moment and demand to know why he was loitering along the beach. He was ready for them—he had raised the hood on his Land Rover, loosened one of the distributor cables to keep it from starting—and was prepared to plead ignorance if an army patrol stopped to "help" him. In that event, he would move on and return as soon as possible, when they were gone.

It was a decent plan, all things considered, but his nerves were still on edge. He knew the methods used by state interrogators when their curiosity had been aroused. A number of his personal acquaintances had disappeared from military custody, while others had emerged alive but broken in their hearts and souls. Siraj al-Mahdi's only brother had been executed, back in 1990, on a trumped-up charge. That incident, beyond the rest of what he witnessed every day, had driven him to help the CIA spy on his country.

It wasn't *his* government, no matter if the men in uniform were Muslims, like himself. Al-Mahdi was no friend of Israel or the West, but it appalled him when the junta practiced genocide against his fellow countrymen. Religious differences aside, he knew that

Muslim Arabs suffered daily from the same brutality inflicted on the blacks down south. The junta cared for power more than anything. Now foreign terrorists had been invited to pitch camp throughout the countryside, their presence and the crimes they plotted in Sudan a constant shame to al-Mahdi and his fellow country-men.

At first he thought the blinking light well out to sea was an illusion. Worse, it crossed his mind that some-thing might have gone awry, that a patrol boat could be lying out there, winking at him, waiting for the coded response that would seal his fate.

He shook off his apprehension, palmed his flashlight and pressed the button with his thumb. Two short, one long, two short. The other light flashed back at him, perhaps a hundred yards offshore. Two more short flashes from his own light, and the Sudanese jogged down the beach to meet the strangers who could get him killed.

[?] [?] [?] [?] [?]

CHAPTER ELEVEN

The tough part had been choosing where to start. Hassan Jubayl wasn't headquartered in Khartoum, but many of his troops and front men operated from the capital, and so Khartoum appeared to be the logical selection. Bolan had considered working as a team, but finally decided they could cover more ground in a shorter time, while minimizing danger to themselves, if he and his two Phoenix Force comrades operated independently to blitz their hit list in Khartoum.

Sudan was one of those peculiar nations with two capitals. Khartoum, with something less than half a million residents, was the country's executive capital, while legislative business was conducted in nearby Omdurman. Siraj al-Mahdi had provided them with names, addresses, everything they needed to get the ball rolling, but the accuracy of his field intelligence would be an unknown quantity until they tested it by fire.

Beginning now.

Twelve hours in the country, and he stood outside a dingy tavern on a filthy side street, breathing in the odors of manure and urine, sweat and misery. The sun wouldn't go down for several hours yet, but Bolan had already waited long enough to find his enemies and hit them with a wake-up call.

The tavern's name was painted on a cracked and fading stucco wall in Arabic. It was illegible to Bolan, but his contact had told him that it read April Wine. The touch of poetry seemed out of place in those surroundings, but it didn't really matter what they called the establishment. It was enough to know that gunmen from the Spear of Allah killed time there, between their stints at training, missions to the world outside and other martial chores. On any given day, al-Mahdi said, between one half and two-thirds of the paying customers at April Wine were die-hard members of the Spear.

Which left the task of separating them from innocent civilians, but Bolan guessed that he could handle that with no great difficulty. He would go in raising hell, assume that anyone who tried to kill him was the enemy and act accordingly.

He wore a baggy short-sleeved shirt as a concession to the baking heat, the square-cut tails outside his pants to cover the Beretta pistol in his waistband toward the back. His folding-stock Kalashnikov was in the bulky shopping bag he carried, standard baggage in Khartoum for those few tourists who were bold or foolhardy enough to brave the climate, hostile atmosphere toward Westerners and the long-running civil war. They had considered wearing native garb, employing stain to darken hands and faces, but the plan was finally discarded as requiring too much busywork for minimal results.

Besides, this way survivors who remembered him would spread the word. Hassan Jubayl would know that he was being hunted by a foreign stranger. With any luck at all, that knowledge just might rattle him, provoke the chief guerrilla into making critical mistakes.

Bolan crossed the narrow street and stepped through the tavern's entrance into smoky darkness. There was native music playing from an ancient set of speakers, while a chubby girl in harem garb worked on the dance of seven veils. She still had three or four veils left to go when Bolan entered and removed his automatic rifle from the shopping bag. She saw it coming, screamed and made a dive in the direction of the bar, her flight more graceful than the dance she had been struggling to perform.

He fired a short burst toward the ceiling, chopping two blades off a sluggish fan that barely stirred the tavern's rancid atmosphere. A glance around the place had shown him half a dozen men, two on their own, the others grouped together at a table on his left. When Bolan opened fire, both loners hit the floor and stayed there, while the quartet flipped their table over, using it for cover, each man reaching for a hidden gun.

He swiveled the Kalashnikov to face them, squeezing off another, longer burst that caught one rising from a crouch and punched him over backward, swept along from there to pock the table with a line of bullet holes and tag another gunman squatting to the left.

Behind the table, one of Bolan's two surviving adversaries yelped in pain, the other popping up to fire a hasty shot in the Executioner's general direction.

It was all he needed, ready with the AK as his target came in view. A short precision burst ripped through the gunner's throat and lower face, spun him and dropped him facedown on the grungy floor.

And that left one.

He was prepared to leave the wounded hardman where he was, a witness who could feed the rumor mill, but fear or desperation brought the young man out from under cover, firing as he rose. One of his hasty bullets zinged past Bolan's face, not bad for reckless shooting, but it wasn't good enough. The AK-47 stuttered one more time, and Bolan saw his target stagger toward the bar, collapsing halfway there to rise no more.

He bent to retrieve the shopping bag, concealed his rifle and retreated from the slaughterhouse.

Round one, but he had far to go before he heard the last bell in Sudan. With any luck at all, he would survive.

He thought about his comrades, wished them well and moved off toward his second target of the afternoon.

IT SHOULDN'T BE SUPPOSED that Muslim law, enforced by troops in uniform, was any more successful at eradicating crime than Western statutes. Punishments were often more severe—the amputation of a thief's hand, for example, or castration for a first-time sex offender who would likely get probation in the States—but Third World law-enforcement personnel were known for their corruption, laziness, brutality and whimsical approach toward justice. Laws forbidding prostitution in the Middle East, for instance, were ignored in much the same way narcotics statutes in Colombia or Mexico. Baksheesh, the cash "gratuity" that had so much in common with *mordida* in the Western Hemisphere, would solve a host of problems on the spot, before handcuffs and booking documents came into play.

It came as no great shock to Gary Manning, then, when he discovered that the first stop on his hit list was a whorehouse. Technically illegal in Khartoum, as everywhere throughout Sudan, the brothel—and perhaps a hundred others like it—was protected from police harassment by the bribes its owner calculated as a flat percentage of the weekly take. Those common men who craved a harem of their own but hardly earned enough for the support of one wife could forget their problems for an hour or two, at fairly reasonable rates. A tourist would pay more, of course, with prices scaled to fit the pallor of his skin, but even so the cost was trifling when compared to prices in the States or Canada.

This brothel was a square three-story building, windowless, and ten minutes from the heart of town on foot. It didn't advertise, had no need for publicity, since its patrons were lured by word of mouth. A major draw was the variety of women housed therein— some Africans, some Asians, with a nubile European or Australian every now and then. No one cared how the women were procured, whether they were sold by starving parents or abducted from the streets of Amsterdam, as long as they performed. Hashish and heroin helped break down their inhibitions, while shame and threats of violence from their masters did the rest. Sudan was listed in a number of reports on female slavery filed with the United Nations, but the government professed to see no problem, casually dismissing the reports as racist lies.

The men who patronized this brothel might suspect its owner's mode of operation, but few would have guessed his driving motive. Ali Nasir wasn't a simple panderer, by any means. In fact, he was a dedicated member of the Spear, whose profits helped support guerrillas at a dozen training camps and in the field. If he derived a certain pleasure from his chosen business on the side, it was a sweet fringe benefit, his just reward from God for a job well done.

A stranger couldn't simply walk in off the street and order sex to go at Ali Nasir's establishment. A first-time client needed references to keep up the standards and ward off problems from the several watchdog agencies who circulated pamphlets and petitions carping on the scourge of modern slavery. It could have been arranged for Gary Manning to present himself in style, receive a tour of the place, but he preferred to crash the party on his own, save time and thus eliminate the need for middlemen who might betray him to the enemy.

There was a back door to the place, unlocked for easy access to a row of rusting trash cans in the alley.

Manning went in with his pistol drawn, a stubby sound suppressor attached, his trouser pockets heavy with grenades. There was no guard to stop him as he paused a moment, waiting for his eyes to make the shift from glaring sunlight to the brothel's murky atmosphere, proceeding cautiously when he was confident that he could handle anything that came his way.

One of the brothel's women was the first to meet him, dark and slender, with a glazed expression in her eyes that could have been hashish or simple hopelessness. The gauzy shift she wore was clearly not designed for modesty.

"Where's your boss?" he asked her, spitting out the phrase in Arabic that he had memorized to help him find the man in charge.

She blinked at Manning, spent a moment staring at his gun, then pointed toward the stairs. He didn't understand a word of her response, but he got the message anyway: upstairs.

He left the woman rooted where she stood, watching him go. If she was going to betray him with a warning cry, he thought, it would be soon. When Manning reached the second floor without a sound behind him, he decided that the lady had to be anxious for her keeper to receive a surprise.

He checked the second floor in haste and found nothing that resembled office space, although many of the doors were closed, with sound effects behind them that assured him they were occupied by working girls. He climbed the last two flights of stairs, had almost reached the third-floor landing when a chunky figure loomed above him, shock and sudden anger mingling on the swarthy face.

The man was reaching for some kind of weapon worn behind his back when Manning shot him in the chest. Two silenced rounds at point-blank range switched off the life-light in the target's eyes before he toppled and hit the carpet with a solid thud.

It was a quiet kill, all things considered, and his quarry in the nearby office cubicle apparently suspected nothing as grim death advanced to meet him. Manning found the office door ajar. He stepped inside to cover two men seated at an ancient wooden desk, one counting money while the other scribbled figures in a spiral notebook.

"Greetings, gents."

They gaped at Manning with the look of bovines bound for slaughter, slack jawed in surprise, the older of them blinking rapidly behind his steel-rimmed bifocals. His hand was inching toward the top drawer on his right when Manning shot him in the forehead, spattering the wall behind him with a clot of gray and crimson.

Pivoting, he caught the younger man half-risen from his chair, his gun hand frozen in its progress toward the holster worn beneath his baggy linen shirt.

"You might as well," Manning said, putting on a smile.

He spoke in English, but his tone conveyed the message loud and clear. The young man whimpered, digging for his weapon, vaulting backward as two parabellum manglers opened up his chest.

Still nothing from the other rooms along the hall, and Manning reckoned he had dealt with all the household staff. He palmed a fragmentation grenade, released the safety pin and lobbed the bomb through the office doorway as he made his exit, moving toward the stairs.

"Danger!" he shouted in Arabic, as he ran downstairs.

The blast behind him emphasized the warning, plaster dust cascading down on his head before he reached the second floor. He heard some women screaming as he passed their rooms, then saw the same one waiting for him at the bottom of the stairs. A smile was in place, and she made no attempt to stop him as he passed her, headed for the alley out in back.

"Thank you," she said in her language, and Manning didn't need a translator for that one.

He nodded as he reached the door and made his way outside.

The blaze of sunlight dazzled him, but he didn't slow down. There was no time to waste. He still had other stops to make before he could regroup with Bolan and McCarter. Other targets begged for a taste of justice long deferred. He might not reach them all, but he would do his best.

SIRAJ AL-MAHDI WONDERED if he had made a critical mistake when he agreed to help these Western strangers in their plot against the Spear of Allah. It had been exciting at the outset, something very different from his normal dealings with the CIA. Most times, he won-

PLAY THE "LUCKY 7" SLOT MACHINE GAME!

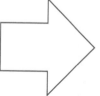

NO COST! NO OBLIGATION TO BUY!
NO PURCHASE NECESSARY!

PLAY "LUCKY 7"
AND GET FIVE FREE GIFTS...

HOW TO PLAY:

1. With a coin, carefully scratch off the silver area at the right. Then check the claim chart to see what we have for you—FREE BOOKS and a gift—ALL YOURS! ALL FREE!

2. Send back this card and you'll get hot-off-the-press Gold Eagle books, never before published. These books have a total cover price of $18.50. But THEY ARE TOTALLY FREE, even the shipping will be at our expense!

3. There's no catch. You're under no obligation to buy anything. We charge nothing—ZERO—for your first shipment. And you don't have to make any minimum number of purchases—not even one!

4. The fact is thousands of readers enjoy receiving books by mail from the Gold Eagle Reader Service™. They like the convenience of home delivery... they like getting the best new novels before they're available in stores... and they love our discount prices!

5. We hope that after receiving your free books you'll want to remain a subscriber. But the choice is yours—to continue or cancel, anytime at all! So why not take us up on our invitation, with no risk of any kind. You'll be glad you did!

SURPRISE MYSTERY GIFT!
IT CAN BE YOURS <u>FREE</u> WHEN
YOU PLAY "LUCKY 7".

PLAY "LUCKY 7"

Just scratch off the silver box with a coin.
Then check below to see the gifts you get.

YES! I have scratched off the silver area above. Please send me all the gifts for which I qualify. I understand I am under no obligation to purchase any books, as explained on the back and on the opposite page.

164 CIM CCNF
(U-M-B-09/97)

NAME

ADDRESS   APT.

CITY   STATE   ZIP

 **WORTH FOUR FREE BOOKS AND A FREE SURPRISE GIFT**

 **WORTH FOUR FREE BOOKS**

 **WORTH THREE FREE BOOKS**

WORTH TWO FREE BOOKS

Offer limited to one per household and not valid to present subscribers.
All orders subject to approval.

THE GOLD EAGLE READER SERVICE: HERE'S HOW IT WORKS

Accepting free books places you under no obligation to buy anything. You may keep the books and gift and return the shipping statement marked "cancel". If you do not cancel, about a month later we will send you four additional novels, and bill you just $15.80—that's a saving of 15% off the cover price of all four books! And there's no extra charge for shipping! You may cancel at any time, but if you choose to continue, every other month we'll send you four more books, which you may either purchase at the discount price…or return to us and cancel your subscription.

*Terms and prices subject to change without notice. Sales tax applicable in N.Y.

If offer card is missing, write to: Gold Eagle Reader Service, 3010 Walden Ave, P.O. Box 1867, Buffalo, NY 14240-1867

BUSINESS REPLY MAIL

FIRST-CLASS MAIL   PERMIT NO. 717   BUFFALO, NY

POSTAGE WILL BE PAID BY ADDRESSEE

GOLD EAGLE READER SERVICE
3010 WALDEN AVE
PO BOX 1867
BUFFALO NY 14240-9952

NO POSTAGE
NECESSARY
IF MAILED
IN THE
UNITED STATES

dered if the information he provided to his contacts even reached America, or whether someone in the Company took time to read it prior to filing it away. The money wasn't bad, all things considered, but he never had a solid feeling of accomplishment, of doing anything to change life in his homeland, where the people kept on dying from starvation and disease, torture and executions, day by day.

There had been nothing like this in the past, where he could see results almost at once, in action on the streets. It was a heady rush at first, but then reality set in. Al-Mahdi understood that he had placed himself at greater risk than ever in the past. If anyone found out what he had done—was doing—with the three white strangers, he could only pray for swift and relatively painless death.

But in the meantime, he had work to do.

Three strangers in Sudan couldn't hope to proceed against the Spear of Allah on their own. Al-Mahdi had tried to make them understand the situation, how Hassan Jubayl had close friends in the junta, men who hated Israel with the passion most reserved for loving wives or mistresses. Sudan exported cotton and gum arabic—of which it was the principal supplier for the world at large—and funneled money into military hardware while its people starved by the thousands. It was the largest country in Africa, more than one-fourth the size of the United States, but barely five percent of that land was arable. The junta didn't care, because its members and supporters owned that five percent. If others—southern blacks, especially—died off from hunger or disease, it saved the army time and money that would otherwise be spent in killing them on sight.

Siraj al-Mahdi was a Muslim, but his private readings of the great Koran did not instruct him to annihilate his fellow man because of race or creed. He wondered, sometimes, what the rulers of his country were frightened of, if they believed in God and were confident that he was on their side. Why couldn't *he* take care of any nations *he* despised, without recruiting young fanatics to plant bombs, strafe children in their classrooms, snipe at aged men and women on their way to market? What was wrong with God, that he needed men—and men like these, of all he had to choose from—to complete his dirty work?

A major flaw in all religions, al-Mahdi thought, was the persistent need of men to cite divine authority for selfish deeds. You want to steal land from your neighbor, take his wife and children, maybe kill him in his sleep and burn his home? First you should have a "holy vision" and declare that God decreed it should be so. When you were done, a simple prayer of thanks would wipe the slate and leave you ready to begin a new campaign.

It was a cynic's view of life, al-Mahdi realized, but he had seen enough in thirty-seven years to understand the ways of power, greed and politics. Men trampled others underfoot because they could; it was analogous to striking poses for a mirror, gloating over how your muscles swelled beneath the skin. How many body-builders could resist the urge to show their strength in public, demonstrate their physical perfection to a world of lesser men and women?

Politics and war were much the same. Not one man in a thousand was content to work behind the scenes, pull strings from hiding and let others take the public credit for his deeds. What was the point in having power if you couldn't flaunt it, bending peasants to your will?

Al-Mahdi understood that he was doing much the same thing. He had a bit of influence, albeit tiny, through his contact with the CIA, and he had used that influence to bring three strangers from the West to kill some of the people he despised. It hadn't happened *quite* that way, but close enough. No matter who conceived the notion, it came out the same.

Unless someone revealed his secret and got him killed.

The best way he could think of to prevent that was to smooth the way as much as possible for his mysterious associates. Right now, they needed targets: names, addresses, anything at all. Al-Mahdi was scouring his brain for further information on the Spear, resisting the temptation to include the names of certain private adversaries on his hit list.

It was risky business, that. It took only one contact or informant to betray him, and the men who would be coming for him in that case had long since purged themselves of mercy. Sudanese interrogators or the Spear, it made no difference in the end. Before they finished with him, he would long for death, tell anything he knew and then some, making stories up if necessary to escape the pain.

The worst part had been starting in Khartoum. If they were fighting somewhere in the desert wasteland of his country, then al-Mahdi would have less reason for the fear he felt inside. Discovery and torture, leading ultimately to his death, wouldn't be foremost on his mind. Three men could run amok out there, get lost forever in a firefight or a sandstorm, and the finger wouldn't point back to Siraj al-Mahdi. In the city, though, with troops and gunmen from the Spear at every turn, there was a greater likelihood that someone would be captured, forced to spill his guts, as the Americans would say. He couldn't expect the Westerners to hold their tongues and suffer endlessly on his behalf, nor were the three of them his only weak points in Khartoum. Al-Mahdi dealt with others on a daily basis, and while none of them knew he was working for the CIA—his queries were couched in general terms—he knew that any one of them could go to the authorities with vague suspicion, and suspicion was enough to get him executed in Sudan.

He thought again that it was time for him to bail out, take cash on hand and flee to Liechtenstein, retire from cloak-and-dagger work before he stepped across some line he could not see and wound up in a cage, condemned to die.

But he couldn't go yet. The strangers needed him, and he had pledged himself to help them. Not for money, though he would be paid, but rather for his country, for himself. Where honor was involved, Siraj

al-Mahdi told himself that profit—even personal survival—took the back seat to a man's performance of
his duty.

This wasn't about the money in his numbered bank
account, and it wasn't about the fear that ate him up
inside. It was about the debt he owed to his ancestors,
to himself.

Siraj al-Mahdi couldn't run.

Not yet, while he had work to do.

McCARTER FOUND a squad of soldiers waiting for him
when he spotted his first target, two blocks straight
ahead. The small house wasn't much to look at—a
square stucco box, its tiny windows barred with black
wrought iron—but the army clearly found it worth
protecting, to the tune of half a dozen soldiers on the
street. Inside, if he wasn't misled, a captain in the
Spear of Allah lived with his mistress and two or three
friends.

McCarter weighed the odds, deciding he could take
the soldiers if he wanted to, surprise them, mow them
down. It would be sloppy, granted, bound to raise
alarms within the house, but he could go from there,
try breaking in somehow to finish off the job.

His orders were another matter, though. He was
supposed to hit the Palestinians and keep on hitting
them until their cadre in Khartoum was finished. Killing soldiers on the street, regardless of their link to
terrorism and the guilt of those who gave them their
assignment, would be more destructive to his cause
than helpful. It would mobilize the army in a flash,

force members of the ruling junta to strike back with everything they had, and that could only jeopardize the chance of reaching out to tag Hassan Jubayl.

Reluctantly McCarter scratched the target from his list, at least for now. He walked back to his rental car and drove for fifteen minutes through the narrow, twisting streets, where beggars jostled street vendors for elbow room. There were five targets on his list, and scrubbing one didn't mean he was giving up, by any means.

He found the second, motored past and parked his car three blocks downrange. It seemed a long walk back, McCarter feeling out of place, as if all eyes were focused on his back the moment that he passed a group of locals in the street. He had no reason to believe that any of them would attempt to interfere with him this evening, and he was prepared to deal with any opposition that arose, but it was still an eerie, fish-out-of-water sensation, moving through the shadows toward his target, carrying his AK-47 in a bulky shoulder bag.

His destination was the storefront office of a tabloid newspaper the Spear of Allah published weekly, bearing tales of Israeli atrocities and courageous Arab resistance in Palestine. They called their rag *Saheeh*—*"The Truth"*—and while McCarter didn't give a damn what anybody wrote or read, the office was a well-known hangout for Jubayl's commandos, thus a target worth his time.

Two of the thugs in question waited for him, lounging on the steps outside the office as McCarter closed the gap to half a block, his right hand slipping casually into the shoulder bag. One of them saw him coming and nudged his comrade. The two of them stood, concerned or curious at the appearance of a pale-skinned stranger in the neighborhood. Their khaki shirts weren't tucked in, tails hanging loose to cover pistols in their waistbands. One of them—the nearer shooter—eased one hand underneath his shirt to find the weapon hidden there.

McCarter gave them points for readiness, but it wouldn't be good enough. He thumbed off the AK-47's safety, a live round waiting in the chamber, and he fired the first, short burst one-handed, making no attempt to draw his weapon from the bag. His bullets shredded canvas fabric, scorched it with the muzzle-flash, his target jerking, collapsing as the first rounds struck him in the chest.

The Briton brought up his free hand to steady the Kalashnikov as he kept firing, staggering the second gunman with a burst from fifteen feet, blood spouting from the wounds that opened in his hip, chest, throat and face.

McCarter sprinted for the office doorway, hurdling prostrate bodies as he ripped the AK-47 from its smoking bag. He cleared the threshold, met a young man rising from behind a desk immediately to his left, a shiny automatic pistol in his hand, and dropped him with a 3-round burst at point-blank range.

They had the presses running in the back room, but gunfire drowned out the racket, alerting two more members of the Spear who had been busy cranking out next week's edition. They rushed to meet

McCarter, more testosterone than common sense, both holding pistols as they cleared the doorway to the room in back. One of them got a round off as McCarter held down the AK-47's trigger and swept them with a blazing figure eight that dropped them both together in a boneless sprawl.

He ditched the empty magazine, replaced it with a loaded one and went to check the press room out. No other soldiers were in evidence, the press still running on its own, disgorging printed sheets of paper in a steady stream. McCarter sprayed the press with armor-piercing bullets, watching it rattle to a halt, and took the time to grab a handful of the printed papers as he moved back toward the office. He scattered the still-warm sheets among the cooling bodies, then slipped his rifle back into its ruined bag before he stepped outside.

The street had emptied of pedestrians the moment that he started shooting. Khartoum's residents had learned enough from years of civil war and harsh repression to evacuate a scene before they could be tagged as witnesses, hauled in for rough interrogation or intimidated into silence. They saw nothing, heard nothing and kept themselves healthy that way.

So much the better for a warrior on the run.

McCarter jogged back to his car, one hand still clutching the Kalashnikov inside his shoulder bag, prepared to deal with anyone who tried to intercept him. He was lucky, and his last glimpse of the target was a fading image in his rearview mirror, corpses stretched out on the sidewalk, barely visible in the descending dusk.

He concentrated on the road and targets still ahead, felt precious time slip through his fingers as he drove.

So many predators, so little time.

But he would keep on trying, to the bitter end.

THE FIRST GRENADE exploded with a crash of smoky thunder, spewing shrapnel high and low around the room. Mack Bolan went in through the shattered window, breathing shallowly and squinting through the smoke in search of moving targets. One man sprawled across his path, facedown and shrapnel torn, but Bolan passed him by, intent on living enemies.

Siraj al-Mahdi had described the loft as a frequent meeting place for Spear of Allah members in Khartoum, where they sat in on lectures, sometimes plotted strategy or simply sat around and told war stories, blooded veterans vying with one another in the details of their personal exploits against Israel and its supporters.

Peering through the window from the fire escape, Bolan had counted seven men before he lobbed the Russian frag grenade and ducked back out of range. The blast had killed or gravely wounded three men he could see sprawled out around him, while another slumped against the wall to Bolan's left, still on his feet but fading fast. The Executioner stitched him with a short burst from behind and watched him fall, then turned to search for other hardmen.

A muzzle-flash sent him diving for the littered floor

as bullets streamed above his head. He went down firing, had no way of knowing whether he would tag his adversary, but the short burst was rewarded by a cry of pain. He came up on his elbows, aimed the AK-47 at a lurching figure several paces distant and unleashed another burst that brought his target down.

And that left two.

He heard them scuttling toward the nearest exit, turned in time to spy them as the door swung open, framing them in pale light from the outer corridor. One turned to fire an aimless pistol shot across the room, and Bolan dropped him with a rising burst that opened him from crotch to sternum.

The last of Bolan's adversaries from the loft had cleared the threshold, racing toward the stairs and ultimate escape. He nearly made it, gaining precious time while Bolan scrambled to his feet in hot pursuit, but then he lost it, slipping on the stairs and throwing out a hand to catch the banister before he fell. The hardman was recovering his balance when death found him, looming overhead and sighting down the barrel of a folding-stock Kalashnikov.

The Palestinian glanced up and saw his doom, threw up an arm as if mere flesh could stop the rain of bullets that descended on him from above. His body jerked from impact, then pitched forward, tumbling through a clumsy somersault before he hit the landing below and sprawled there like some giant's cast-off toy.

Clean sweep.

Bolan went out through the window and hustled down the fire escape. It would require some time and nerve for neighbors to investigate the racket, more time for police to get the message and respond. He would be long gone by the time the first official vehicles arrived, moving toward his next mark in the war against Hassan Jubayl.

CHAPTER TWELVE

Hassan Jubayl had put off picking up the telephone as long as possible. With each new update on the deadly violence in Khartoum, he waited for a word that one of his commandos had been lucky, had succeeded in disabling or killing one of their unknown opponents. He needed something to let him sort out the situation and discover who was tracking down his people like a grim avenging angel.

He had waited, but the word he longed for didn't come. His men were dying in Khartoum, more than two dozen of them at last count, and there was nothing he could do about it from his base of operations at Sannar. At the beginning of his sojourn in Sudan, Jubayl had judged it wiser to remain some distance from the capitals, and he was doubly thankful now for that decision. If he had been quartered in Khartoum, he might be dead by now, along with the young men who had died so far.

It galled him, even so, that he should have to ask Marawi Bol for help. It was embarrassing, especially as the request would come within a day of his assurance to the colonel that there were no problems with the Spear of Allah's operations in Sudan. Now he would have to eat those words, look like a weakling who couldn't defend himself. And even worse, if that was possible, he would look foolish, running to the junta for assistance when he couldn't even name his enemies.

Jubayl could almost see the colonel smirking now, his deep voice sticky sweet with mock concern: How could he help him? Enemies? Of course, they would be taken care of. Where could they be found? Who were they?

And to that, no answer.

Twice he reached out for the telephone, and twice withdrew his hand, as if he feared the contact would contaminate him. The disease of cowardice was always fatal, and it spread like wildfire through the ranks of fighting men whose leaders were infected. There should be some other way for him to solve the problem, take his soldiers to the streets and hunt the bastards down, but that in turn would violate his contract with the junta in Khartoum.

The Spear of Allah was a welcome guest, as long as it confined its violence to the state of Israel and its allies, striking anywhere outside Sudan. Within the country, members were allowed to train, bear arms, defend themselves if they were physically attacked, but no one in Khartoum or Omdurman would be inclined to sit and watch while Palestinian guerrillas mounted street patrols and started searching house to house for faceless enemies. Jubayl didn't have men enough to pull it off, in any case—less now than yesterday, in fact.

He had no choice but to request the army's help. It didn't matter if Marawi Bol was laughing at him, making jokes at his expense, as long as their elusive enemies were brought to heel. Unchecked, he worried that the gunmen who had killed two dozen of his troops might sweep Khartoum, move on to strike at other sites. The longer they survived, the more harm they inflicted on his war machine, the more Jubayl would suffer, even after they were dead.

Negotiating with the Sudanese was like a game. You had to deal from strength, or no one in the junta would respect you. They were interested in reputations, body counts—in short, results. Why should the generals spend their stolen money on guerrillas who were slaughtered in their own backyard, without inflicting any damage whatsoever on the enemy?

In that sense, asking for Bol's help was risky. There was no doubt he would take it as a sign of weakness, no doubt he would seize the opportunity to gloat and sneer. Jubayl could live with that, as long as he wasn't commanded to pack up and leave Sudan. The list of countries willing to accept his soldiers had been dwindling lately. Jordan had become selective in the choice of rebels who were welcome in its Bekaa Valley, and Iranians effectively controlled that outlaw's paradise, in any case. The president of Syria still funded Palestinian guerrilla armies, but he was reluctant to be seen with them or have them found within his country. Libya was unpredictable, Khaddafi's moods as transitory as his lucid moments. In Algeria, well, that was still a possibility, at least, but it would mean uprooting all his soldiers and equipment, moving fourteen hundred miles to find new quarters—and the move itself would be conditional upon negotiations with the politicians in Algiers.

It would be better all around if they could just stay where they were. Jubayl could live with some embarrassment to pull that off, secure in the belief that once his present adversaries were eliminated, it would be no time at all before he scored fresh victories to justify the junta's faith in his crusade. The bloody mess in Paris hadn't fazed Marawi Bol; he had ignored it, laughing with the Palestinian about Amal al-Qadi's raid on the Museum of Modern Art.

Jubayl had laughed along with him, all the while counting money in his head. A daring strike at the United States increased his stock immeasurably with the Sudanese. The generals were bullies, hopelessly infatuated with the fantasy that might makes right. They had no sympathy for underdogs, but could admire resistance fighters who accomplished feats beyond the ordinary, winning in defiance of the odds. Conversely they despised all weaklings and losers, and wouldn't appreciate invited guests who brought more violence down upon their capital.

Still, there was no alternative. The terms of his agreement with Khartoum required Jubayl to let the army handle any problems he couldn't resolve by swift internal discipline. Defiance of that rule would put him on the junta's hit list. It would be more sensible for him to pack his gear right now, and flee Sudan that very night.

This time, before Hassan Jubayl reached out to touch the telephone, he rose and poured himself a brimming glass of wine. His religion forbade him to drink, but that didn't stop him. He could use some at the moment.

With any luck, the wine would keep him from choking when he had to eat his pride.

MARAWI BOL WAS SMILING as he dropped the telephone receiver back into its cradle. He chuckled to himself and spun a full 360-degree turn in his high-backed swivel chair. It was delicious, listening to bold Hassan Jubayl plead for assistance, men and guns to save his precious Spear of Allah from an enemy he couldn't even name.

Pathetic amateurs, the colonel thought. Jubayl amused him, sometimes, with his raids in Israel, even recent forays to America, but there were times when Bol still questioned the decision of his government to fund the Spear of Allah and provide it with a base of operations in Sudan.

Like now, for instance.

Thinking of the bloodshed in Khartoum, Bol immediately lost his smile. He didn't mind the violence, per se; his homeland's civil war would soon be ten years old, and he would never have attained a colonel's rank at thirty-five without domestic turmoil to provide combat experience. What troubled him this evening was the knowledge that Hassan Jubayl couldn't protect himself and that a paramilitary team of strangers was at large and killing with impunity.

Marawi Bol was the liaison officer between the junta and Jubayl's toy soldiers. Anything that went awry in that relationship would ultimately fall upon the colonel's shoulders, and there would be no excuse for failure if the violence spread, if someone from the foreign press began to file reports on how Sudan invited terrorists to train within its borders, then couldn't protect them from reprisals by their targets.

He suspected Israel first, the devious Mossad, but that was more an ingrained reflex than a logical deduction. Who despised Hassan Jubayl enough to kill his men on sight? The list undoubtedly included most Israelis, plus substantial numbers of Americans and British, French and Germans—even certain Arab leaders he could name. The Spear of Allah had insulted Arafat, Abu Nidal and members of the PLO on more than one occasion. Men like those took grudges to the grave and cared little more for ethnic brotherhood.

Too many suspects, Bol thought. The way to do it was to grab informers off the street, squeeze them until they gave up something he could use. It was unlikely that a stranger could move freely, unobserved, around Khartoum. The Palestinians could mix, of course— some of the darker Jews, as well, if they spoke Arabic—but no one from the West. They would be spotted, scrutinized, remembered. All he had to do was find the proper witnesses and make them talk.

Of course, that was the rub.

Years of civil war and ethnic cleansing, martial law

and torture, hasty treason trials and public executions, had inclined most Sudanese to keep their mouths shut and avert their eyes when they saw anything resembling trouble. Some of them would fight to save blood relatives or spouses, but the native population of Khartoum—of all Sudan—couldn't care less about the Spear of Allah, whether Jubayl's soldiers lived or died. Bol shared that complacency, but it was still his job to cope with any problems that arose from operations of the Spear within his country, and his job—perhaps his very life—depended on how well he handled this emergency. A failure could result in reassignment to the southern front, where rebels loved to lie in wait for army officers, take them alive if possible and see how long they could be made to scream before they died.

No, thank you.

He would help clean up this mess Jubayl had made, then he would suggest to his superiors that they withdraw their invitation to the Spear of Allah, let Jubayl look elsewhere for his sanctuary and support. The Spear contributed precisely nothing to Sudan, beyond a hint of danger that was countered by the threat of UN sanctions for supporting terrorism. He could make a case against the Spear, but he had to mend the damage first, in order to speak with full authority to his superiors.

How to begin?

Sweep the streets. It was the surest place to start. Pick up the usual informers, men and women who would sell themselves, their children, for a few coins or some minor privilege. One of them had to know something. All Bol would have to do was make them understand the benefits of sharing...and the risks of keeping secrets from a man who held their lives like peanuts in his hand.

One squeeze, and they were gone.

That kind of power was an aphrodisiac. It warmed his blood, sometimes, just knowing he could spill the blood of others with a word to his subordinates, no one to question him or interfere as long as he didn't conduct himself outrageously and spark some kind of public demonstration in the streets. In that case, if the foreign press got wind of what was happening and he was deemed a personal embarrassment to his superiors, Bol would have a problem. In the meantime, if he kept his nose clean, relatively speaking, he could do no wrong.

And while he watched out for the junta's interests in Khartoum, he was accumulating funds on the side, enough to tide him over if his job and life were threatened unexpectedly. He could evacuate Khartoum on thirty minutes' notice, and be safe in Chad—where he had cultivated friends—before the army knew where he was going.

Always think ahead—it was the one rule of survival in Bol's world, and he had seen enough formerly smug soldiers stand before a firing squad to know that he wasn't immune. This business with Hassan Jubayl might put some more against the wall, if he contrived to play his cards right, but he didn't mean to be among them when the shots rang out.

He was a wiser man than that, his rank—the very fact of his survival in the midst of so much palace politics—a testimony to the fact that he had grown adept at thinking on his feet. Or on his knees, if there were certain asses that required a tasteful kiss from time to time.

Please those above you; manage those below. That simple rule had seen him through hard times, and would again if he but kept his wits about him.

He had to move against the enemy, and smartly if he meant to clean the situation up that night, the following day at the latest. Any more delay, and he would have to answer some uncomfortable questions from the men upstairs.

And he didn't relish that prospect.

Not at all.

If anyone got burned because of this, Bol was determined that the heat should fall upon Hassan Jubayl. It was the way things worked around Khartoum.

Shit rolled downhill, and there was always someone waiting at the bottom of the slope.

THE ROOM WAS nearly small enough to rank as claustrophobic. With the window closed for safety's sake and no air-conditioning, the atmosphere was muggy, body heat from four men mingling with the baked-in heat that had accumulated through another scorching day and dissipated slowly, even hours after dark. A single naked light bulb lit the room, but poorly, dimming frequently in a salute to Khartoum's poorly maintained power lines.

Mack Bolan and his Phoenix Force comrades sat around a smallish table with Siraj al-Mahdi, maps and sketches spread in front of them. The table was a cheap contraption, metal tubes and fiberboard, a thin layer of plastic on the top, resembling those found in so many American kitchens during the 1950s. Bolan had no eye for the decor this night, nor was he troubled by cramped accommodations. He had combat on his mind and wouldn't be distracted from his purpose.

"Here you find the nearest camp," al-Mahdi told them, pointing on a large map of Sudan. His index finger came to rest two inches west of Ad-Duwaym, some eighty miles below Khartoum. "There are some others, but you have to travel farther. This is fairly close."

"How many men in camp?" McCarter asked.

The contact agent shrugged. "It varies," he replied. "With several camps to choose from, Hassan Jubayl does not put—what is the expression?—all of his hens in one basket."

"Eggs," Bolan corrected him. "Eggs in one basket."

"Ah."

"An average number, then," McCarter pressed.

The Sudanese stared at the map, as if he hoped to find an answer printed there. "No more than fifty, with instructors."

"Fifty," Manning echoed.

"Much less, sometimes," Siraj amended. "It is difficult to say."

"But fifty, tops?" Bolan asked, frowning at the man across the map.

The little Sudanese was quick to nod. "The Spear of Allah's membership is frequently inflated by the press. They take Jubayl's assertions at face value and believe he has five thousand men. It makes him more newsworthy, yes?"

"How many does he really have?" McCarter probed.

Another shrug. "Perhaps four hundred hard-core fighters. There are always volunteers who wish to join, and sympathizers who are old or weak, afraid to fight. Jubayl counts everyone and multiplies by ten."

"You hope," McCarter said.

"My information is reliable," al-Mahdi answered stiffly. "I have eyes inside the Spear."

"You trust those eyes?" Bolan asked.

"They have not betrayed me yet."

"First time's the charm," Manning said.

Al-Mahdi's voice went up an octave as he answered. "I did not invite you here, nor did I volunteer to serve your great crusade. If you are troubled by the risks involved, feel free to leave at any time."

"Relax, Siraj," Bolan said. "No one's calling you a liar. You can understand that we need firm intelligence."

"Of course," the Sudanese replied. "I have been satisfying your Central Intelligence Agency for some time now."

"It's not my Agency," Bolan said, "and I'm not

collecting information for the files. Our heads are on the block with this if your reports are wrong."

"I trust my source," al-Mahdi insisted. "Of course, if *he* has been deceived somehow…"

He left the comment dangling, spread his hands as if to say that there was nothing more for him to do. Bolan recognized the dilemma and McCarter's concerns, but at the moment he was focused on the Spear of Allah and Hassan Jubayl. They hadn't come this far and dared so much to throw it all away because they couldn't get a final head count on the personnel of a guerrilla training camp.

"How are the roads?" Bolan asked.

"Passable. The maintenance is poor, but with so little rain, sandstorms are the most persistent problem. That and the patrols."

Bolan nodded. They had already seen glimpses of how the junta protected its terrorist allies in Khartoum. Out in the countryside, where internecine warfare was a fact of daily life, the armed patrols would be alert for any strangers, anything suspicious in the least. Three white men driving through the hinterlands would certainly be stopped if they were seen, at least detained for questioning, and when their arsenal was found…

He stopped that train of thought before it traveled any further down a dead-end track. Defeatism was contrary to Bolan's nature. If the army spotted them en route to strike Hassan Jubayl's base camp, they would confront that problem in due time. Right now, he knew that it was better to dismiss the prospect of disaster, focus more completely on the task at hand.

If it was fifty guns, so be it. They would do their best with what they had. He reached out for the sketches that al-Mahdi had obtained from his connection in the Spear of Allah.

"Now," he said, "let's talk about the camp."

CHAPTER THIRTEEN

Ad-Duwaym stood on the western bank of the White Nile, a hundred miles south of Khartoum. To the west, caravan routes crossed the Kurdufan Desert, mile after mile of sand, hardpan and scrub brush baked by a sun as relentless as death in the daytime, covered by a magnificent canopy of stars at night. The road Siraj al-Mahdi had described as passable ceased to exist a few miles west of Ad-Duwaym. It gave way to a dirt-and-gravel track that shook the army-surplus jeep until it rattled, making Bolan wish they could afford to stop and take another bladder break. Dust rose behind them in a cloud, and gravel clanged beneath the vehicle's undercarriage.

They had begun their journey after nightfall, and there was no moon, so he wasn't concerned about the dust. They drove with the headlights off; McCarter was fitted with a pair of infrared night-vision goggles, driving as he would have if it had been daylight on the Kurdufan. From time to time, he swerved to miss a pothole; otherwise, their track ran arrow straight across the wasteland, toward the target they had chosen for this night.

McCarter killed the engine a little over a mile from contact with the enemy. Beyond that point, noise could have given them away, and they were close enough to finish the approach on foot. Each man wore desert camouflage and carried a Kalashnikov, along with side arms, knives, garrotes, grenades and bandoliers of ammunition for their weapons. Bolan and McCarter carried RPGs, as well, with rockets tied across their backs in canvas slings.

It was a half hour past midnight when they came within sight of the training camp. The place was blacked out by design, to minimize the threat of aerial attack or satellite surveillance. Theoretically the Spear of Allah's soldiers were secure in Sudan, but the Israelis had been known to strike at terrorists around the world, from Syria and Jordan to Uganda, the United States and South America. A flight of Phantoms skimming low across the Red Sea, banking southwest from the coast, might take Jubayl's guerrillas by surprise some night.

They took turns with the goggles, scoping out the camp, before they chose positions. Bolan would be on the east, McCarter on the northwestern perimeter, with Manning on the south. Three men couldn't surround a camp of any size, but they could damn well cover most of it, provide for interlocking fields of fire and close to give the enemy a taste of hell on earth while he was groggy, fighting up from sleep in an attempt to save himself.

The next ten minutes were a waiting game for Bolan, checking out the sentries while he killed time as

Manning and McCarter scuttled through the midnight shadows to the vantage points from which they would initiate their strike. He fed the RPG one of its fat, nose-heavy rockets, double-checked his AK-47 and sat back to watch the men he was about to kill.

At times like this, the brain kicked in with questions, uninvited by the conscious mind. Was it wrong to kill from ambush, even slaughter adversaries in their sleep? Morality and warfare often parted company, as Bolan understood from long experience. Regardless of a soldier's goals, the tactics of a given situation might be ruthless, brutal, totally devoid of mercy. Such had always been the way of war, and if he harbored any doubts about the course of action they had chosen, all he had to do was think about the victims slaughtered by Hassan Jubayl and company, from Israel to the States. More to the point, he thought of victims yet to be.

It was enough to let him lift the RPG and brace it on his shoulder, peering through the sights. He couldn't see the Phoenix Force warriors from his position, but there had been time enough for them to take up their positions, mark initial targets and prepare to fire on Bolan's signal.

Any second now.

He squeezed the trigger on his RPG and let the rocket fly.

AFIF MATALKA WAS the Spear of Allah's second-in-command, after Hassan Jubayl. Amal al-Qadi had been favored in the past for his audacious strikes against the enemy, but he was gone now. Losing him, the circumstances of his death, had damaged their prestige, but there was some good to be found in anything. Al-Qadi's death had cleared the path to power for Afif Matalka. Even now, as he was lying on his cot and staring at the canvas tent above him, he was scheming ways to make the Spear his own.

Jubayl had done his best, of course, but it was time—

The first explosion dumped Matalka from his narrow cot, facedown on hard-packed earth. He blinked, coming up on his hands and knees as sentries started to shout back and forth on the perimeter and someone opened fire with an automatic weapon. He reached for his Uzi submachine gun, thinking of the recent violence in Khartoum and wondering how it could find him here.

There was no time for pondering that problem as he struggled to his feet. Another blast ripped through the camp, and someone started to scream, cries of mortal agony. Matalka had heard those sounds before, had caused a number of his enemies to scream that way himself. It didn't frighten him, so much as set his teeth on edge. He thought of the effect it had to be having on his soldiers, and he wished the wounded man would simply die.

He started to reach for the light he kept beside his bed, then caught himself before he switched it on. If there were enemies around the camp, he wouldn't give them any better targets through rank negligence.

One of his sergeants burst into the tent, half-dressed

and breathing heavily, prepared to wake and warn Matalka if the noise of battle hadn't done so. Many guns were firing now, and more explosions lit the night with leaping balls of flame.

"See to the men!" Matalka snapped. "If we cannot defend the camp, make ready to evacuate!"

"Yes, sir!"

The sergeant vanished, with Matalka trailing several steps behind him. Peering from the entrance of his tent, he saw the camp in turmoil, several tents on fire, with the communication hut collapsed in smoking rubble. He could see no corpses from his vantage point, but that meant nothing in the circumstances—darkness and confusion, smoke and fire, men running everywhere. It would have been miraculous if no one had been killed or wounded, and he didn't believe in miracles.

Matalka clutched the Uzi, wishing that it made him feel more confident. In all his years of raiding Jewish settlements and striking urban targets in the West, he had been hardened to the rigors of guerrilla warfare, trained to hit and run. He had been training others in those skills and waiting for relief, a summons to Khartoum, where he would help Jubayl chart new directions for the Spear and gradually position himself for a leadership bid.

But at the moment, all the Palestinian could think of was survival, living through the next few moments, finding some way out of the chaotic, hellish scene before him.

He would have to drive, of course, and that knowledge directed his attention toward the motor pool, a long tent, open on all sides, where trucks and jeeps were parked to shield them from the desert sun and high-flying eyes in the sky. So far, the vehicles hadn't been damaged. Each had keys in the ignition; all he had to do was reach the tent, select his wheels and make his run before a bullet or some flying bits of shrapnel cut him down.

In these conditions, Matalka thought, he was as likely to be killed by his own men as by the faceless enemy. There was no time for planning, in the normal sense, but he could still use caution, make his way across the camp by stages, killing if he had to, hiding where it served his purpose better.

He would take it one step at a time.

As he cleared the threshold of his tent, Matalka crouched in the shadows, the Uzi braced against his hip. When the moment came, he charged across the open ground and glimpsed someone sprawled to his left, ignoring the body as he kept on running toward the motor pool. Off to Matalka's left, the mess tent had become a staging area of sorts, a number of his soldiers crouching there and firing automatic weapons toward the camp's perimeter.

At what?

He couldn't say, and was less interested in the identity of his assailants at that moment than in his own prospects for escape. Almost against his will, Matalka glanced back toward the mess tent just in time to see a rocket streaking from the darkness, detonating with a clap of thunder, scattering his men like so many broken mannequins.

The shock wave knocked Matalka down. He dropped his Uzi, scrambled for it and was on his feet again in nothing flat. Each step he took was one step closer to salvation. All he had to do was keep his wits about him and—

His thoughts evaporated as the world exploded in his face.

McCARTER'S SECOND ROCKET blitzed the mess tent, flinging bits and pieces of his human targets in all directions. Number one had taken out the communications hut and anyone inside, instantly severing the base commander's capability of calling out for help.

So far, so good.

He fed the RPG a final rocket, shouldered it again and scanned the camp downrange in search of targets. There was no need for night-vision goggles any longer, with the flames that had caught hold among the tents and plywood structures in the compound. It wasn't as bright as day, but he could see the soldiers of the Spear of Allah running to and fro, some of them firing aimlessly off into the darkness, attempting to defend themselves against an adversary they hadn't yet seen.

He lined up on a hut that had the look of a command post, standing near the middle of the camp, its tin roof painted beige to roughly match the sand. It wouldn't fool a satellite, but they were trying, anyway. He sighted on a window with a bulky air conditioner installed and squeezed the trigger, sending rocket number three to close the gap between him and his enemies.

The CP hut disintegrated as the rocket burst within. The roof was airborne, like a giant flying disk, spinning through the air before it finally surrendered to the pull of gravity and came down on a pair of soldiers who stood gaping at it, stunned. McCarter doubted whether it would kill them, and he didn't give a damn. He was out of rockets, and several of the riflemen down there had marked the last one's progress, pointing up the rise toward where he sat.

They started to fire at him, still uncertain of their target in its finer details, peppering the desert with converging streams of automatic fire. McCarter didn't duel with them; it would have been a futile exercise, his muzzle-flashes giving them a chance to narrow down their aim. Instead, he scurried backward, put the gentle rise of ground between himself and his attackers, moving to his right some twenty yards before he turned back toward the camp.

There was no shrubbery to speak of, nothing in the way of cover that would mask his progress, but he counted on the agitation of his enemies to help him out in that regard. McCarter counted five of them, by muzzle-flashes, standing in a group and spraying fire toward the position where he had been sitting when he launched the rockets on them from above. It took another moment for the Palestinians to realize no one was shooting back, and by that time, the Briton had come level with them, to their left, and turned in that direction, closing up the gap.

He could as easily have passed them by, pushed on into the camp, but it made no sense for him to leave five guns at his back, prepared to swing around and follow him the moment he revealed himself again. Conversely, if he could eliminate this group, he would have cut the Spear's gross strength by ten percent.

He ran as if his life depended on it, counting on the racket from their guns to cover his approach. One of the gunners, pausing to reload, glanced to his left and saw McCarter coming through the shadows. He blinked and squinted, trying to decide if the man was friend or foe. The Arab was still working on that problem when McCarter shot him in the chest, three rounds from thirty feet, and slammed him backward into the sand.

The others recognized their fatal error then. It was a manic scramble, four guns swiveling to face the commmando, one of them still spitting bullets as the shooter panicked to the point that he couldn't release his trigger for the time it took to turn and aim. McCarter followed his example, hosing them with automatic fire in one long burst, without finesse, the bodies jerking, twitching, dancing as his bullets ripped through flesh and fabric. They were going down, a couple of them still returning fire with lifeless fingers locked on AK-47 triggers, but the guns spewed bullets skyward, wasted on the stars.

McCarter wasted no time checking pulses. They were dead or dying—hurt bad enough that none of them would be returning to the fight—and he left them where they lay. He stood upon the outskirts of the camp, one tent burning close enough for him to read by firelight if there had been anything for him to read.

But all he saw right now was the handwriting on the wall.

He had a job to do, bold comrades to support, and any breather he allowed himself would come at their expense. It was impossible to count their adversaries in the tumult of the camp, but he and his companions were still outnumbered. The simple act of letting down his guard was tantamount to suicide.

Reloading on the move, McCarter made his way into the killing ground, his nostrils flaring at the old, familiar smells of gunpowder and smoke and burning flesh.

It smelled like home.

LIEUTENANT MUNI NAJRAN mistook the first explosion for a distant thunderclap and glanced up to check the stars above his open staff car to make sure that his patrol wasn't in danger from a flash flood in the desert. There was little rain that time of year, but when it *did* fall, it came down in sheets that filled old streambeds, flooded gullies, decimated caravans and sometimes carried away armored vehicles. Such rains were few and far between, but seeing one, surviving it, made a believer out of any man.

The skies were cloudless, though. The young lieutenant ordered his driver to stop and switch off the car's engine while he listened. Behind them, the ar-

mored personnel carrier and the flatbed truck carrying
the rest of his patrol stopped short, their engines idling
as the drivers tried to figure out what he was doing.

Najran retrieved the dash-mounted radio microphone and ordered the other two vehicles to switch off
their engines. A moment later, when silence had descended on the little column, except for the ticking of
heated metal as it cooled, he stood in his seat and
listened, scanning the horizon with binoculars.

A second blast was too far away for him to feel the
shock wave, but he had a general fix on the direction.
Turning to the north, he lowered the binoculars and
simply listened.

There! That sound was gunfire, automatic weapons
blasting in the distance. Glancing down, Najran saw
that his driver heard it, too. The privates seated in the
rear of his staff car were at alert, hands clasping rifles
as they watched him, waiting to discover how he
would react.

"That way!" he told the driver, pointing, mouthing
orders into the microphone as he sat down. Three engines growled to life, and the patrol turned northward,
following the sounds of battle on a rough collision
course.

The lieutenant knew where they were going, where
the action had to be. The Spear of Allah had a "secret" training camp a few kilometers due north of his
position, and while he was relatively new in his command, he understood the way things worked between
the army and assorted Palestinians or other terrorists
who trained and hid out in Sudan, with tacit blessing

from his government. The "visitors" were told to be discreet, behave themselves, watch out for bad publicity that would embarrass their most gracious hosts. They should avoid contact with news reporters at all cost and take precautions to prevent spies from recording their activities. The latter was impossible, of course, but at the very least, the Palestinians were warned to stay away from obvious displays of firepower.

In practice, that restricted training for nocturnal missions to the sort of action where they ran around with empty guns, lobbed dummy hand grenades and stabbed or strangled mannequins in silence. They were definitely not supposed to set off bombs or rockets in the middle of the night, much less unload their rifles and machine guns as if they were in some kind of festival, without a worry in the world.

Najran had no idea what he would find when he reached the Spear of Allah's compound. If the terrorists were deliberately flaunting rules they all knew very well, then it would be his job to chastise them, disarm the culprits without bloodshed if he could and file an incident report with his superiors before he went off duty in the morning. That report would certainly provoke a reprimand from someone in authority, though he had no good reason to believe the Spear would be expelled. Its leaders had friends in Khartoum; they served a common cause in their determination to eliminate Israel.

The thought that troubled him, that raised the goose bumps on his arms despite his long-sleeved shirt and

the relative warmth of the night, was a question of
what he would do if the shooting meant something
else. Suppose an enemy unknown was striking at the
Spear right now, determined to eradicate the camp?
Suppose the raiders were Israeli, violating Sudanese
territory to punish the Palestinian extremists?

What then?

There was no easy answer to the problem. He would
fight, of course; that much was obvious. But there
would be no hope of reinforcements rushing to the
scene and helping out if he should find himself outnumbered. Even if he made the call to Al-Ubayyid
now, without examining the situation for himself, it
would be forty minutes to an hour before help could
arrive by air. And if the reinforcements traveled overland...well, the lieutenant wouldn't dwell on that
eventuality.

There was no reason to believe the Israelis would
stage a raid like this, when they were talking peace
with neighbors to the north. The Spear had enemies
enough within its own exile community to spark a
firefight; everybody knew that much. The lieutenant
hoped he could deal with the situation.

THE PALESTINIAN HAD BLOOD smeared on his face,
and his eyes were glassy, as if he were dazed or
drugged. That didn't stop him from recognizing Gary
Manning as a stranger, though, or rushing up to intercept him with a long knife in his hand. It was a brave
but foolish gesture, flying in the face of common
sense, and Manning ended it with one clean shot be-

tween the eyes, before his enemy could close to striking range.

The point where he had crept into the compound was obscured by drifting smoke from tents and huts that had been set afire by the initial high-explosive rounds from Bolan and McCarter. Manning had delayed his entry to the camp until that first bombardment was completed, waiting for the shrapnel storm to pass, but he was in it now, without a clue to where his comrades were. The RPG grenades had scattered casualties around the camp, some moving fitfully, while others lay still, but the big Canadian focused his thoughts on the living, those who posed a challenge to him now.

They were outnumbered, certainly, but he didn't believe Siraj al-Mahdi's estimate of fifty soldiers in the camp was accurate. From what he had observed before the battle started, forty seemed more like it, and perhaps a third of those went down in the first moments of the battle, killed or wounded by grenades, incoming bullets, even friendly fire. If they were lucky, handled it correctly, they could still come out on top, despite the odds.

It wouldn't be the first time Manning had been on the winning side when things looked bad.

He saw two Palestinians advancing through the pall of smoke, both watching out for enemies, not yet conscious of his presence. He had the AK-47 braced against his shoulder, sighting down the barrel, when they spotted him, and it was already too late for them to save themselves. He dropped them both with one burst, watched them fall together in an awkward tangle, arms and legs entwined, their bodies twitching as the life ran out of them.

He was advancing in the general direction of the motor pool, a point of rendezvous they had agreed upon before they separated to begin the raid, when something at the corner of his eye demanded his attention. Turning toward the south, he squinted, picked out bobbing specks of light on the horizon, drawing closer by the moment.

Headlights?

Reinforcements!

Even as he searched his mind for other explanations, Manning knew he had to have got it right the first time. There were several vehicles approaching—two or three, at least—and logic told him that the only persons drawn to battle in the middle of the night were men with guns who had some motive for supporting one side or the other. And since Bolan and McCarter were his only fighting allies in Sudan, it stood to reason that the new arrivals would support their enemies.

He made a guess at distance, called it half a mile or so and decided two minutes remained before the vehicles reached camp.

Manning grabbed the compact walkie-talkie from his belt and thumbed down the transmitter button. "We've got company approaching from the south. Two vehicles, at least. Look sharp!"

The voice that crackled back at Manning from the small box in his fist was Bolan's, sounding miles away, with gunfire in the background for an eerie stereo effect.

"Head for the motor pool," the Executioner said. "I'll meet you there ASAP."

"Affirmative," McCarter replied from somewhere in the darkness and confusion of the slaughter pen.

"Don't leave without me," Manning added, but he was talking to himself, the radio already snuggled in its hip pouch as he took off jogging toward the motor pool.

Another hardman tried to stop him, charging with his AK-47 held in front of him as if it had a bayonet attached. The man was close before his footsteps and his wheezing breath betrayed him, the Canadian almost too late to block the thrust and nail him with a buttstroke to the face. The guerrilla staggered, went down on one knee and tried to rise again. Still, he didn't attempt to fire, and Manning understood his piece was jammed or otherwise disabled.

Fair enough.

A 3-round burst from six or seven feet away ripped through the young man's chest and dropped him sprawling on his back, legs folded under him in such a manner that it would have hurt if he were still alive.

No problem there.

The big Canadian dismissed his latest kill and kept on moving toward the line of sheltered vehicles, now forty yards away.

TWO PALESTINIANS had taken it upon themselves to guard the motor pool, whether in service to their unit or in hopes of dodging bullets, Bolan neither knew nor cared. He came in while their backs were turned and shot them once each, ignoring them thereafter as he went to check the vehicles.

Each vehicle had a key in the ignition, making Bolan wonder if the Spear of Allah had some kind of training manual for getaways. He had been lucky in New Jersey, and his luck was still holding.

The sound of running footsteps stopped him, made him turn, the AK-47 rising into target acquisition, but he stopped the trigger pull as Gary Manning entered from the south end of the tent. McCarter got there seconds later, dusty, soot stained, with a bloody crease across one cheek that looked to Bolan like a bullet graze. All three of them were in one piece, regardless, and the time had come for them to retreat before the unknown reinforcements made escape impossible.

"They've all got keys," Bolan said. "I was thinking we should take a jeep."

"Makes sense," McCarter replied. A truck would slow them down, produce less speed, increase the odds of breaking down before they put clear ground between themselves and anyone pursuing them.

"We need to take these others out," Bolan announced, nodding toward the vehicles their enemies had lined up under canvas.

"Right," McCarter said. "You cover me, I'll start the barbecue."

He moved along the line of rolling stock, unscrewing gas caps and tossing them away. When he had done the job on every vehicle except the last jeep on the left, where Bolan stood with Manning, he came back and crouched beside the two sentries sprawled in their own blood.

"They won't be needing these," McCarter said, and used his knife to cut their khaki shirts away with swift, efficient strokes. He handed one to Manning and told him, "Wicks. Let's get a move on, shall we?"

Still, the Spear of Allah gunmen hadn't spotted them. It seemed incredible, but in the chaos of the moment, hardmen running every which way, others stopping dead and pointing toward the headlights fast approaching from the south, no one appeared to have a clear fix on their enemies. They were disoriented and distracted at the moment, and with any luck at all, that edge would be enough to see the Stony Man warriors clear.

"Fire in the hole!" McCarter barked as he came loping down the line of vehicles, a lighter in his hand, wicks blazing as they dangled from the gas tanks of two trucks behind him. Manning had a couple of the others lit, and Bolan threw himself behind the last jeep's steering wheel, one hand on the ignition.

As it responded to his touch, Bolan shifted into first and released the parking brake. He felt McCarter pile into the back, glimpsed Manning as he gained the shotgun seat, and they were rolling, no headlights, their sudden charge surprising several nearby Palestinians, leaving them standing there, frozen, before they understood exactly what was happening.

They were too late to head them off, but they were firing at the jeep from all sides, bullets glancing off the fenders, sizzling past Bolan's face as he ducked and drove. There should be a diversion coming...any...second...*now!*

The motor pool went up in fire and thunder, trucks and small four-wheelers detonating like a string of giant firecrackers. He saw the fireball in his rearview mirror, gunmen flattened by the shock wave, others running to escape the heat.

How many dead and wounded? Never mind.

He concentrated on his driving, heard his companions firing back at snipers in the dark. Beyond the camp's perimeter, the desert waited for them, dark and hostile, menacing.

And on their track, three sets of headlights locked in, giving chase.

CHAPTER FOURTEEN

Lieutenant Najran had lingered in the Palestinian guerrilla compound only long enough to learn that they had been attacked by someone from outside, an enemy who had escaped in one of their vehicles prior to blowing up the rest. He got a pointer in the general direction, and they were off in hot pursuit.

His quarry drove without lights, but Najran and his troops weren't trying to hide. Their high beams cut a swath of brilliance through the midnight wasteland, wobbling when they hit rough ground or had to swerve around a boulder, always coming back on track. He wondered if his soldiers felt the same excitement that had gripped him, and if theirs was also mingled with a taste of fear.

It would have helped if he had some idea whom he was chasing, or at least how many of them were involved. The Palestinians had been disoriented, stunned that anyone would have the nerve to raid their compound in the desert. Najran had no idea how many of them had been killed or wounded; it wasn't his primary concern. When he was finished running down their adversaries, he would stop back at the camp and take more notes for his report, but he wasn't about to loan them soldiers for the funeral detail.

If they were so intent on living in Sudan between their raids abroad, the least they could do was clean up their own mess.

The lieutenant wished he had a weapon other than the pistol on his hip. It was a curiosity, he thought, that each promotion to a higher rank reduced a soldier's personal ability to fight. Of course, he understood the concept: privates and the like did all the heavy grunt work and the front-line killing, while their officers remained behind the lines, directing them to victory. But there were times—like this, for instance— when he wished a junior officer's equipment would include an AK-47, or at least a submachine gun.

His hands were trembling, and he clutched his knees to keep the driver at his side from noticing. Najran wasn't a virgin, in the military sense: he had seen combat in the south, pursuing Christian rebels, razing villages. It had been butcher's work, and several of his men were killed in skirmishes with the guerrillas who refused to take their orders from the junta in Khartoum, but he had always known that he was on the winning side. Technology, as backward as it was in the Sudan, was on his side. With armored vehicles and automatic weapons, the occasional helicopter with machine guns and infrared spotting devices, there was no way he could lose.

But he could still get killed. Oh, yes.

The fear had dogged him through his tour of duty in the south, and while Najran believed he had concealed it from his men, he couldn't hide it from himself. Each time he strapped on his pistol and went to lead another night patrol, he felt it in his stomach, squirming like a parasite that sapped his strength and will. He still went through the motions—there was no alternative but resignation in disgrace—but he was always worried by the thought that he might fail if there was trouble, break down on the firing line and show his men the kind of coward that he truly was.

But not this night.

His quarry had evacuated in a jeep, which meant that even if they sat on one another's laps, there would be less than half a dozen men involved. Three or four seemed more likely, and while they were clearly fearsome warriors, evidenced from the havoc they had wreaked among the Palestinians, Najran had them outnumbered eight or nine to one. There would be no advantage of surprise for them this time, no self-styled freedom fighters dreaming in their tents. It would be interesting to see how they performed against a welltrained military force out in the open, when they had no place to run and hide.

Of course, he had to catch them first.

Najran wondered if the raid had anything to do with the reports of violence in Khartoum. Both cases had involved the Spear of Allah, and he had no faith in blind coincidence. If he could catch or kill the men responsible for raising hell around the capital, Najran would be the hero of the hour, pulling off a coup that colonels in Khartoum would envy from their air-conditioned offices. It could mean decoration, maybe even a promotion.

Once again, the nagging voice came back at him: he had to catch them first.

And once he had them, he would have to keep from blundering across the line of fire. The medals and promotions would mean nothing to a dead man.

He would have to stay alive.

THE HEADLIGHTS WERE a mile or so behind them, holding steady. Bolan counted three sets when they broke formation, but he couldn't tell what kind of vehicles they were without a closer look. Three jeeps would mean a dozen guns, at most. If they were trucks or APCs, the total could be five or six times that.

Were they guerrillas? Regulars? It made a difference, both in training and in hardware, not to mention radio communications that could bring all kinds of reinforcements down upon them, maybe even airborne, if the proper orders were relayed.

It would have helped, he thought, to know where they were going. McCarter was driving now, so Bolan could plan their route. The escape had worked out fine, except that they were driving blindly through the desert, westbound to nowhere, with a minicaravan of hostile gunmen on their track. The maps that he had studied in Khartoum told Bolan that the desert west of Ad-Duwaym went on for something like six hundred miles without a break, until you entered Chad—that was, unless you hit a chain of mountains in the Darfur district, which would force you to turn north or south. More desert, then, and still nowhere to hide.

Not that it mattered. They wouldn't make one-third that distance without stopping to refuel, and once they stopped, the enemy would overtake them swiftly, make it all or nothing in the middle of a wasteland where the jeep would be their only cover.

The reinforcements turning up had been a wild card, absolutely unpredictable. He couldn't blame their strategy, but still it rankled, having come this far and dared this much, to have it finish in the middle of the night, with only foreign stars to watch them die.

But they weren't finished yet, by any means. They still had room to run, and if those *were* three jeeps behind him, Bolan would have bet the farm that he and his companions could eliminate a dozen gunmen, regulars or otherwise.

They had already done as much this night.

As if in answer to his thoughts, McCarter said, "I think we're screwed."

"How's that?"

"They must have hit the petrol tank back there. The needle's dropping like a stone."

"How long?" Manning asked.

"Ten or fifteen minutes. Maybe less."

"Terrific."

"What we need," Bolan said, "is a place to make a stand."

"We need a bloody miracle," McCarter told him.

"We'll have to make our own. Look sharp, now. Anything at all."

"In case you missed it," the Briton stated, "it's a little flat out here."

"Turn on the lights."

"You mean it?"

"Does it matter now?"

"I reckon not."

The headlights blazed, illuminating hard-packed earth in front of them, scrub brush that looked like dry, dead twigs unless you put it underneath a microscope. The high beams helped him scan their course, and it would make no difference in regard to their pursuers. Either way, in ten or fifteen minutes the enemy would have a sitting duck to practice on.

Unless they found some kind of cover first.

The desert wasn't absolutely flat. Bolan knew that from experience. The earth was scarred in places, with dry riverbeds and gullies, broken by slabs of rock thrust up from below, in some ancient upheaval before the dawn of man. The question now was whether they could find that sort of cover soon enough to make it count—and whether it would help them if they did. Against a dozen guns, it might be useful, but against three truckloads, with support troops summoned on the radio...

They had to find a hiding place before he judged it suitable or otherwise. Whatever they came up with, it had to beat a standing fight on open ground.

He clutched his AK-47, staring out beyond the headlights into darkness, trying to forget about the headlights closing from behind.

AFIF MATALKA SHOUTED orders at his men until his voice began to fail, and still they were disorganized, like children in a playground, startled by a sudden cloudburst. They had managed to extinguish all but one or two small fires; the others had burned themselves out or been smothered with buckets of sand. Most of the smoke had dissipated, but there was still the reek of burning oil and gasoline, scorched canvas and the roast-beef smell of bodies seared by flame.

They had the dead lined up on one side of the camp—nineteen so far, and several of the wounded would be joining them before long, if Matalka was any judge. They had no medical facilities beyond first aid, and no means of transporting wounded men to Ad-Duwaym. The soldiers might return to help when they were finished chasing his attackers, or the officer in charge might think he had done enough already, tracking those who razed the camp, without providing transport for Matalka's wounded men. Whichever way it went, the Spear of Allah's would-be second-in-command had no recourse, nowhere to shift the blame.

It was his problem all the way.

He could attempt to mitigate the damage, for all the good that it would do. No one had stopped the raiders in Khartoum, where they had twice as many men as he had in the training camp. He had posted guards as usual. Was it his fault the raiders came equipped with rocket launchers and sufficient nerve to turn the compound upside down?

Three men, he thought, and mouthed a bitter curse. That was the worst of it. Matalka had seen the jeep as it sped out of camp, three silhouettes against the bright flames from the motor pool. Their search had found no dead or wounded strangers in the camp, which meant that there were only three to start with, or the rest had slipped away on foot, unseen.

Three men to kill nineteen and wound eight more, to wreck the camp and all its vehicles.

To make Afif Matalka look like an incompetent poseur.

He had nine soldiers fit for work or battle, most of those with minor cuts or bruises from the fighting, all of them dismayed by the apocalypse they had survived. There had been nothing in their training to prepare them for this night. *They* were supposed to be the raiders, charging out of darkness to surprise their enemies in sleep. They had rehearsed the moves a hundred times, from crawling on their bellies under concertina wire to lobbing dummy hand grenades through bedroom windows, but they didn't train to fight pitched battles in defense of military installations. It wasn't their job.

He thought about the news he had to deliver to Hassan Jubayl and was glad the raiders had destroyed his communications gear. There would be no escaping it, of course, but he could stall for time, attempt to find some hint of silver lining to the storm clouds looming dark above his head. It would be difficult to hide his failure, but he had to try.

Matalka wished he were more seriously wounded, something more dramatic than the small cut on his hairline and the bruise below one eye. If he had been shot, for instance, then at least Jubayl could never doubt that he had done his best to save the camp, their men. This way, it might appear that he had found a place to hide while those around him gave their lives up for the cause.

It was too late to shoot himself. The others had already seen him, would come running at the sound of gunfire. He was stuck with the pathetic wounds he had, but he could still claim he was dazed or knocked unconscious. There was no one to dispute him, and at least one of his men had seen him flattened by the shock wave from a rocket as it struck the camp.

Matalka wondered if the man who helped him to his feet was still alive. It hardly mattered, since the confusion of the moment—all that smoke and blood and panic—had prevented him from recognizing who the soldier was. If he began to ask around, it would become a joke.

He was on his own.

He hadn't come this far up the ladder without learning how to doctor a report, present himself as more heroic than the cold, hard facts allowed. It was a skill that every freedom fighter learned if he survived that long. The suicide commandos were immune to criticism in their graves, but those who lived to fight another day—and planned to keep on living—soon discovered ways to tailor facts, make them more palatable to the brass.

The present situation was a challenge, granted. He could banish any thoughts of a promotion for the next few months at least, but there was still a chance to save himself from censure, ward off any kind of drastic punishment. If he could just persuade Jubayl that he had done his best in an untenable situation, saved as many of the soldiers as he could... Their inexperience and lack of discipline would help him there, the fact that they hadn't tested under fire.

Still, he was in command, and the responsibility was his. It would require some fancy footwork to defend himself.

With any luck, he might come out of it alive.

McCARTER SAW the dark shape looming on their left, perhaps a hundred yards ahead. "What's this?" he asked, and swung the jeep in that direction, switching off the lights a heartbeat later. As the dash went dark, he saw the fuel gauge with its needle grazing the empty mark.

It was all he had to know. Whatever hope this new break in the desert landscape offered, it was all that they could get in the circumstances. It was this or nothing.

"Rocks," Manning said, leaning forward from his place in the back seat. "A pile of rocks."

It was, in fact, a giant slab of stone thrust up from somewhere underground and fractured over time, until it made a heap of boulders, strewed about with smaller stones, deep fissures running through its heart. It was too small for anyone to label it a hill, but larger than the average pile of rocks.

With a glance back toward the headlights drawing closer all the time, McCarter said, "We're out of gas,

or damn near, anyway. If you want to run for it, I'd
say we've got another mile or two, at most.''

"We might as well stay here," Bolan said, jumping
clear and moving toward the jumbled slab of stone
before McCarter switched off the grumbling engine.

The Briton grabbed his AK-47, wished he had the
RPG and half a dozen rockets, but he would make do
with what he had. The stone was smooth beneath his
boots, cool to the touch as he reached out to find a
grip and started to climb, looking for a niche that
would provide both cover and mobility for fighting.
When the sun rose, they would bake here in the rocks,
but that wasn't a problem in McCarter's view. It had
to be hours yet until dawn. Smart money said they
would be dead by then.

He heard a scuffling sound of boots as Manning
scrambled up behind him. Bolan had a place picked
out already, on the south face of the promontory, nestled in with jagged slabs behind him, rising like a
shield. The boulders would deflect incoming fire, all
right, but they were also prime for ricochets.

It helped to hold the high ground, granted, but their
rocky fortress was so isolated that it would take little
effort to surround them, come at them from all four
sides at once. They had a limited supply of ammunition and no water for the daylight hours, if it turned
into a sunbaked siege. A crafty enemy could sit back,
out of rifle range, and throw up tents on the perimeter,
contain them with his snipers, waiting for the desert
sun to rise and broil them where they sat. With tem-
peratures above 110 degrees and nothing in the way

of shade, McCarter knew they would fall prey to sunstroke well before the day was over. After that, a raw recruit could wander in and finish them at point-blank range, no sweat.

It wasn't how he planned to die, but then again, the details had been fuzzy any time he thought about the end. McCarter never saw himself as dying with his boots off, in a bed, but he had managed not to linger over details in the moments when he let his morbid daydreams drift that way. A blade or bullet, a grenade or speeding car, it all came out the same. One moment, you were on your feet and breathing, fighting for your life, all systems go; the next, they had you stretched out on a slab, with shiny instruments laid by to see what made you tick when you were still alive.

Before he let the sun deprive him of his wits and strength, McCarter knew that he would find a way to end it, take his battle to the enemy on open ground and drop a few of them before they cut him down. It was a better way than hiding like a woodchuck in a hole and stretching out the time to no effect.

But first, before it came to that, he and the others were prepared to give their enemies one hell of a reception. If the bastards kept their lights on, it would be a help, turn the advance men into silhouettes as they approached the rock pile, with the lights behind them, shining bright. Come daylight, if they lasted that long and their ammunition held, they could drop man-size targets anywhere within a hundred yards on open ground.

Whichever way it went, the men who came to kill

him wouldn't have an easy time. With all the odds on their side, they would still be forced to work for it, spill blood and sweat to take their prize.

And after that, then what? Would Hal Brognola send the rest of Phoenix Force to make things right? What form would payback take when he was gone?

No matter.

He could hear the engines now, the headlights glaring in his eyes, three vehicles approaching from the south, with greater caution, slowing down.

McCarter sat behind his weapon, index finger on the AK-47's trigger, and began to search the desert flats for someone he could kill.

LIEUTENANT NAJRAN COULD feel his stomach knot when his quarry turned on their headlights, swerving off the straight track they had followed for the best part of an hour. They had to know that he could see them, and that meant they were desperate or they had some kind of plan in mind.

In either case, it meant that they would stand and fight.

Najran shouldn't have been afraid, considering the odds, but he couldn't avoid a certain sense of apprehension as his driver homed in on the headlights, holding steady when they were extinguished once again.

"Take care," he told his driver. "It could be a trap."

He felt the sergeant looking at him, knew the man was frowning, but he didn't glance in that direction, wouldn't let himself be baited. His subordinates would follow orders, even if they thought he was too cautious. It was better, Najran thought, to take some extra time and do the job correctly, with a minimum of friendly casualties, than to rush in and risk a massacre by being unprepared.

A dark blot on the skyline, close to the abandoned jeep, told him his quarry had found cover of a sort. Najran couldn't have said exactly what it was, perhaps a rock formation of some sort, but it would complicate the problem of surrounding them. He knew that they had automatic weapons and grenades. With cover, they could make a stand, perhaps repulse his first attack. How would his men behave once some of them were dead or wounded?

He was reaching for the dashboard-mounted radio before he caught himself. If he called in for reinforcements now, before a shot was even fired, he would appear ridiculous. Those officers who presently respected him would change their minds, and any who nursed doubts about his courage would see weakness in his hesitancy to attack without supporting troops.

Three men, he thought, or four at most. How could he fail to overrun them with the troops he had?

Still, it was better to be careful, not throw lives away unnecessarily. He wasn't friendly with his men, preferring distance and respect to fraternizing with the troops, but he wasn't prepared to throw their lives away for nothing, either. It wouldn't look good to his superiors, if three or four men decimated his command. Worse yet, Najran knew that each soldier killed or wounded brought him that much closer to a private confrontation with the enemy.

He had his driver stop some fifty feet behind the jeep, their high beams showing every detail of the vehicle. It was abandoned, clearly, passengers and driver having taken to the jumbled heap of stone a few yards farther on. His headlights barely grazed the lower reaches of the outcropping, and there was no sign of the enemy from where he sat.

"What shall we do?" his driver asked.

Najran considered snapping at the sergeant, telling him to mind his business, but it would have made him seem…disturbed. Instead of glaring at the sergeant, he replied, "Turn off the engine. I want silence."

As the staff car's engine died, the drivers of the vehicles behind him took it for a signal, switching off their own. A sudden stillness settled on the desert, broken only by the sound of heated metal ticking as it cooled.

The lieutenant sat and waited for a few more moments, finally realizing that nothing was about to happen there unless he *made* it happen. Turning in his seat, he faced the riflemen who sat behind him.

"You two check the jeep," he said, "then scout those rocks ahead."

They glanced at each other, frowning, but obeyed the order, scrambling from the staff car, moving forward with their AK-47s ready, leveled from the hip. He saw them circle warily around the jeep, one of them peering underneath it in the headlights' glare, then they proceeded toward the rugged slabs of stone.

When they were ten or fifteen feet beyond the jeep, a muzzle-flash erupted from the rock heights above, and both men went down, writhing in the dust.

The unmistakable report of a Kalashnikov rang loud in the lieutenant's ears. He ducked below the dashboard of his staff car, felt the sergeant close beside him as another burst of slugs whined through the darkness.

Groping for the microphone above his head, he found it, thumbed the button down and started to shout to his troops.

"Close in! Attack! Attack!"

CHAPTER FIFTEEN

Bolan knew that the easy route would have been to sit tight and let the pointmen go the distance, scramble through the rocks, get close enough for knives or close-range pistol shots. That way, he could have bagged two extra rifles and whatever ammunition they were carrying. But the Executioner chose to drop them on the flats before they got that far.

It was a demonstration to his enemies, first blood. With any luck at all, the Sudanese commander would think twice about a rush before he had a chance to scout the ground and make a plan. Time was all they had now, stretching out the game, unless their adversaries made a move so strange and ill conceived that it would somehow tip the balance.

From where he crouched among the rocks, Bolan could make a fair guess at the force opposing them: two men surviving in the staff car, out in front, immediately followed by an APC designed to carry ten men in a pinch. It looked like twelve to fourteen in the flatbed bringing up the rear, and he would have to count the driver, if it came to that.

His second burst had rattled off the military staff

car, maybe damaging the engine; Bolan didn't know or care. Another time, in a different situation, he would have considered ways to spare at least one of the vehicles for their escape, but at the moment, driving out of there was the last thing on his mind. Survival took priority, and Bolan knew the odds were long.

Not that he minded facing larger forces; that was SOP, and with the Phoenix Force commandos to support him, Bolan would have guessed that they could take the Sudanese patrol in other circumstances. At the moment, though, they were pinned down, and no doubt soon to be surrounded. If the officer in charge was cool and kept his wits about him, he could wait them out, sit back and let them fry in daylight, while his snipers covered them and reinforcements came to finish off the job.

He was about to fire another short burst at the staff car, to try to shake them up, when several automatic weapons started blasting at him from the truck and APC. He ducked back under cover, listened to the bullets striking rock above him, whining into darkness as they ricocheted.

His comrades let the firestorm rage, aware that dueling with the enemy at that range and in the dark was simply wasting precious ammunition. They would wait for solid targets, man-shapes moving through the glare of headlights, and make every bullet count.

But in the meantime, they were forced to duck and cover, while incoming fire etched abstract patterns on the stone around them. Bolan didn't try to count the guns. It was enough for him to know that *they* were wasting ammo now, and when they came for him—

He froze, the new thought chilling him. He shifted in his niche and risked a glance around the slab that sheltered him from gunmen to the east. One look was all he needed to reveal a line of soldiers, six or seven strong, advancing from behind the vehicles, all firing from the hip or shoulder as they came. It was a fairly decent plan, as such things went: the concentrated fire to keep his head down, while foot soldiers crossed no-man's-land to strike at killing range.

It was the kind of plan that Bolan might have tried himself if circumstances were reversed. In this world, though, the best that he could do was warn his comrades, speaking through his walkie-talkie to avoid the kind of shouting that would help his enemies fix targets in among the rocks.

Close quarters, then, if Bolan and the others let them get that far. There was a chance to beat them back, but that meant taking chances with the fire that raked their sanctuary, high and low.

So be it.

Bolan rose and sighted on the middle of the line advancing toward him at a steady pace, and opened fire with his Kalashnikov.

THEIR ENEMIES WEREN'T *all* attacking from the west, as Gary Manning soon discovered for himself. Bolan warned him, saying, "We've got company. Look sharp!" He braced himself to rise, return some of the fire that peppered his position from the westward side, but even as he made the move, he heard a scuffling sound of boot heels on the rock immediately to his left.

He swung in that direction, squinting through the night, recoiling as a bullet struck the rugged stone beside him, throwing sparks and slivers in his face. He glimpsed a shadow rushing at him, more behind it, and he opened up with the Kalashnikov as he recoiled, his shoulders flattening against the rocky slab that formed one angle of his sniper's nest.

The first rounds from his AK-47 hit the pointman, spun him like a dervish, muzzle-flashes blasting from the soldier's automatic weapon as he fell. Behind him, others cried out in alarm, perhaps in pain, as friendly fire stitched through their ranks. They stumbled backward, slipping, sliding on the rocks, a couple of them firing aimlessly in Manning's general direction as they fled.

He almost missed the other one, advancing under cover of the wild fire from his friends. The sneak attack from Manning's blind side could have worked if his opponent had been able to refrain from shouting as he made the final lunge. Some kind of macho thing, perhaps, to boost his courage, or it could have been a trick absorbed from Chinese kung fu movies, but in any case, it gave away the slim advantage of surprise.

The soldier was already close enough to kill if he had simply used his rifle, hosing the rocky cleft where Manning stood his ground. Instead, he rushed to close the gap for hand-to-hand combat, the wooden butt of his Kalashnikov aimed right at Manning's skull.

For a split second, the big Canadian wondered if the Sudanese had orders to take prisoners, but that wouldn't explain the others shooting at him when they charged. That left it to a private whim, one soldier acting on his own, perhaps in hopes of taking home a hero's honors if he brought one of the raiders in alive.

There was no time to think about it further, as the human whirlwind came at Manning in a rush. The Phoenix Force commando was quick enough to save his face, the AK-47 slamming into stone where flesh and bone had been a heartbeat earlier. He heard the wood crack, swung his own piece like a cudgel up into the soldier's rib cage. Bone cracked, and the Sudanese staggered, gasping painfully as he lurched backward, bringing up his rifle to defend himself.

It was a close thing, going in. The soldier couldn't miss him at that range, and Manning knew he was as good as dead if he allowed the other man to fire. He stepped in close and blocked the rising weapon with his body, swung his own Kalashnikov against the soldier's face as if he were about to knock a baseball clear out of the park. The impact slammed his adversary's head against a boulder close behind him with a thick, wet, cracking sound.

The soldier's legs turned into rubber, and he folded, dropping to an awkward squat, his back against the nearest slab of rock. It was the kind of situation where you didn't take chances, and a bullet through the forehead satisfied Manning that his grappling adversary wouldn't rise again.

The echoes of that shot were ringing in his ears

when other weapons started hammering at his position from the slope where his retreating enemies had disappeared from view short moments earlier. The first few rounds were high, but it wouldn't take long for them to find the range. Once they had him spotted, pinned down in his hole, it would be no great trick to creep in closer, maybe finish him with hand grenades.

Grenades!

Like Bolan and McCarter, Manning carried several Russian frag grenades clipped to his webbing. He had used none in the camp, when there were targets for his rifle all around, but there would never be a better time. Almost before the thought had time to register, he palmed one of the metal eggs, pulled out its safety pin, wound up the pitch and let the bomb fly.

The toss was less for distance than precision. He couldn't risk standing to mark the muzzle-flashes, but he knew approximately where they were and calculated from that knowledge, easing off a little on the pitch and going more for altitude than distance. Counting off the seconds in his head, he ducked back under cover, hugged the cool, rough stone and waited for the blast.

It came, complete with smoke and fire, its shock wave swiftly dissipated in the open air. Down slope, he heard one of his adversaries screaming, and he wished the wounded soldier luck—all bad. He hoped that others had been taken out by the explosion, but it would have been too much to count on for a single blast to clear the slope.

Still, he had bought some time, some breathing

room. His enemies were stunned, disoriented. It was time to make his move.

He rose from cover, sighting down the barrel of his AK-47, looking for a target in the smoky darkness of the desert night.

NAJRAN WAS CROUCHED behind his staff car, with a pistol in his trembling hand. He risked a glance around the fender, saw the darkness split by muzzle-flashes from his line of soldiers as they closed in on the enemy position. There were other flashes, too, from up there in the rocks, and even as he watched, Najran saw one of his soldiers stagger, going down, immediately followed by another.

He ducked back and hugged the cool flank of the staff car as a bullet sizzled overhead. It wasn't working out as he had hoped, but he couldn't quit yet. He would allow his troops a bit more time to do the job before he summoned help.

Besides, he couldn't reach the radio from where he was, and going for it would have meant exposure to the snipers hiding in the rocks.

He inched around to face the sergeant, who was crouched beside him with a submachine gun in his hands. He fixed the other man with a determined eye and said, ''Go get the radio.''

The sergeant glared at him, stopping short of telling him where he could stick his order. Moving in a clumsy ducklike manner, the soldier headed around the left side of the vehicle, advancing toward the open door. It gave him partial cover, and he kept his head down, reaching back inside the car to snare a walkie-talkie from between the seats.

Just then, some kind of an explosion echoed from the outcropping in front of them. Someone screamed, and the sergeant raised his head to look around just as Najran peered from his own secluded hiding place. Both missed the flash of the explosion, but they witnessed its effect on the advancing troops, their whole line wavering, intimidated by the blast and the ensuing screams, beginning to fall back.

"Go forward, damn you!" the lieutenant shouted from his hiding place.

The sergeant rose and fired a short burst from his submachine gun, just above the heads of those uncertain warriors. He was aiming toward the rock pile, granted, but they got the message loud and clear. Proceed as ordered, and at least they had a chance to overcome the enemy. Defy an officer, retreat despite his order to advance, and they were looking at a court-martial, assuming they weren't gunned down as cowards on the battlefield.

The ragged line stood fast for several seconds more, then started toward the rock pile once again. Najran ducked back to cover as the shooting started with renewed intensity, already counting his reserves and wondering how he should use them in the second wave if this one failed to do the trick.

He had perhaps a dozen men to fill the second line, assuming he could get them to do anything at all. Each one was listening or watching as his comrades made the first assault, and they had seen a number of their company cut down, heard screams of agony after the hand grenade went off. Some would be hesitant to put their own lives on the line if they regarded the battle as crass futility. There was an outside chance that one or two of them might openly defy him, challenge his command, and he would have to be prepared to deal with them from strength.

The sergeant waddled back to join him, carrying the compact two-way radio, and handed it over. The lieutenant was about to call for reinforcements when he noticed that the radio felt strange—too light, as if he held an empty metal shell in his hand. A closer look showed him the reason: just above the walkie-talkie's mouthpiece, he made out a tidy hole where something had punched through the metal; in the back, loose wiring dangled from another hole, this one at least three inches in diameter.

A bullet had destroyed the radio, which meant that he would have to fetch another from the truck or pass an order to the APC and have it relayed back to Al-Ubayyid. Either way, it meant more risk, exposure to the bullets that got past his line of soldiers, striking one vehicle or another, raising spurts of dust when they struck earth.

"This radio is broken," he informed the sergeant.

"Right."

"I need another one."

Again his driver seemed about to answer him, refuse the order, but the sergeant had been too long in his uniform to suddenly defy an officer in circumstances

where refusal to obey an order meant he could be shot
down on the spot.

"Yes, sir."

He started moving toward the APC in his peculiar
duckwalk, shoulders hunched, the submachine gun
clutched against his chest. When he was almost there,
the sergeant straightened a bit, perhaps believing he
was covered by the APC, and that was when it happened. Najran was staring at him when the bullet
struck between his shoulder blades, slammed him face
first against the armored vehicle with force enough to
break his nose.

Not that the nose job mattered now.

Najran sat trembling as he watched the dead man
fall, knew he would have to make that walk himself
if there was any hope at all of bringing reinforcements
to the scene. The longer he delayed, the worse that
trek would be.

But there was something wrong with Najran's legs.
They wouldn't move.

The lieutenant sat there, frozen in his spot, and felt
hot tears of shame pour down his cheeks.

McCARTER SAW the first wave coming, watched the
soldiers break off into squads and ring the outcropping
where he and his companions were making their stand.
He didn't fire at once, allowing his targets to move in
closer, lessening the odds of wasted shots. They were
within a hundred feet when someone in the second
wave wised up enough to douse the headlights of their
vehicles, but he had their positions marked by then

and tracked their progress via starlight, covering their line of march with his Kalashnikov.

One of his comrades started to fire first, above him and behind, but McCarter held steady, straining for the sound of running feet approaching from his front. Four soldiers had been detailed to that side before the lights went out, and he was ready for them now. A scrape of leather on the rock below alerted him, man-shapes lurching in the night, and he cut loose on them from thirty feet.

His first rounds took the pointman, staggered him and sent him sliding back downhill. The soldier's weapon discharged as he fell, a spray of bullets chipping stone around McCarter, but the Phoenix Force commando held his ground. A second burst knocked that one out of play forever, while the troops behind him scrambled in a search for cover on the barren slab of stone.

The Briton followed them by sound and shadows, sighting on a muzzle-flash when one of them tried to lay down a screen of cover fire. The soldier didn't duck or weave, but rather held his mark, unloading from the hip, until McCarter cut him down. The short burst from his AK-47 knocked the gunner backward, tumbling through a clumsy somersault, his weapon spinning in the opposite direction, clattering on stone before it slid away.

And that left two survivors of the charge, more cautious now, determined not to give themselves away by careless noise or movement. Still, they had to reach him somehow, root him out and finish it. He was ready when they started to climb toward him, one on either side.

They almost got it right. Within the limits of the situation and their training, he would probably have given them an A for effort, but the limitations make or break a soldier in the field. One slip, one sound, can spell disaster in a combat situation, and the young men sent to kill him had been schooled by drill instructors who weren't concerned with climbing rock piles silently at midnight. Other skills were deemed more vital to the soldiers who patrolled the wasteland of the Kurdufan: desert survival, fighting with support from armored vehicles, the proper method for assaulting native villages, perhaps some sniping on the side.

But gaps in training never really showed until a person met a problem in the field. This night, McCarter was their problem, and the Sudanese were definitely second-best.

The climber on his left was making better progress, inching closer, scraping on the rock face like a giant beetle. On McCarter's right, the other uniform was several yards behind his comrade, trying to catch up, his weapon grating on the stone and on the Briton's nerves.

He took the closer target first, prepared to do it with a 3-round burst and swivel instantly to bring the second soldier under fire. If he was quick and accurate enough, it would be over in the next few seconds, and he could prepare to meet the second wave.

The sound of racing engines startled all concerned. McCarter glanced back to his rear to find out where

the sound was coming from. If reinforcements had arrived already, they were finished. Fresh troops meant
they could be attacked from all four sides at once,
while they defended only three. Defeat would be in-
evitable, and defeat meant death.

But he could damn well take these bastards with
him, come what may.

The climber on his left was less than twenty feet
away. McCarter shot him in the face and sent him
tumbling back downhill, arms flailing, his equipment
rattling on the slope. The proximity of death unnerved
his comrade on McCarter's right, and when he turned
to bring the second soldier under fire, his target was
already scrabbling backward, lunging for the deeper
shadows that would offer him at least some minimal
protection.

Then the lights came on.

The first two vehicles to join the rest were motorcycles, followed closely by a pair of dusty jeeps.
McCarter kissed the climber off and sighted on the
closer of the cyclists, index finger taking up the
AK-47's trigger slack, when suddenly the bikers
opened fire with submachine guns, spraying bullets at
the startled soldiers down below.

DON'T LOOK A GIFT HORSE in the mouth.

The old saw came to Bolan in a flash as he beheld
the new arrivals hosing his enemies with automatic
fire. The regulars were taken by surprise, but they
fought back, unloading on the new arrivals at a range
so close that it was difficult for them to miss. Both

sides were taking hits down there, vehicles skidding to a halt, men sprawling on the ground, before he understood exactly what was happening.

One of the motorcyclists was illuminated for a moment by the headlights of the jeep behind him, long enough for Bolan's mind to register his ebony complexion. They were rebels, striking at the junta's soldiers when and where they could, guerrilla style. He had no way of knowing whether their arrival on the scene was chance, or if they had been following the Sudanese patrol, but it made little difference. These men were fighting, dying, when they could as easily have waited in the outer darkness for the troops to finish Bolan and his friends, then picked them off at leisure when their guard was down.

It was a wild, chaotic scene down there, but Bolan did his best to help the rebels. Selecting targets was the risky part, when most of them were simply shadows grappling in the dark. He stayed away from soldiers fighting hand-to-hand, incapable of telling who was who or dropping one without some risk to his opponent. It was easier to spot the solitary targets, khaki clad and framed by headlights.

Bolan spotted one such, rising from behind the army staff car, his semiauto pistol leveled at one of the motorcycle riders, cranking off a hasty round before he found his mark. He was about to try again when the Executioner shot him in the chest and dropped him out of sight behind the vehicle. The biker glanced back toward the rocks and flashed a dazzling smile before he gunned his dusty cycle, put it through a sharp one-eighty, spewing sand in all directions, and reversed his track. He wore some kind of compact submachine gun on a sling around his neck, and he unlimbered it to fire a strafing burst as he roared past the flatbed truck.

The odds were close down there, perhaps a slight advantage to the regulars, and Bolan calculated that the fight could still go either way. On either side of him, the Phoenix Force commandos had begun to snipe at targets on the eerie desert battlefield, their choices indicating that they had the general scenario worked out. Still, with the rebel vehicles in motion, circling, headlights sweeping, dust clouds rising, passengers unloading for a closer shot at their appointed enemies, it made for risky business. Bolan was about to warn his comrades off when he heard still more engines, drawing closer by the heartbeat, and he hunkered down to see which side the new arrivals represented.

More headlights, a truck and two more jeeps this time. He couldn't see the passengers, their uniforms or race, but they were barely on the scene before they started to fire at the army regulars, their rifles and a light machine gun flashing, adding a surreal, kaleidoscopic aspect to the action down below.

It lasted only moments after that. The regulars were cut off and surrounded, suddenly outnumbered two or three to one. They fought and died, a handful throwing down their weapons toward the end, but their opponents weren't interested in taking prisoners. A final volley from the rebel firing line, and stillness settled on the smoky killing ground.

What now?

Their rescue from the soldiers, Bolan realized, was strictly incidental to the ambush that was one more skirmish in Sudan's long-running civil war. For all he knew, the rebels would decide to turn around and kill the white men they had saved, eliminate three witnesses. He stayed well under cover as the gunmen gathered.

One of them separated from the others and moved forward. Bolan recognized the motorcyclist he had assisted moments earlier, still smiling as he walked up to the base of the Executioner's stony fortress. Bolan straightened enough to show himself above the waist, making no effort to conceal the rifle in his hands.

"A white man," the cyclist said, grinning like a man who'd won the lottery. "Do you speak English?"

"Right the first time," Bolan replied.

"You might as well come down," the rebel said, "unless you plan on walking home from here."

CHAPTER SIXTEEN

The rebel camp was situated eighty miles to the south-east of Al-Ubayyid, on the banks of a tributary feeding the White Nile. Military aspects of the camp were well disguised, the layout tailored to resemble any other native village from the air and even from a cursory inspection on the ground. Patrols passed through the area, twice a month on average, and while the soldiers sometimes stopped to search or throw their weight around, they had discovered no incriminating evidence in eighteen months.

That was a tribute to the ingenuity of rebels who had constructed the community and dared to put their wives and children in harm's way to make the place resemble a civilian town.

"They are no safer if we send them farther south," Manute Yousef explained to Bolan as they sat beside the cooking fire and ladled fragrant stew from wooden bowls. "At least this way, we have a chance to fight for them if the patrols decide to rape or kill them for the color of their skins."

Yousef had been elected leader of this rebel band, as he explained, because he had more formal education than his comrades, and he was the first man from his village—miles away—to kill a soldier of the junta. He had killed three of them, in fact, when he surprised them in the midst of an attempted rape. His sister was the victim, and Yousef had only a machete to oppose three soldiers armed with automatic weapons. He had killed them, all the same, and when the deed was done, the other members of his village helped to strip the bodies and drop them in a river where the crocodiles were always hungry. There had been no turning back from that day forward, though a number of his people had preferred to move away and change their names, instead of following the course that led to all-out war against the junta in Khartoum.

"Have you made any progress?" Manning asked him as they sat beside the fire.

"We're still alive," Yousef replied. "Some of us, anyway. The men we lost tonight will live on in our songs and in our memories. They will not be forgotten, even by our children's children. Someday we will have our country back and live in peace."

The stew was tasty, even if the contents were a mystery best left unquestioned. Bolan swallowed, wiped his mouth and told their host, "You saved our tails back there. We can't thank you enough."

"You fight the strangers, I believe," Yousef said, "men who use our country as a staging area for crimes in other lands."

"That's right."

"We would be happy to ignore them, but they make themselves our enemies by taking arms and money from the government," their host went on. "You have repaid our help by killing them. If you kill more before you leave, so much the better."

"You've had dealings with the Palestinians, I take it," McCarter said.

"Yes, indeed. Sometimes, when they get tired of practicing on wooden targets, soldiers from Khartoum direct them to our villages and grant them leave to murder anyone they wish. They call it practice. We consider it an act of war."

The bitterness in Yousef's voice was obvious and understandable. "Have you gone after them before?" Bolan asked.

"Not so much. It may seem harsh, but in the scheme of things, the people they have murdered are a handful in comparison to victims of our 'lawful' government. We kill them when we can, of course, but mostly we oppose the army. When the generals are removed from power, executed for their crimes, the strangers will find somewhere else to play their games."

"You take it all in stride," McCarter said.

Yousef shrugged. "The war has lasted for years, and before that, there was always trouble with the Muslim people in the north. Not all of them, you understand, but those who wind up in control. Such men crave power for their own. They hate to share. They look at us and see a kind of vermin they must kill to make their homes and fortunes safe. These mice fight back, though. They were not expecting that."

"There should be something we can do to help," McCarter said.

Yousef thought about it, staring at the fire. At last, he said, "We had another target scheduled for tonight, before we heard the soldiers shooting at you. If you really want to help us..."

Bolan saw the others watching him and nodded.

"What's the deal?" he asked.

HASSAN JUBAYL PICKED UP a heavy crystal ashtray from his desk and flung it at the nearest wall. It didn't shatter, but the stucco wall was gouged and scarred from impact where it struck. He cursed bitterly, then kicked a trash can across the room.

He had received Afif Matalka's news at last, now that the sun was up, long hours wasted, and there was no hope of tracking down his enemies. A squad of soldiers had pursued them from the camp, but they hadn't returned, and now he understood that *they* were dead, as well.

Who *were* these demons that tormented him?

Matalka was no help, though he had glimpsed them for a moment, racing past him in a stolen jeep. There had been three men, or so he said, but there was little more to add. A search of the perimeter revealed two RPGs, but they had been dispensed by thousands to guerrilla fighters all around the world, before the Soviet regime and Eastern European satellites collapsed. Jubayl himself had Russian rocket launchers in his arsenal. It told him nothing as to the identity of his assailants.

He had trouble, now, not only from the strangers who were hunting him, but also from Marawi Bol. Jubayl's liaison with the junta had been visibly concerned by the attacks around Khartoum, more by the prospect of adverse publicity than any casualties the Spear of Allah had sustained. It was a different story in this morning's light, with soldiers dead and no scapegoat available to take the blame. If someone wasn't punished soon, Bol might well decide to blame the Spear and take it out on them. It was a way for him to save face with his masters, and he was nothing if not geared to preservation of his own position in the government.

Jubayl knew how the system worked, and he couldn't complain. The junta's ideology and lack of moral principles allowed him to find sanctuary and support within Sudan; if those same traits worked to his disadvantage now, when there were difficulties, it was his task to resolve the problem quickly and efficiently before it cost him everything.

But how?

His men had gotten nowhere, asking questions in Khartoum, and the interrogation teams Bol dispatched had likewise come up empty-handed. That meant nothing in itself, except that Jubayl's enemies were good at covering their tracks. Still, if he couldn't find a way to stop them soon, repay them for the damage and embarrassment they had inflicted on him, he was bound to lose support from the commanders in Khartoum. They wouldn't willingly give arms and cash to losers, much less when the effort cost them soldiers of their own.

Jubayl had toyed with the idea of making an example of Afif Matalka. He could execute his first lieutenant, let the others see what happened to a man who failed the Spear of Allah. But on second thought, he deemed such action to be premature. Matalka was frightened at the moment, rightly so, and fear could be a solid motivator. If Matalka got a second chance to face the men who had humiliated him, he would do everything within his power to destroy them, knowing that it was his last chance to perform and prove himself.

And if Matalka should fail a second time, Jubayl would have no hesitation in presenting him as an example to the other members of his private army. Any system that rewarded failure—or ignored it in a crisis situation—sowed the seeds of ultimate defeat within itself.

Meanwhile, Jubayl had tightened personal security. He had no way of telling where his faceless adversaries would strike next, but he didn't intend to fall before their guns by way of negligence. If he was running out of time, at least he meant to take all steps within his power to protect himself.

And in the meantime, he still had a broader war to fight. The Zionists in Tel Aviv still ruled his homeland and his people with a rod of iron, supported by donations from America. His first and foremost duty was to press the fight against Israel at any cost. If he allowed himself to be distracted from the cause, his enemies had won already. He would be disgraced, pathetic in his own eyes and in the opinion of his men.

A warrior who thought more about himself than his appointed mission was a failure from the start. Hassan Jubayl didn't intend to fail, not while he lived.

Danger or not, the holy war went on.

AT FIRST, Manute Yousef had harbored doubts about the three white strangers. They were adversaries of the junta, clearly, but that fact alone didn't mean they were friends of his. Even within the rebel movement, there were tribes and factions that couldn't cooperate, though life depended on it. Some of them were dead today, wiped out because they focused too much on some petty problem of their own and let the common enemy sneak up on them when they were unprepared.

At last, he saw their very strangeness, their incontestable status as outsiders, in a wholly different light. If they came from outside Sudan, from whichever Western nation they named, the fact of their *difference* proved that they weren't traitors dispatched from Khartoum. There had been other would-be spies for the regime, but Yousef or his aides had rooted each one out and dealt with them in the only manner infiltrators understood—brute force. Their bodies had been spirited away and buried secretly. They might be found eventually, through a sandstorm or some other fluke of nature, but Yousef would be long gone by then, one way or another.

Manute Yousef hadn't gone to the Palestinian guerrilla camp to check out their story; he didn't have to.

By the time the sun rose, rousting warriors from their blankets, word of mouth had spread the story of a massacre. It was remarkable not for its ferocity or body count, but rather for the choice of targets. Someone, he was told, had taken a dislike to Palestinian resistance fighters in Sudan, not only at their camp, but in Khartoum, as well.

Such men would fight, but Yousef couldn't guarantee that they would win. So what? None of the men who followed him had any guarantee that they would see another day. The knowledge of their own death, lurking just around the corner, made them more determined fighters in a pinch, and Yousef liked it that way. They would fight like devils to the bitter end, while many others in the south were conditioned to defeat, prepared to pull up stakes and flee whenever someone glared at them and snapped his fingers.

For himself, Yousef could take or leave the Palestinians, as long as they did all their killing somewhere else and didn't practice on his people. There were blood debts owed this day, and while a number of them had been paid last night, he wouldn't mind another chance to watch the Arabs die or run away.

But he would have to deal with first things first. His *real* war was against the junta in Khartoum, with its oppressive rules and grim commitment to a war against his brothers.

Never mind.

There would be blood aplenty when he led his soldiers and the three Americans against the military base near Kusti. Al-Ubayyid would be closer, but he knew the soldiers there were on alert by now, infuriated by the loss of fighting comrades. Word would spread, of course, but officers commanding at a distance from the Kurdufan would think about what happened, tell themselves that some young officer had made an error on patrol that cost his men their lives. And that wasn't entirely wrong, of course, as Yousef would admit. It took a rebel strike team to destroy them, though, and as the news spread southward it would bring them new recruits, young men—and possibly some women—who desired an opportunity to serve their race or faith by standing tall and proud against the enemy.

His circle of advisers—some of them, at least—expressed concern that the three strangers might recant their promise when they saw the Kusti base, but Yousef had a feeling they were wrong. These men had seen it all, and they were long accustomed to ignoring odds. Yousef had seen them fight, however briefly, and he had observed their scars.

These weren't men who quit or ran away.

The final test would come when they were at the target, facing soldiers whose disdain for human life was legendary in Sudan. There was a difference, though, between sadistic butchers and committed men at arms. One killed for profit or for pleasure, seeking out the path of least resistance, while the other spilled blood by necessity, found no real pleasure in it, but continued in defiance of the hardships he encountered.

It came down to spirit versus numbers, heart against hardware. Yousef couldn't be certain which side would prevail, but he knew which side he was on.

And he would die defending it, if that was what it took to bring the junta down.

MARAWI BOL GLARED at the telephone upon his desk, despising it for all the bad news it had brought him in the past few hours. He wasn't particularly sorry for the Spear of Allah's soldiers slaughtered in the desert; there was even some relief that the attacks had shifted from Khartoum. He could live with that, perhaps claim credit for inducing those responsible to leave the capital.

But then, there were the *other* casualties.

A squad of regulars had been wiped out, along with the expendable guerrillas. Bol knew none of them, wouldn't have recognized them if they passed him by on the parade ground, but that was beside the point. They had been soldiers, agents of the junta, and their deaths had to be avenged.

That task came down to him, and if he didn't finish it with all deliberate speed, the brass above him would be looking for another man to handle it. His job was hanging by a thread, and the thread was stretched across a razor blade. His next mistake could be the last.

Worse yet, he could be penalized for someone else's failure, purged and punished for the foibles of Hassan Jubayl. No matter how Bol despised the fact, their fates were linked for now. To sever them, reclaim his own identity, he would be forced to deal with those who were bedeviling the Spear of Allah.

And he had to do it soon.

There was no room in Khartoum today for slackers. Rather, there was no place for an officer who hadn't learned the art of looking busy, keeping up a bold front of activity that made him seem efficient to the men who mattered. Much of it was pure illusion: victories against opponents who were frequently unarmed civilians, body counts that were inflated to impress the brass, perhaps the odd report of skirmishes that never happened. In Sudan, the civil war had dragged on for so long that both sides craved good news, and those on the receiving end of false or modified reports were often so relieved that they would never look beyond the document itself, made no examination of the facts.

Bol suspected it had been the same, to some extent, with the Americans in Vietnam. He was a child when Saigon fell, but there were always lessons to be learned from history. If he could learn from the mistakes of those who had confronted rebels in the past, avoid the pitfalls that had claimed their lives or ruined their careers, so much the better.

In the present situation, though, it seemed to him that nothing short of hard results would do the trick. He couldn't bluff when his superiors demanded bodies, even public executions of the men responsible for killing close to thirty soldiers in a single night.

Where could he start?

The bad news, other than his own embarrassment, was that he had no more clues today than he had yesterday—which meant that he had none to speak of whatsoever. There was still the word of two or three survivors, from the early raids around Khartoum, that he was looking for white men—Americans or British, French or something else, he had no way of knowing. No one left alive had heard the gunmen speak, except for short phrases in Arabic that could have been memorized from any tourist phrase book.

It was useless information, more because of what Bol couldn't do in his search for the elusive gunmen. He couldn't announce that several Europeans or Americans were running wild around Sudan, eluding his patrols and killing soldiers, killing visitors who were protected by the government. That kind of news would make the junta seem ridiculous. If they couldn't corral three foreigners who would stand out in any crowd, how could the leaders of Sudan maintain control, suppress the armed rebellion of their fellow countrymen? That was a question asked too often in what appeared to be an unending civil war. The last thing his superiors desired was more adverse publicity, more questions from the very people who supported them in office.

It was one thing to display a group of prisoners when they were whipped, disarmed and waiting for the firing squad. Acknowledging that they were still at large was something else—if not a frank admission of defeat, at least a signal that the confidence some people still had in the junta was misplaced.

Bol would have to solve all that, and quickly, if he meant to keep his rank…and it could well be worse than that, he realized. If he should fail, it wouldn't be the first time that an ineffective officer was made to take the fall for others, offered to the populace as an example. If he didn't watch out, Bol could wind up standing where the foreigners should be, against a wall festooned with bullet scars and rusty stains.

He could not let that happen. If he found himself with no alternatives, then he would dump the problem on Hassan Jubayl, accuse the Spear of Allah and its competition—Hezbollah, perhaps, or Jihad—of waging fratricidal warfare in Sudan, endangering the people's army with their power plays.

It might not stick, but it was damn well worth a try.

And in the meantime, while he built his case in private, he would spare no effort to locate and punish the elusive foreigners. With any luck at all, Bol might come out smelling like a rose.

"NO SECOND THOUGHTS?"

They were alone when Bolan spoke, the rebel tribesmen having left them to their own devices in a thatch-roofed hut with walls constructed out of something that resembled adobe. Manning and McCarter glanced at each other briefly, and the former SAS commando answered for them both.

"The army's been supporting terrorism, and they're after us, regardless. We've already killed some. This could throw them off the scent and give us time to finish it."

"Just so you're sure."

"No problem," Manning said.

Bolan told himself that it wasn't the same as killing cops. From the beginning of his one-man holy war, the Executioner had balked at drawing down on the police of any land, no matter how corrupt or brutal they might be. It was a point of honor, laying off the badge that some, at least, had worn with pride as fellow soldiers in a struggle that would never end. He also knew that Phoenix Force and Able Team didn't share his aversion to eliminating officers who murdered, brutalized or dealt in drugs, and that was fine. It was a personal decision, each man for himself. He could no more tell Manning and McCarter what to think or feel than he could make the moon reverse its course in outer space.

With combat troops, it was a different story. A fine distinction, maybe, since both groups wore uniforms and put their lives at risk for tax-supported salaries, but Bolan's years in Southeast Asia and the urban wars that followed had impressed him with a subtle difference. Cops, at least in theory, were committed from the day they volunteered to fight evil, stand up for civilized society, uphold law and order on the streets. A military force, meanwhile, was ruled by politics, its rank and file oath bound to follow orders anywhere they led, whether the end result was liberation of a country or some shocking act of genocide.

Police, in short, were paid and sworn to see that justice would prevail, and when they wielded deadly force, it was in that pursuit. An army, on the other hand, was the blunt instrument of politics, the sharp end of diplomacy, more interested in means than ends. The soldiers who enlisted to support a government involved in terrorism, genocide or any other crime against humanity were willing tools of evil.

They were fair game for the Executioner.

"You reckon he was right about the numbers?" McCarter asked.

Bolan shrugged. Manute Yousef estimated there could be as many as a hundred guns against them when they struck the army camp at Kusti, but they would be taking twenty rebels, in addition to Yousef, the Phoenix Force warriors and himself.

"It's hard to say."

"We shouldn't do too badly," Manning interjected, "even so."

"That's bloody optimistic," McCarter said. "'Not too bad'!"

"I always try to see the bright side," Manning told him, putting on a crooked grin.

"I've noticed that about you."

"We should try to get some rest," Bolan said, glancing at his watch. They wouldn't leave the village until nightfall, driving south in convoy, and he felt the tension of the past few days in every fiber of his being.

"It's too bloody hot to sleep," McCarter said. "This lot should snag some air conditioners next time they get the chance."

"Put that in the suggestion box," Manning told him.

"I've got your suggestion box right here."

He left them to it, recognizing their good-natured bickering as a release of tension, and retreated to the cot he had selected for himself.

Too hot for sleep?

He wasn't sure, but it could do no harm to try.
The Executioner lay down and closed his eyes.
He hoped he wouldn't dream.

CHAPTER SEVENTEEN

Manute Yousef stood with his two lieutenants and the three white men—the latter daubed with war paint now, so that they almost looked like members of the tribe—and tried to think of something he should say. They knew their business, had rehearsed the moves on a scale model prior to starting on the long drive south, but it was different, he knew, when you were facing guns and stood to lose your life.

"Remember your positions and the signals," he instructed, speaking more to his men than to the foreigners. Gut instinct told him those three would remember what they were supposed to do if they were handcuffed, blindfolded and set on fire. They had the grim air of professionals about them, men to whom the guns and bloodshed were a calling rather than a situation forced upon them by prevailing circumstances.

Both of Yousef's men responded with a nod and spoken promise to attack on time, according to instructions they had memorized. Each would be leading six men into battle, no more than a rifle squad, while six more followed Yousef when he led the charge. The three white men were on their own, a separate force, attacking from the fourth side of the camp.

Yousef couldn't help thinking of the enemy. If he was right in guessing at the population of the Kusti base, they were outnumbered five to one. Surprise was on their side—or would be, if the plan went off without a hitch—but those were still harsh odds.

And it had been a long, harsh war.

Yousef stood watching as his officers retrieved their soldiers from the shadows, leading them through darkness, moving cautiously to take up their positions on the north and west. His squad would be attacking from the south, while Belasko and his comrades took the east side of the camp. He had no doubt that they could fight as well as six or seven men, but it was still a moment that he dreaded, sending them to face an enemy who wasn't rightly theirs.

Still, he would take the help they offered him, and gratefully. He was in no position to let sympathy or foolish pride prevent him from attacking when he had a golden opportunity to deal the junta an effective blow. And if they lost their lives while helping Yousef's people, he would offer up a prayer of thanks to the gods for providing him with bold and selfless friends, requesting that the gods make room for them in Paradise.

The soldiers Yousef led this night were young men, five in their midtwenties, one just turned nineteen, but all were veterans of Sudan's long civil war. Each had a score to settle with the government, for friends and family members murdered, property destroyed or sto-

len by the state, youth wasted in pursuit of vengeance
when they should have been enjoying life and raising
families. Yousef knew them each by name, knew their
histories and had no fear that they would let him down
when it was time to face the enemy. Almost certainly
some of them would meet their deaths this night, but
that couldn't be helped. The struggle was what mattered, more than any single man or woman. If he ever
let that central fact escape him, Yousef would lose
track of why he fought, why he had spent the best
years of his young life killing people he didn't even
know.

It was a grotesque life, he realized, but it was all he
had. The government had taken everything from him
but the will to fight, and he would use whatever time
remained to him in paying back his blood debt to the
butchers in Khartoum. Some would have called him a
fanatic, and he had no solid argument to counter that
description, but his critics never took the time to see
where he had come from, all that he had lost, to think
of *why* he fought. If they could only understand, what
then?

Yousef purged his mind of philosophical concerns.
He stood upon the threshold of another desperate battle with a handful of the men he trusted most in all
the world—and three white strangers, whom he also
trusted, if for different reasons.

Those men had seen evil, smelled its fetid breath
and staked their lives in opposition to its progress.
They might die this night, but they would never break
and run away.

Yousef would have bet his soul on that.

He checked his watch and saw that it was time. A glance back at the others showed him they were ready, waiting for the order to advance. He didn't speak, but urged them forward with a gesture of his hand, and started to move toward the camp where they would find at least a hundred of the enemy.

BOLAN WAS READY when the shooting started, sprinting toward the camp that sprawled in front of him, two hundred yards across, with tents and Quonset huts set up in rows, a minitown erected in the middle of the wasteland.

Somewhere on his left, McCarter would be keeping pace, while Manning was positioned on his right. They had fanned out deliberately to give themselves a better chance of getting past the sentries in one piece, prevent some lucky gunner with an automatic weapon from dropping all of them at once. Each man was adept at fighting on his own, and they could still support each other in a pinch if it came down to that.

The keys to living through a clash with overwhelming odds were speed, audacity and preparation. If you killed the lights and tossed in the advantage of surprise, it just might be a winning hand.

The hour was late enough that most of their opponents ought to be in bed, if not asleep, and their reaction time to an attack would be extended as they grappled with their clothes, their weapons, trying to reorient themselves. As for the sentries walking post around the camp, all he could do was hope they let their guard down far enough to let him draw first blood.

Beyond that, it was anybody's game.

Yousef's men had RPGs, one launcher to a squad, and Bolan hung back, waiting for the rockets to explode before he rushed the camp's perimeter. It took only a moment, comets streaking in from three directions, detonating almost simultaneously at the center of the compound, and the rush was on.

It was enough to shake the sentries, throw them off their stride and give the raiders a fighting chance. No rockets had been fired on Bolan's part of the perimeter, so the sentries turned to stare inside the camp just when they should have been most sensitive to danger from without.

They wouldn't have a second chance to do it right.

The first short burst from Bolan's Kalashnikov caught a distracted soldier who stood directly in his path, and dropped the man facedown in the dirt.

Target number two began to turn to face the painted warrior charging at him from the outer darkness. This one was almost quick enough, but then his feet got tangled up in the maneuver, and he staggered just enough to spoil his aim as he squeezed off a short burst from his SMG.

He never recovered, as hot rounds from Bolan's AK-47 ripping through his chest and blowing him away. The killer wore a stunned expression as he toppled over backward, sprawling on the hard-packed ground.

The way was clear, at least for Bolan, though he

still heard gunfire to his left and right, Manning and McCarter fighting their way through the line and into the camp. He had faith they would make it, confidence born of observation and experience, but his conscious mind was occupied with the minutiae of personal survival.

Smoke and flame billowed in front of him, with men running back and forth, as if they knew where they were going, while their officers stood still and shouted orders no one seemed to hear. A rocket plowed into the motor pool, well off the beaten track from any squad's attack zone, and the first three vehicles went up like Roman candles in the night, fuel burning brightly as it spread from ruptured gas tanks in a lake of fire.

He had selected marks with Manning and McCarter, drew the communications hut himself, aware that any calls for help had to be cut off before the camp could summon reinforcements. They had long odds as it was, and the arrival of another hundred men—much less an armored cavalry detachment—would eclipse their rout of the previous night, at the Spear of Allah's camp.

And it would get them killed, damn right.

He saw his target through a drifting pall of smoke and dust, corrected slightly for a hard collision course and put on speed. Two soldiers blocked his path unwittingly, their dark eyes going wide, surprised and startled into fleeting immobility at meeting one of their opponents in the flesh. There was no possibility of Bolan being taken for a fellow Sudanese—not with his greater height, his painted face and battle garb—

but they lost precious time recoiling from the sight before them, thinking how they should react.

For Bolan's part, it was instinctive, firing from the hip and dropping them together in a tangled heap without a break in stride.

The commo hut was just in front of him, roof bristling with antennae, thick black cable snaking through a port in one wall, out of sight to Bolan's left. He fired a short burst at the cable, saw it fly apart, then continued to the hut. Its door faced eastward, opening as he got there, a confused and frightened man emerging to discover what had happened to his power.

The Executioner shot him in the chest, three rounds to make it stick, and stepped across the twitching corpse to make his way inside the hut.

McCarter DUCKED his head involuntarily as yet another RPG grenade went off. He was conditioned that way, dodging shrapnel at the first sound of a blast, regardless of the fact that he was still well out of range. Old habits were enough to save a life sometimes, and in the present bloody circumstances, he could see no reason for a change of style.

A solitary lookout glanced back from the fireworks long enough to glimpse McCarter coming at him from the shadows. There was nothing he could do about it, not from that position, but he made the effort anyway, half turning at the waist and swiveling his gun to bring the stranger under fire.

Too late.

McCarter had the man sighted in before his quarry

glanced around and saw death coming. When the sentry tried to bring him under fire, McCarter got there first, a short burst from his AK-47 rocking his adversary. The hardman dropped to one knee before going over on one side. His eyes were glazed in death now, looking through McCarter at some distant point no living man would ever see.

He canned the battlefield philosophy and kept on moving toward the hulking Quonset hut that he had drawn when they were choosing targets back in the darkness. It was more imposing here, up close and personal, but every structure of its type had certain built-in weaknesses. Most such buildings had two doors, arranged in shotgun style, but this one had a single exit, thereby making an attacker's job much easier.

McCarter didn't know if he was moving toward a barracks or a storehouse, but it made no difference to his plan in either case. Empty or occupied, the hut had been slated for destruction, and he wouldn't leave a crucial job undone.

He kicked the door in, crossed the threshold in a crouching rush, prepared for anything except the stillness that enveloped him. Before him stood racks of weapons in a double row. To either side, he spotted wooden crates of ammunition and grenades, perhaps more weapons mixed in with the rest of it.

He made a quick check for explosives and found plastique on his right and halfway down the line of crates. Wisely the detonators in their foam-lined boxes had been separated from the explosives by some twenty feet, and it required some time for him to find them, plus a dry-cell battery, jog back and hook the whole thing up. Ten seconds on the timer, and McCarter palmed his walkie-talkie as he beat a swift retreat.

"Fire in the hole!" he warned. "Hit the deck!"

Almost before he had a chance to take his own advice, the hut seemed to swell, like something made of rubber, a grotesque balloon with air or water pouring in. It burst a heartbeat later, with a sound like heavy-metal thunder, slinging slabs of corrugated steel around the camp, smoke billowing, the secondary blasts of ammo and grenades continuing for what seemed an eternity.

The shock wave knocked McCarter sprawling, left him facedown in the sand, ears ringing from the blast. He felt as if he had been drop-kicked by a giant, but there was no lasting damage. He remained prostrate for several moments until the echoes of the blast began to fade and smoking shrapnel stopped raining around him. It was eerie how the powerful explosion brought a momentary silence to the killing ground, soldiers of both sides shaken, awed, but then the sounds of combat started up again, guns rattling, bullets whining overhead.

McCarter scrambled to his feet and glanced back at the crater where the Quonset hut had stood short moments earlier. It was impressive, but he had no time to stand there and admire his handiwork.

He told himself that several Sudanese, at least, had to have been killed or wounded when the plastique blew, but he couldn't have proved it. There were bodies scattered everywhere by now, and it was his job to increase their number, not to stand around and meditate on the effects of his fireworks display.

McCarter checked his AK-47, making sure the piece hadn't been damaged when he fell, and went in search of other enemies to kill.

CAPTAIN AKIL UMARHA knew disaster when he saw it, and the scene displayed before him met all the criteria: bodies scattered everywhere, vehicles burning on the far side of the camp, lights out from loss of power, muzzle-flashes winking in the darkness, tracers burning through the night like tiny meteors, a blackened crater where his arsenal had stood.

Disaster.

It wasn't a rout—not yet, at least—but it could come to that if he didn't find some way to regain control.

Umarha didn't know who was attacking his command, and the identity of his assailants wasn't critical. They would be rebels, obviously, and it made no difference which tribe or faction they belonged to. He could tell all that from looking at the corpses, questioning survivors.

His enemies were good; that much was obvious from the way they organized themselves and closed to killing range, struck at selected targets, rather than unleashing random sniper fire on the perimeter. He couldn't judge their numbers in the present circumstances, but there were enough of them to turn the whole camp upside down, provoke his soldiers into firing aimlessly at shadows, shooting anything that moved.

The captain kept a bullhorn underneath the desk in his command post, but the building was some fifty yards away, and he didn't feel good about his chances if he tried to cross that no-man's-land alone. One thing about command—you quickly lost the knack for front-line fighting and relied on others to perform the risky tasks.

Unless you had no other choice.

Umarha ran back to his sleeping quarters in the three-room bungalow that was his residence in camp and retrieved the pistol belt that hung across a chair beside his bed. It was the only weapon in his quarters, since he never really thought the base at Kusti would be jeopardized by a direct assault. Now that the rebels had conspired to prove him wrong, it was too late to curse himself for lack of preparation for emergencies.

He slipped the belt on, buckled it, drew the pistol from its holster and worked the slide to put a live round in the chamber. As he moved toward the door, a rifle bullet struck the wall immediately to his left, punched cleanly through and passed within six inches of the captain's face. He was already sweating, but he felt a cramping in his bowels now, praying that he wouldn't soil himself.

Umarha's soldiers needed him, and he couldn't allow himself to fail them out of fear. It would have made his whole career—his very life—a mocking lie.

He met a squad of riflemen just passing by his quarters on a dead run as he stepped outside. Umarha shouted at them, brought them back, projecting calm with every bit of strength that he possessed. They stood before him anxiously, some of them barely dressed, their faces marked with dust and perspiration. One of them was bleeding from a small cut under his left eye.

"We must get organized," he told them, "to repel these savages! You men will come with me to the command post."

There was no point leading them to the communications hut, since he could see that it had been destroyed, but there were walkie-talkies in his office, battery powered and thus independent of the camp's failed generators. He wasn't convinced the signal from a hand-held radio would reach from Kusti to the nearest army post, but it was worth a try.

In fact, it was his only hope for bringing reinforcements to the scene.

Umarha took his place among the soldiers as they started off toward the command post, letting them surround him. They looked apprehensive, clutching at their weapons, anxious for a chance to shoot instead of being shot at by invisible opponents. Dead men strewed along their line of march were mostly friends and comrades, though Umarha saw one face, lightly powdered with a layer of dust, and recognized the southern rebel by his faded denim pants. It reaffirmed the captain's first impression, but did nothing to inform him how many more rebels they would have to kill before the nightmare ended.

If the rebels defeated the soldiers... But he couldn't make himself complete the thought. A rebel victory would mean the end of his career. Assuming he somehow escaped alive, the generals in Khartoum would need a scapegoat, someone to accept the blame for failure, and the ranking officer in charge would be a logical selection. If Umarha didn't wish to be a sacrificial lamb, he had to do something quickly to reverse the damage already inflicted on his camp.

And to do that, he needed help.

They were a few yards from the CP, when a soldier on Umarha's right cried out a warning, and the captain spun in that direction, gaping as a rocket hurtled toward them. Someone grabbed his sleeve and pulled him down, the rocket's course of travel veering at the final instant, taking it directly to his office doorstep. The command post went ballistic as the rocket detonated, walls pushed outward, tin roof wafting skyward on a tongue of flame. The shock wave slammed Umarha backward, driving the air out of his lungs.

He tried to rise but couldn't feel his legs. Around the level of his waist, it seemed that something warm and wet was soaking through his shirt. Around him, frightened-looking soldiers knelt and stared.

Captain Akil Umarha felt the heavy pistol in his hand and smelled defeat.

Before the young men watching him could move, he raised the handgun to his head and fired.

THE FIRST GRENADE fell short when Manning pitched it, opening a crater in the arid ground between him and the gunners who had pinned him down. It gave them food for thought, though, and they started to withdraw, intent on circling around his flank while keeping him in place with probing fire, to get in closer for the kill.

The last thing Manning planned to do was wait for them to pull it off. He palmed another frag grenade, released the pin but held the safety spoon in place as he got to his feet. Instead of running for his life, he charged them, firing the Kalashnikov one-handed, left arm cocked to make the toss.

The soldiers saw him coming and couldn't quite believe their eyes, one man attacking four. They all let go at once, but it was nervous fire, unaimed. A couple of the bullets tugged at Manning's clothes and one nicked his ear, but he was too far in to scrub the plan and try another angle of attack.

He saw one soldier fall, blood spouting from his chest, the man beside him visibly recoiling from the sight. The other two were edging backward, trying to avoid this madman with the war paint on his face but they had stalled too long. He threw the frag grenade and went down on his face, in a continuation of the move, his AK-47 tracking, spitting death, before the lethal egg went off.

This time, the pitch was right on target. Two of Manning's enemies were airborne in a flash of smoke and flame, the third man staggering, dropping to his knees, one hand clapped to his forehead where a ragged shrapnel wound spilled crimson through his fingers. He still clutched his weapon but had lost the will to use it. Manning dropped him with a 3-round burst and went in search of other prey.

He passed the tangled bodies of a rebel and a soldier, locked together with their hands around each other's throat, eyes bulging, tongues extruded from between dry lips. They could have been wax dummies in a house of horrors, but the fear and fury on their faces would have challenged any sculptor.

Headlights bobbing toward him, through the middle of the carnage, startled Manning. He had seen the motor pool go up in flames, but it was obvious that at least one vehicle had been exempted from the firestorm. The big Canadian watched it coming, recognized the jeep by size and shape, picked out the silhouette of a machine gun mounted on the rear deck, with a soldier crouching over it, prepared to fire.

The headlights found him, pinned him, but he broke the spell and rolled out to his left before the .30-caliber projectiles started swarming after him. Manning came up with his AK-47 spitting, fired a short burst at the gunner, then decided he should focus on the driver if he meant to stop the jeep.

Twin headlights glared at the Phoenix Force commando, muzzle-flashes winking at him from above those glowing orbs. He tried to think of them as dragon's eyes, aimed where he would have if the jeep had been a living thing, then raised his sights a foot or so and held the trigger down. His bullets cracked the windshield, chipped the steering wheel and nailed the driver to his seat. The vehicle began to swerve, the rear-deck gunner losing balance for a moment, firing at the ground and then the stars. Before he could recover, Manning had him spotted, squeezing off another burst that emptied his rifle's magazine and swept the shooter from his perch, another rag doll sprawling in the dust.

The jeep rolled on without him, racing with a dead man's foot on the accelerator, breaking up a skirmish line of soldiers, crushing one who wasn't quick enough to save himself. The others scattered, running for their lives, and Manning took advantage of the chaos, hastily reloading, rushing in pursuit, the AK-47 spitting 3- and four-round bursts as he dropped first one runner, then another, sparing no one from his wrath.

Two rebels joined him midway through the wild charge, and they were laughing as they cut the soldiers down. Years of fratricidal conflict ruled out any thought of mercy, calling for repayment of old debts in blood.

Before their running targets reached the far side of the camp, two other rebels met them, cut them off and pinned them in a deadly cross fire. Manning watched them die, helped kill them, but he took no pleasure in it, turned away when gleaming knives were drawn to cut the dead men's throats.

It wasn't his war, he told himself. He was only passing through.

But he was in too deep to see the other side.

IT HADN'T BEEN INTENDED that the rebel force should seize and hold the military base at Kusti. Rather, they had come to raise some hell, inflict as many casualties as possible and disappear before the junta's reinforcements could arrive and trap them at the scene. It came as no surprise to Bolan, therefore, when the walkie-talkie on his web belt crackled with instructions to pull back.

The problem was that his adversaries had him pinned down with triangulated fire.

It was no mean achievement in the circumstances, three excited soldiers spotting Bolan in the midst of so much chaos, firing on him from diverse positions until they spotted what was happening and took advantage of their luck. Now they were closing in to make the kill.

His cover was the smoking ruin of the generator hut, still warm from the explosion of a rocket that had left the camp in darkness. Bolan used the silent, blackened generator housing as a shield against incoming bullets from the shooters on the north and northeast fronts, while part of a surviving wall helped screen him from the rifleman who had him covered on the south. The cover didn't stop them firing, though, and they came close enough with well-aimed rounds that Bolan had to keep his head down, minimizing his ability to answer with his own Kalashnikov.

It seemed an odd place to confront his death, and while he wasn't giving up, the Executioner had long since made his peace with God or whoever was handling details for the universe at large. Still, if he had a chance to turn the tables on his enemies...

He risked a glance around one blackened corner of

the burned-out generator housing, just in time to see one of the shooters scurry closer, dropping prone after he had gained a dozen yards. At that rate, if the other two were keeping pace, they would be right on top of him within the next few moments. And, if Bolan lingered where he was, Manute Yousef's strike team would depart without him, logically assuming he was dead. The Phoenix Force commandos might remain behind to look for him, but that would only further jeopardize their lives.

He had to break the stalemate, and he had to do it now.

With little left to lose, he went for broke. A quick check on the AK-47's load confirmed that the magazine was nearly full. He palmed a frag grenade—the last one, Bolan noted—and released the safety pin. Coordination was the key, and if he blew it, there would be no time to wonder how or why.

He burst from cover, lobbed the frag grenade in the direction of the gunner on his left, to southward, while the others scrambled to recover from the first shock of surprise. They had been counting on a rush-and-smother play, from all appearances, but it had blown up in their faces. He heard the hand grenade go off, but he was focused on the rifle in his hands, the human targets that were ducking, weaving, firing at him as they tried to compensate for being caught out in the open by their would-be victim.

Bolan nailed the closer of the two with four rounds to the chest and torso, spinning him, the soldier's automatic weapon firing all the way to impact with the ground. There was no telling where the bullets went, but it didn't matter, as long as *he* went down and stayed down.

That left one shooter on his feet. Something had to have snapped inside him, pushing him beyond raw panic in the face of death. He charged at Bolan, screaming, firing from the hip, as if he had a hundred men behind him and was confident of victory.

The AK-47 met him with a stream of deadly manglers, lifted him completely off his feet and slammed him backward to the ground. He lay there, twitching for a moment, boot heels drumming on the sand before the whole machine shut down and he went limp.

The soldier he had blasted with the frag grenade was wobbling to his feet when Bolan turned, no mean achievement in the circumstances, with his left leg nearly severed at midcalf. The guy was using his Kalashnikov to brace himself, its muzzle in the dirt, and he could only stand and gape as Bolan put a mercy round between his eyes.

And it was time to go.

He started working back toward the perimeter and the rendezvous where Yousef's soldiers were expected to regroup. Along the way, he glanced at rebel bodies on the ground, gave up on counting them, but still checked faces where he could, afraid that he would see Manute Yousef among the dead.

But he didn't.

The rebel chief was waiting for him when he reached the rise of ground a hundred yards outside the

Kusti compound. Manning and McCarter stood beside him, their faces mirroring relief as Bolan joined them.

"Nice of you to make it," McCarter said, covering his apprehension with a show of sarcasm.

"I didn't want to miss my ride," Bolan told him.

"We must go," Yousef stated, "in case they managed to call in reinforcements."

"Suits me," the Executioner replied. "I'd say we've worn our welcome out with these guys, as it is."

CHAPTER EIGHTEEN

Hassan Jubayl felt numb, as if he had been beaten to the point where pain became irrelevant and Nature dulled the senses in a final show of mercy to the doomed. Within the past few hours, he had experienced rage, fear, incredulity, and rage again, until it seemed there was no feeling left inside him, no reaction he hadn't explored, wrung dry and tossed aside.

The scathing tirade he had suffered from Marawi Bol had been the final straw. Jubayl longed to respond in kind, defy the colonel openly, but he couldn't afford that kind of self-indulgence at the moment. With his troops in disarray, at least a quarter of them dead or wounded, it would be irrational for him to push his luck against the junta.

It could cost him everything that he had left.

The Palestinian commander paced his study, scowling, looking for solutions to his problem, but he came up empty. He could think of nothing that would help him in the present situation, nothing that would get him off the hook.

Bol assumed the raid at Kusti was connected somehow to the prior acts of violence directed at Jubayl and his commandos. There was no clear evidence to prove it, but he knew the colonel needed scapegoats, someone to divert attention from himself now that the junta had lost soldiers of its own. If he could blame Jubayl, however indirectly, for provoking the attacks, the colonel might be granted breathing room, some time in which to clean up the problem.

But that, Jubayl could tell him from experience, would be no easy task.

The Palestinian wasn't concerned, just now, with what the junta chose to do about its enemies. The plan would have its impact on the Spear of Allah, but he didn't think Khartoum would waste its time or soldiers coming after him, when there were still so many rebels out there, begging to be hunted down and killed. Reprisal raids were more Bol's speed, exacting vengeance on the helpless to repay his enemies for their unbridled arrogance.

Assuming that the junta voted to expel Jubayl and his commandos, they would have some warning. He had seen to that by bribing certain officers around Khartoum, maintaining records of their illegal transactions so that he could ruin them if they attempted to betray him. Although never one to trust his fellow man unduly, Hassan Jubayl believed his spies would warn him of a drastic move against the Spear. His movement had survived worse things than being driven from a country by some disillusioned general or king. They would survive again.

Unless, of course, their unknown enemies got to them first.

It was the uncertainty that drove Jubayl beyond distraction, to a point where he couldn't decide if he should weep or scream. In all his years with the resistance, waging endless war against the Zionists in Tel Aviv, avoiding the Mossad and gunmen from the Wrath of God, it was the first time that he had been hunted without knowing who his stalkers were. Identity was half the battle, for he knew that killers ran to type. The Jews had certain tactics they preferred, as did the Americans, the Britons and so on. Still, Jubayl had never before been pursued in quite this way, and it unnerved him, made him worry that he might not have the strength or courage to maintain control.

He would begin, he decided, by ignoring the attack at Kusti. Rebels in Sudan had been assaulting junta outposts for the best part of a decade; there was no good reason to assume the raid concerned his men in any way. With that decided, he could concentrate on strengthening his own defenses, getting ready for a hostile move from any quarter, be it generals in Khartoum or gunmen he hadn't been able to identify.

Three men had razed the camp at Ad-Duwaym. He was confident of that from the reports of his surviving troops, and while the fact made Jubayl's soldiers look like clumsy idiots, it also gave him a degree of confidence. If his opponents had more men, they surely would have used them on the raid. Since only three turned out, it stood to reason that the force that hunted him was strictly limited in size.

Three men.

Hassan Jubayl would gladly have recruited three

such killers for himself if it were possible, but at the moment, he was more concerned with stopping them.

He thought the hardsite at Sannar should do the trick.

If they were fool enough to track him there, he would find out what they were made of, read the future in their entrails when his men were finished with them.

There would be no tricks this time, no grand surprise to throw his men off guard. Jubayl himself would take charge of defensive preparations at the camp. He would inspect each man and weapon personally, making sure that all were ready and prepared.

There would be nothing left to chance.

This time, he couldn't afford to lose.

THE ATMOSPHERE in Manute Yousef's camp was jubilant, despite a loss of men approaching twenty-five percent in the previous night's raid. The rebels were accustomed to such casualties, and while they mourned the loss of friends and loved ones, they were also heartened by the knowledge that the junta had lost many times that number for each slain tribesman.

It was victory enough for now.

Mack Bolan and his Phoenix Force comrades had been up since shortly after dawn, preparing for the last phase of their campaign in Sudan. They wouldn't linger with the rebels any longer than it took to feed themselves, stock up on ammunition and obtain a vehicle. Sannar was still two hundred miles away, and they would have to make their way across the White

Nile, unobserved by spotters or patrols, before the target was within their reach.

No easy job, but they would pull it off somehow.

The ammunition was no problem. Yousef had already offered them whatever they could carry, plus an RPG launcher and rockets. As for wheels, if Yousef's people couldn't spare a vehicle, then Bolan meant to beg a ride and find one of his own somewhere along the way. There had to be other vehicles that could be obtained by one means or another.

"You've thought about the river?" Manning asked.

"What's on your mind?"

"Well, according to this map, they've got only one bridge across, unless we go back through Khartoum." He pointed at the map spread out before them. "That's at Kusti, maybe half a mile from where we were last night. I might be wrong, but something tells me we'll have trouble passing muster over there."

"Too bloody right," McCarter said.

"We'll find a way," the Executioner assured them. "Catch a river ferry, rent a boat—hell, steal one if we have to."

"They'll be watching for you."

Bolan turned to find Yousef standing in the entrance to their hut, his face etched in a thoughtful frown.

"We'll have to take that chance," Bolan said.

"I have friends who might be useful, if your mind is quite made up," the rebel leader said.

"It is."

"Then we must lay our plans with special care. Two

raids within as many days is not the normal way we operate.''

"You've done enough already," Bolan said. "More than enough. We're square."

"My country has been long at war," Yousef answered, moving closer to the table where they sat around the map. "We fight today because the soldiers in Khartoum think we are slaves to be manipulated in accordance with their whims. They hate us for the color of our skins, and for the fact that we reject their version of God. We hate them for the crimes they have committed, all the kinsmen we have lost.''

"I understand that," Bolan said.

"Then you must understand, as well, that there can be no peace between my people and the junta's friends, if they be Palestinians or Russians, the Iranians, whatever. We would gladly seize an opportunity to fight the Spear of Allah, even if you were not here to help. The fact that we work well together makes it easier to fight them now.''

"I wouldn't count on that," Bolan said. "After last night, every soldier south of Khartoum will be hunting you, not us.''

"But we are Sudanese," Yousef replied, "no matter how the generals wish it was not so. The soldiers see black faces every day on their patrols, on city streets and country roads. Three white men—now, *that* is a sight to make them stop and take a closer look.''

"He's got that right," McCarter said.

"What did you have in mind?" Bolan asked.

"A charade," Yousef replied. "We have certain

friends who might surprise you. The appearances can be deceiving, yes?''

"So I've been told."

"It is a deal, then?"

Bolan glanced back at his Phoenix Force comrades, saw McCarter shrug, while Manning frowned and nodded.

"It's a deal," he said, and hoped Yousef wouldn't regret it to his dying day.

COLONEL MARAWI BOL had surely suffered worse days, but he couldn't recall one now. Perhaps in childhood, there had been a more humiliating moment than this morning's dressing-down by his superiors, but it was lost to memory. His cheeks still burned with shame, transmuted into fury as he thought of ways to punish those who had placed him in an untenable position.

It wasn't *his* fault that rebels had been able to surprise Akil Umarha's troops at Kusti, but the gutless captain had found nerve enough to shoot himself when he was wounded in the fight. That left Bol, as his immediate superior, to bear the brunt of condemnation from the generals in Khartoum. He could investigate, attempt to blame specific soldiers for some act of negligence or cowardice, but it would only make him look like he was trying to relieve himself of personal responsibility.

What he required this day, instead of slick political maneuvers, was a solid victory against the rebel bastards who had brought this shame upon his head. A brisk offensive in the neighborhood of Kusti would suffice for a beginning, round up anyone and everyone who had the smell of treason, kill those who resisted and interrogate the rest until one broke and gave him names. If he could net the rebel leadership, Marawi Bol could turn the Kusti raid from a disaster to a coup of sorts, but he would have to do it soon, before the rebels had another chance to strike and make him look more foolish to the brass.

The colonel had reminded his superiors of his assignment to the Spear of Allah, as liaison with the Palestinians. It seemed a solid answer for their insults, until they began insisting that the Kusti raid was somehow linked to the assaults at Ad-Duwaym, and in Khartoum. There had been no convincing them that they were wrong, and frankly, Bol wouldn't have been surprised if it was true. There was too much coincidence involved for any other explanation to make sense.

And that was why he blamed Hassan Jubayl for his misfortune.

There would come a reckoning for all his enemies, Bol decided, but he had to watch his step, take care of one thing at a time. Before he could eliminate the Spear of Allah, for example, he would have to make the generals understand that all their admiration of Jubayl had been misplaced. Once his superiors began to recognize the man for what he was—an opportunist and a parasite—the colonel would receive his orders to eradicate the problem.

It required a deft touch, though, that kind of office

politics and infighting. One careless step, and he could make himself look bad, wind up relieved of his command or worse. In the prevailing circumstances, where his reputation had already taken several solid blows, it wouldn't do for him to act precipitously. Every move required sound strategy, to guarantee that there were no more critical mistakes.

He thought of sending soldiers to Sannar, where they could watch Jubayl under the guise of helping him defend himself, but it was more important to pursue the rebels who had razed the Kusti camp. Once that crusade was under way, he would have time to think about the Palestinians.

And every move he made, from that point forward, would be planned to help himself. The generals in Khartoum made noise about their hatred of the Zionists, and while Bol had no good reason to dispute those feelings, he was still convinced that everything the junta's rulers did and said was calculated and premeditated from the standpoint of self-interest. He had learned that lesson early, as he moved up through the ranks, and he wouldn't forget it now.

The rank embarrassment Bol had suffered in the past two days might even now prevent him from attaining entry to the general staff, but he wasn't prepared to let himself become the sacrificial lamb, to cover up for someone else's lapse in judgment. It hadn't been *his* decision to invite the Spear of Allah to Sudan and make its soldiers welcome there, to shower Hassan Jubayl with cash and military hardware. He didn't object to Jubayl's use of terrorism as a diplomatic tool, but rather to the Palestinian's apparent feeling that the Arab world owed him a living and should pay his way through life while he pursued a personal agenda, bringing grief and worldwide condemnation down upon his hosts.

There was an outside chance, he realized, that Jubayl would resist leaving Sudan. In that case, as a loyal defender of the government and Muslim faith, Bol would have no choice but to respond with military force, as much as necessary to prevent the impudent outsiders from defying law and order.

But one thing at a time.

He turned and focused on a large map that was mounted on his wall. Each native town and village in the neighborhood of Kusti had been marked, the shifting population centers constantly updated so that he could always find his enemies at will.

He started counting villages, projecting totals, estimating how many divisions he would need to make his sweep.

And for the first time in the past three days, he smiled.

THE PLAN WAS relatively simple. They needed uniforms and vehicles, the second item on their shopping list admittedly more trouble than the first. Manute Yousef knew a man who knew a man, and so it went from there. When volunteers were called for to retrieve the gear, McCarter raised his hand.

They almost turned him down, owing to the color of his skin, but then Yousef thought about it and decided he could tag along if he stayed out of sight. The drive back to Khartoum was risky, but coming back would be worse, if they succeeded in their quest. By that time, any glimpse the soldiers or civilians had of any white man in the company could spell a sudden and disastrous end.

The back end of the covered truck was like an oven, and McCarter was regretting his decision by the time they put five miles behind them. Still, he had known hotter days, and there was shade back there, a canvas water bag that helped replace some of the moisture he was losing through his pores.

Their destination, as McCarter understood it, was a district on the southern outskirts of Khartoum, where sympathizers of the rebel cause were known to stockpile "military surplus" items still in good repair. They stole the army uniforms from factories and laundries, sometimes from delivery trucks, and sometimes took the trucks, as well. The trade in stolen military vehicles was strictly limited, since mere possession was a capital offense. The rolling stock was carefully concealed, kept for a day when it would find some special use.

Like now.

He waited in the truck, the AK-47 close beside him, while Yousef's man picked out the address he was looking for, then went in to talk with someone and negotiate the deal. It crossed McCarter's mind that they could be in trouble if the army knew about this contact, posted lookouts with a radio to summon backup as required. Two rebels with him in the covered truck, and two more in the cab, made lousy odds if they were suddenly surrounded by a rifle company.

McCarter took another sip of lukewarm water, poured some in his hand and splashed his face, as if to wash away the morbid thoughts. Beyond a certain point of readiness, it did no good to dwell on each and every thing that could go wrong. The pessimism that resulted from such introspection led to doubt, and doubt to fear. It was a vicious cycle, and he forced himself to think about the southward trip instead, while staying on alert.

They needed more than uniforms and vehicles to make Yousef's daring plan a reality. They would require at least four Sudanese of Arab parentage to dress as soldiers, play the part of drivers on their trek to neutralize the Spear of Allah's hardsite at Sannar. Black faces wouldn't pass inspection at the army checkpoints, any more than white. To carry off the bold charade, they had to trust in Yousef's Muslim friends and hope that none of them were agents of the junta in disguise.

A quarter hour passed before the leader of their little team returned with two companions. Peeping through a small slit in the canvas covering the truck bed, he could see the other men, both Arab in countenance, who stood beside the vehicle. They talked for several moments more, McCarter sweating freely as he watched them, one hand on his AK-47. Then they finally got into an old, beat-up sedan, pulled out and started to roll eastward, with the truck behind them.

Ten minutes later, they stopped once more, this time

outside a giant, sunbaked warehouse. Once again, he waited in the truck while others went inside to close the deal. When next he peered out through the perforated canvas covering the truck, he saw an army staff car and a pair of APCs emerging from the warehouse. In the open car, two Arab types in standard military uniforms were visible, and he assumed the drivers of the APCs would also pass inspection in a pinch.

A high-pitched whistle sent his black companions scrambling from the truck. McCarter took the water bag and followed them, glancing all around the warehouse parking area before he jogged across the blacktop to the nearest APC. At once, he wished that he were back inside the truck, instead of sitting in a mobile kiln, but then the air conditioner kicked in and brought a measure of relief.

They kept the armored shutters closed, and while he couldn't see a thing outside the APC, McCarter told himself they had to be headed back toward the rebel village. On the floor in front of him, clean khaki uniforms were neatly folded, stacked, shirts separate from the pants, in cardboard boxes. There were easily enough to clothe a dozen men, with boots heaped farther down the aisle.

So far so good.

If they were intercepted on the drive south, they had increased protection from the APC, machine guns mounted in the turrets that would help them deal with any opposition. Now the only task remaining was to load the troops and drive two hundred miles, across the White Nile and no end of hostile ground, to reach their target at Sannar.

A piece of cake, McCarter told himself.

And wondered why he thought at once of devil's food.

SIRAJ AL-MAHDI DIDN'T have a telephone at home. He took the call from Mike Belasko at his "office" in a pawnshop operated by a friendly fence, and didn't speak until he had attached the compact scrambler given to him by his contact from the CIA. It left Belasko's voice clear to Mahdi, but would render their discussion useless gibberish to anyone eavesdropping on the line.

"Are you secure?" Bolan asked.

Al-Mahdi frowned and said, "I think so, yes."

"You might consider a vacation," the American suggested. "Get away from all this heat and find a cooler place to stay."

The Sudanese knew there was more to the suggestion than a simple weather bulletin. "I will consider it," he said, not asking what the American had planned or even where he was. The daily headlines told al-Mahdi more than he had ever wished to know.

"Before you pack," Bolan said, "I need to find out who our Spear man talks to when he needs a favor from the junta."

That was easy, but al-Mahdi took his time, considering the question. It was never wise to make your job seem too simple, as if it could be done by anyone at all. A wise spy cloaked himself in the mystique of someone who was sly, courageous, nothing short of brilliant at extracting information from reluctant sources. Thus, he made himself seem more important, and increased his value to his sponsors.

"In Khartoum," he said at last, "there is an officer assigned to deal with controversial guests. A colonel named Marawi Bol. He has an office in the city, separate from the army headquarters, where visitors are not on public view when they arrive. His home is on the outskirts of the city. Do you need the addresses? Directions?"

"If you've got them handy," the American replied.

Al-Mahdi read them off from memory, described the most direct means of approach to each location, with an alternate or two, in case of trouble. Even as he spoke, he understood that he was giving up the colonel to Belasko and his comrades, probably condemning him to death, but so many men had been killed in the past few days that one more hardly made an impression.

Still, a colonel!

It was definitely time for him to take that long vacation he had planned, get out that very night, if possible, and let the final paycheck find him when he got to Europe.

Bolan's voice cut through his private reverie. "I think that's all I need," he said. "And I was serious about that change of scene."

"I understand. Thank you."

"Back at you, guy. Don't let your guard down for a while."

It was the last advice he needed, but al-Mahdi felt the big American's concern. "I won't," he said. "Goodbye."

He cradled the receiver, shut down the scrambler and disconnected it, returned it to his pocket, where the bulge was barely visible.

So much to do, so little time.

THE BOGUS ARMY CARAVAN set off at dusk, eastbound, in the direction of the White Nile crossing outside Kusti. It was dangerous, revisiting the scene that way, but Yousef had come up with half-a-dozen cronies who would front the expedition—four men in the staff car and two drivers for the APCs. If they were stopped for any reason, and inspectors started looking at the troops inside the armored vehicles, there would be hell to pay.

And that would be the end, Bolan thought, riding in the forward APC with Manning and McCarter, plus nine rebels dressed as army regulars. The uniforms were simply frosting on the cake, unnecessary once they reached their target, but Yousef went for method acting, and the Executioner wasn't about to argue with him when his plan had worked so far.

It beat a three-man river crossing and a frantic search for wheels on the east bank, and no mistake. While Bolan had objected to the use of rebel troops to fight the Spear of Allah, he was glad to have the extra guns along. Yousef's commandos had already proved themselves, and there was no doubt they would give their all against Hassan Jubayl, as they had done for years against the junta ruling from Khartoum.

It was a brutal kind of war, where fellow countrymen fell out on racial and religious lines, to kill one another in the name of God and ethnic purity. No matter how often he saw the symptoms and results, Bolan would never cease to marvel at the way in which blind faith, supposed to ease the trials of life on earth, could turn men into killers with a mission, doggedly believing that their violence was inspired by the divine.

In this case, it had been an easy choice as to which side to support. The ruling junta was a brutal clique that practiced genocide and fostered terrorism overseas, while their opponents—though the instigators of rebellion in Sudan—were fighting to protect their homes and families from being crushed beneath the Muslim juggernaut.

He didn't have the answers for Sudan—indeed, wouldn't have absolutely sworn he knew the questions—but if his campaign against Hassan Jubayl had helped the rebels out in some small way, so much the better. As for those who died on his behalf, as some would surely do this night, what could he do or say? Each warrior made the choice to stand and fight or walk away. It wasn't Bolan's place to slight their courage by suggesting that they could have made a wiser, more enlightened choice.

He snapped back to the present and found Yousef staring at him from the metal bench directly opposite. The rebel leader frowned and said, ''A penny for your thoughts.''

"I'm thinking that the river is our major obstacle," Bolan said. "If your men convince the soldiers at the checkpoint we have clearance, there should be no problem getting to Sannar. And if they don't..."

He left the statement hanging; he didn't need to finish it. He saw the knowledge in Yousef's eyes, in those of Manning and McCarter as they watched him, weighing Bolan's words.

"The written orders are a decent touch," McCarter said. "For authenticity, I mean."

And on the other side, Bolan thought, they could just as easily be botched. He couldn't read the documents that had been written out in Arabic, and while Yousef told him they were fine, a bit of healthy skepticism kept him on the edge, prepared for anything.

Still, it could work, and he wouldn't have climbed inside the APC if he believed they had less than a fighting chance. With armor, extra guns, an element of shock when they revealed themselves, he thought they just might pull it off.

In any case, the move was worth a try.

Whatever odds they faced at the encampment near Sannar, they had a better chance with thirty guns than three.

The rest of it came down to courage, skill and luck, a combination he had backed before when things were tight and there was no clear way around a sticky situation. It had worked so far, and he could only keep his fingers crossed, hope that it worked again.

If not, well, there was only one alternative to victory.

And that was sudden death.

CHAPTER NINETEEN

The easy thing would have been for Hassan Jubayl to stay away from camp, leave the defensive preparations to his various lieutenants while he found himself a hideout in Khartoum. But he had chosen to present himself before his troops and let them see him in the flesh, see that he wasn't frightened of their enemies and didn't run away.

Of course, he *was* afraid—well, apprehensive—but there was all the difference in the world between perception and reality. If he could make his soldiers think he was a man of steel, then they would fight with more determination to defend him when the time came. Oddly soldiers didn't seem to mind the sacrifice if they were killed on the behalf of supermen, but they resented dying for a weakling or a coward. And in all the years Jubayl had been dispatching men to die for Palestine, not one had ever asked him why a superman should need the help of normal flesh and blood.

Psychology was wonderful that way.

The heat inside his bungalow had been oppressive when he reached the camp, but sundown and the air conditioner that he had mounted in his bedroom window helped to cool things down. By midnight or before, the brutal desert would have cooled enough that men would slip on their jackets before they left to walk their beats on the perimeter, and steaming coffee would be welcome, where a glass of beer or ice water was all they craved short hours earlier.

Jubayl was starting to relax a little when the runner came to tell him that a line of military vehicles was drawing closer to the camp, approaching from the west. He bolted from his tent and trailed the private to the camp's lone observation tower, going up the ladder swiftly with his mind in a chaotic swirl.

He thought first of Marawi Bol, and wondered if the colonel had some treachery in mind. It seemed unlikely that he would dispatch a force to guard the camp, impossible that he would do so without sending word ahead. If he was planning an attack, though, trying to surprise the camp and rout its soldiers, take Jubayl back to Khartoum in chains, then it made perfect sense for him to keep his targets in the dark.

There was another, simpler explanation: it could be a regular patrol, out hunting rebels, whose commander had decided to stop by for small talk, or to ask if Jubayl's spotters had seen anything worth passing on. Such visits were unusual, but not unheard-of.

They would have to wait and see.

The lookout tower was equipped with a machine gun, pintle mounted to command a sweeping field of fire below. It would do little good if they were driving armored vehicles, of course, but if they came with infantry...

He caught himself before the paranoia ran amok, and settled in to find out what was happening. Field glasses let him track three dusty vehicles as they approached the camp, a staff car out in front, two armored personnel carriers behind it. Small for an attack force, he decided, but it was the right-size convoy for a regular patrol.

He wanted to relax, forget about his troubles for a while, but there was something that set his teeth on edge. What was it? He didn't believe in premonitions, but there had been times when instinct saved his life. It wouldn't hurt to wait another moment, watch and see what happened when the staff car reached his outer guards.

The soldiers knew whom they were dealing with. The lowest private in the district had to know about the Spear of Allah, had to have understood that they weren't to be molested or harassed. They had the junta's blessing, after all...or did they?

The staff car slowed, moved closer at a snail's pace, finally stopped with guards on either side. The Palestinians didn't present their weapons with a threatening demeanor, but they held themselves prepared, in case—

Bright muzzle-flashes suddenly erupted from the staff car, automatic weapons cutting down his sentries. With a clash of gears, the driver stood on his accelerator, racing into the camp.

The lookout beside Jubayl bent to his machine gun without waiting for the order, squeezing off a burst in the direction of the speeding vehicle. Jubayl bailed out and left him to it, scrambling down the ladder to the ground.

His mind was racing, and his heart was pounding in his chest, but he couldn't afford to panic. Not if he intended to survive. His men were under fire, and he could only trust that they would fight as he had trained them, to the death.

As for the Spear of Allah's leader, it was his sworn duty to remain alive and fight again another day.

INSTEAD OF SOUNDING muffled by the armor that surrounded him, the first shots were amplified for Bolan, sitting in the APC. He felt the vehicle lurch forward, was reminded vaguely of the bad old days in Vietnam, but there was no time for a flashback as another automatic weapon opened up, somewhere above them, raining bullets on their vehicle.

"The tower," Yousef said, frowning.

They knew exactly where it was, from checking sky-spy photos of the camp and listening to men from Yousef's team who had observed the place firsthand, against a day like this, when they would have to take it on. The tower had at least one man on its observation deck, and from the sound of bullets rattling off the APC, he had some kind of light or medium machine gun, with a fair supply of ammo he wasn't afraid to burn.

"At least he isn't firing AP rounds," McCarter said.

"Small favors," Manning answered. "Once we step outside, he won't need armor-piercing bullets."

"But he can't be everywhere at once," Bolan said, reaching for a loaded RPG.

"That's risky," Manning observed.

"So's breathing," Bolan told him with a grin. "I'll roll out to the right, you two go left and keep him occupied. I need ten seconds, give or take." He turned to Yousef, adding, "If it doesn't work, you'll have to think of something else."

"I'm working on it."

Their APC veered left inside the gate, the other breaking to the right in a deliberate scheme to keep from bunching up their forces, making it a simple shooting gallery for the defenders. Any second now, they would be stopping, troops unloading in a rush. The tower gunman would be going crazy, staring down his sights at an embarrassment of targets.

With any luck, that fleeting hesitation—plus some cover from the men of Phoenix Force—would be the fine edge Bolan needed to resolve their problem.

"Go!"

The APC stopped dead, and someone threw the back door open, rebels piling out and breaking off to either side as they touched down on solid ground. Bolan was right behind them, carrying the RPG, with his Kalashnikov across his back, turning sharply to his right and hearing the bullets whispering around him as he ran.

His Phoenix Force allies came out firing, hosing the lookout tower with their AK-47s as they ran around the left side of the APC. It was a stretch, in terms of range, but they were close enough to make the shooter hesitate, lift off his trigger for a moment, ducking back until he understood they couldn't reach him where he was with what they had.

The lull was all Mack Bolan needed, bringing up the RPG and peering through its sights almost before his comrades hit the ground. When his target took a momentary breather, flinching backward from the sound of automatic rifles down below, it was the moment that the Executioner was waiting for.

He squeezed the launcher's trigger, felt the backblast scorch the earth behind him, hotter than the desert sun would ever be. The fat, nose-heavy rocket wobbled slightly in its flight, but pinpoint accuracy wasn't called for in the present situation. Close would do it, with a ten-by-ten enclosure mounted on an observation tower, and the five-pound missile went in close enough.

The tower shuddered, blossomed like some giant flower with a chunky stem, the bloom of golden flame unfolding thirty feet above the ground. There might have been a scream there, in the middle of it, but he couldn't say for sure. Debris of every kind and shape was raining to the ground, all of it trailing smoke and flames, while MG ammunition started to go off like popcorn in the heart of the inferno.

Call it round one for the challengers, but they were still a long way off from any kind of victory. He had destroyed one man, one gun, but several dozen others were already firing at them from all sides. The camp reminded Bolan of an anthill when you pry the top off with a stick, except that these ants had Kalashnikovs and submachine guns.

Even so, it still came down to pest control.

The Executioner stepped back to drop his launcher on the rear deck of the idling APC, then went in search of vermin to exterminate.

MANUTE YOUSEF SAW the lookout tower blow, and heard a cheer go up from two or three of the commandos trailing him across the battleground. It wouldn't hurt for them to be encouraged, but he hoped a lucky shot didn't give them unreasonable expectations, either. They were still outnumbered, still more likely to wind up in shallow graves than at a party celebrating victory. If they could only keep their focus on the task at hand, they had a chance, but nothing more.

Two Palestinians were just emerging from a tent in front of him and to his right. They had confused expressions on their faces, tousled hair that told him they had been asleep, but both were armed with automatic weapons. Yousef shot them both before they had a chance to fire, the nearest of his soldiers joining in to make the targets dance with bullets ripping through their flesh.

He moved on, knowing that his men were fanning out behind him, dealing with the enemy as they were found. Throughout the camp, a steady roar of gunfire filled the air with smells of cordite, overheated oil, spilt blood and swirling dust.

Fear also had a smell that Yousef recognized but

couldn't have described to save his soul. Not strictly perspiration—you could tell a frightened man from one who had been lifting weights or working in the sun—but fear-sweat was a part of it. As for the rest...the superstitious child inside him thought it might be possible to smell a frightened soul, but he would never try to frame that argument in words. It smacked of witchcraft, and he was supposed to be a modern military leader, even though his war was being played out in a country where the old religions vied with Christianity and Islam for the hearts and minds of millions.

The grenade came out of nowhere, landing almost at his feet. Yousef recoiled, was turning, poised to flee, when one of his young soldiers rushed past him and threw himself atop the lethal sphere. Another grabbed Yousef by the arm and dragged him backward, hurled him to the ground. The blast was muffled by a lid of human flesh, and when he struggled to his feet, peered through the drifting smoke, the rebel leader found that he couldn't recognize the man who saved his life.

Tears stung his eyes, more rage than grief, but there was room enough for both emotions in his heart this night. He wished that there was time to stop and bless the young man who had sacrificed himself, but standing still and waiting for another hand grenade or bullet would have been an insult to the soldier's memory, his final choice to die in Yousef's place.

The proper way to pay him back, he thought, was to destroy his killers, face them down and wipe them from the earth like so much mildew on a dust rag.

Drop them where they stood, or chase them down and kill them if they tried to run away.

As if in answer to his thoughts, a flying squad of Palestinians charged through the battle smoke, all firing as they ran. A gasp of pain behind Yousef told him another of his men was hit, but there was no time at the moment for first aid. He cut a blazing swath with his Kalashnikov, the bullets ripping flesh and snapping bones, while other guns joined in around him, numbing Yousef's ears in seconds flat. He felt a bullet graze his thigh, a burn like dry ice on his flesh, then another plucked at his collar, missing his jugular by a fraction of an inch.

He kept on firing, heedless to the danger, feeling somehow that the sacrifice already made on his behalf had rendered him invincible. It was absurd, he realized, but in the heat of battle, feelings sometimes mattered more than icy logic. Holding down the trigger of his AK-47, he ran out of targets at the same time he ran out of bullets, reaching for another magazine, reloading on the move.

"This way!" he shouted to his men.

They charged like madmen, emptying their magazines, then reloading as the bullets flew around them. Some were hit and kept on going, dropping only after six or seven bullets tore their flesh, but most kept after Yousef, echoing his war cry, blasting anyone and anything that moved. The Palestinians fell back before them, grudgingly at first, then scattering like frightened children in the face of something that they couldn't understand.

And Yousef's men pursued them, ran them down and shot some in the back, killed others when they turned to make a last-ditch stand. They marched through sand turned muddy with the spilled blood of their enemies and never lost momentum, pausing only when they stumbled into outer darkness, with the burning tents behind them, realizing they had cut the camp in two.

Yousef was grinning fiercely as he turned and started back into the hellgrounds. It seemed that he could fight all night, or until a bullet found his heart and brought him down. In either case, there would be no relief, no quarter for his enemies.

Of eight men who had started with him, five were on their feet, some of them slightly wounded, none apparently inclined to sit back on the sidelines and relax.

"Come on!" Yousef shouted to them, and they followed him once more, into the valley of the shadow.

Killing all the way.

McCarter lobbed a frag grenade into the generator hut and ducked back as it blew, the corrugated metal walls shot through with shrapnel in a flash. The camp went dark at once, except for leaping flames that were devouring a number of the tents and plywood bungalows.

Across the compound, he could also see the staff car from their little convoy burning. It had taken countless hits, the fuel tank rupturing, gasoline igniting from a tracer or a ricochet. He wondered what had

happened to its occupants, but there was no point
dwelling on it. They were either dead or still alive,
and there was nothing he could do about it, either way.

McCarter heard the Palestinian advancing in a rush,
and turned in time to fire a quick, low burst that cut
his legs from under him. The terrorist held a long,
curved dagger thrust in front of him, and even as he
fell he reached with the blade, its sharp point zeroing
on the Briton's throat.

The Phoenix Force commando stumbled backward,
triggering another burst that caught the blade man
halfway to the ground and flipped him over on his
back. There was a dazed expression on the Arab's
face, as if his mind couldn't conceive of failure, even
as it died.

Tough luck.

Death came to every man in time. The trick was to
postpone it for as long as possible, and then to take
as many of your adversaries with you as you could.

McCarter turned his full attention to the compound's motor pool, a double line of vehicles along
the south edge of the camp, a long tarp mounted to
protect them from the baking desert sun and from the
prying eyes of spy planes or surveillance satellites.
The latter effort, as the Briton knew from viewing
photographs, was only intermittently successful, and
he knew exactly where to go when he was finished
taking out the generator hut.

Aside from frag grenades, he had three pounds of
plastique, broken down in half-pound charges, each
with a simple timer wired to blasting caps, already

mounted, ready for a touch to start the countdown to doomsday. As he ran in the direction of the vehicles, McCarter watched for sentries who might try to intercept him, shot one who was seemingly surprised to see him, with his guard down and his weapon dangling at his side. The stream of bullets swept him off his feet and punched him backward, through the open flaps of a two-man tent that instantly collapsed on top of him, a canvas shroud.

A few more yards, and he was in among the vehicles, apparently unseen. Another rapid check to make sure no one was approaching on his blind side, and he got to work, removing plastic charges from his shoulder bag, the first one wedged against the fuel tank of a flatbed truck. McCarter set the timer, gave himself five minutes and moved on.

His next stop, skipping several vehicles, was to apply a lump of plastique to the gasoline cans mounted on the rear deck of a dusty army-surplus jeep. He checked his watch and set the timer to approximately coincide with number one, then moved down the line.

McCarter fixed his third charge to the undercarriage of an armored car, again as near as possible to the protected fuel tank. He was rising from a crouch beside that vehicle when scuffling movement close behind him made him turn, his AK-47 rising in a firm one-handed grip.

The Palestinian stood there uncertainly, wide-eyed and wondering what he should do with this demented-looking stranger dressed in desert camouflage. He had a submachine gun, though, and that was all the ID that McCarter needed to identify a lethal enemy.

He fired before the gunner could put his jumbled thoughts in order, stitching a line of bloody holes across the Arab's chest and dropped him where he stood.

The numbers were falling rapidly, though, and he had to set the last three charges in a hurry, estimating on the timers, knowing that the several detonations wouldn't be precise. It hardly mattered, with the vehicles packed in together as they were. Once one went off and spread its lake of burning petrol, most of them would go.

He fixed the last charge, set the timer counting down from thirty seconds and bailed out of there.

McCarter traveled fifty yards before the first explosion tore the night apart behind him, and the shock wave rushed him, swept him off his feet. He just had time to clutch his rifle to his side, and then the world turned upside down, a swirl of dust and smoke that took his breath away.

THE RAPID-FIRE disintegration of the motor pool saved Gary Manning's life. He had dispatched two Palestinians with point-blank bursts from his Kalashnikov, when number three came up behind him in a rush and clubbed him with a rifle butt across the shoulders. The big Canadian went down on his face, rolled over, clutching at his AK, and froze at sight of the guerrilla aiming the barrel of an automatic rifle at his face.

Long out of practice with his prayers, he was braced to try an all-or-nothing burst, no time to aim, when hell on earth erupted less than thirty yards away. The first of several blasts caught his assailant by surprise and lifted him completely off his feet, a stunned expression on his face, and dropped him in the dirt close to Manning.

It was a scramble, after that, the desert heaving underneath them as the nearby vehicles kept detonating, one after another, fuel tanks adding secondary blasts and lighting up the desert night. The wind that seared them both was like the breath of Hell, but Manning shrugged it off and struggled to all fours, his target too close for shooting as he swung the AK-47 like a club.

The Palestinian, struggling to rise himself, took Manning's first swing on the forehead, rocking backward on his haunches, crimson gushing from a scalp wound as he fought to keep his balance. It was all in vain, as Manning followed with a butt stroke to the face that crushed his adversary's nose and knocked him sprawling, barely conscious, totally unable to defend himself.

It would have been an easy thing to leave him then, and let the fates decide if he should live or die, but Manning thought about the others in his party—Bolan and McCarter, Yousef's rebels—any one of which could pay the tab in blood if this one roused himself and went back to the fight. Considered in those terms, the choice was simple, no real choice at all. A 3-round burst at something close to skin-touch range, and Manning left the broken rag doll sprawled behind him as he rose and went to find more human prey.

It was a brutal killing game, without apologies, no room for chivalry if Manning and his friends were going to survive against the odds. Some missions hinged on surgical destruction of equipment, buildings and the like, but this raid was about destroying men, the selfsame terrorists who claimed the right to kill anyone they chose as a sacrifice to their holy cause.

The shoe was on the other foot this night, and mercy had no place in the proceedings. There were no civilian noncombatants in the Spear of Allah's base camp, no misguided innocents who liked to hang around with killers for a thrill when they had nothing better on their social calendars. These Palestinians were dedicated murderers across the board, and Manning was prepared to deal with them on their own terms.

It was the only language die-hard predators could understand.

He looked around the field of death and saw the staff car that had led their convoy, bullet-scarred and burning, fifty yards in front of him. He moved in that direction, hoping to identify survivors from among the Sudanese who had been riding in the car. But hope evaporated when he saw one of them slumped behind the steering wheel, already charred, another sprawled beside the vehicle, with blood soaked through his khaki shirt from several bullet wounds. The other two were nowhere to be seen, and Manning wished them well, without believing he would ever see the pair of them alive.

For every inch of progress, the Phoenix Force commando understood, somebody paid the price.

He thought of Bolan and McCarter briefly, wondered where they were, if they were still alive, then pulled his mind back to the here and now. Distractions on the field of battle were the quickest way to lose it all, and Manning was an old hand at survival.

Even so, he thought, nobody lived forever. You could stretch your luck so far, and then—

The Arab gunner popped up almost in his face, like something in the fun house, snarling as he thrust at Manning with a bayonet. The big Canadian sidestepped and parried with his AK-47, whipped the muzzle back against his adversary's face and opened up a cheek with the rifle's sight. Before the Palestinian could get his balance back, a bullet drilled his forehead and turned the rear part of his skull into a trapdoor, spewing out the contents in a liquid rush.

The man staggered, going down, and Manning stepped across the prostrate body, moving on without a backward glance. Another second and it could easily have been the other way around.

But he was still alive, still hunting.

And before the bastards brought him down, there would be hell to pay.

HASSAN JUBAYL HAD FELT blind panic seize him when the motor pool went up, vehicles detonating like a string of giant firecrackers and launching streams of burning gasoline across the velvet sky. He felt his hope turn black and wither in that searing heat, his plan of getting out destroyed in seconds flat.

He would be trapped inside the camp unless...

The rush of hope hit him like a drug. He almost felt euphoric, had to stop himself from crowing in excitement and attracting every enemy within a hundred yards.

He still had no idea if they were fighting soldiers sent by Bol to kill him, or some impostors wearing army uniforms and driving military vehicles. It hardly mattered now that he had another chance to save himself.

They didn't park the motorcycles with the jeeps and trucks, since only certain members of his team were trained to ride them, and they liked to keep the cycles close at hand for tearing up the desert when they had free time. Jubayl knew where they were—four motorcycles, scattered here and there around the camp—and he could find them even in this chaos.

If they hadn't been destroyed.

The thought came close to freezing him, but he kept moving past the burned-out tents and bungalows, the scattered corpses of his men. Approximately half his total fighting force had been collected at Sannar, but he could get along without them if he had to. There were always new recruits lined up to join the Spear of Allah, boys and young men fresh from Palestine who nursed some grudge against the Jews.

Recruiting troops wasn't his problem at the moment. He would have to stay alive if he was going to direct the Spear in any further strikes against the

Zionists, and his survival would remain in doubt until Jubayl could find himself a vehicle and break out of the camp.

His heart sank as he glimpsed the bungalow where one of the four motorcycles was kept. A rocket or grenade had struck the plywood building, setting it on fire, and while the flames were mostly out now, having starved themselves of fuel, he feared that nothing in the vicinity had managed to survive the blast and fire.

Still, it was worth a closer look. Jubayl pressed on, dropped to his hands and knees as stray rounds started swarming overhead and finished in a crawl that brought him to the back side of the burned-out bungalow.

Incredibly he found the motorcycle lying on its side, tipped over by the blast but seemingly untouched by fire or shrapnel. Once he got it upright, he was able to inspect the bike and verify that there were no holes in the tires or gas tank, no visible damage to the engine. He climbed aboard and pressed the starter, offering a silent prayer of thanks when the engine sparked to life beneath him.

He wasn't an expert rider, and the present circumstances made for tricky navigation, but Jubayl had nothing left to lose. If he fell down and broke an arm or leg, it would make little difference, since his enemies were bound to kill him if he lingered in the camp. One death was no worse than another, and he much preferred to go down fighting—or, in this case, running—than to simply stand and wait until a bullet or a bit of shrapnel cut him down.

He didn't switch on the motorcycle's headlight. The engine's noise was ample to attract unwanted notice, and he didn't need the extra advertisement of the bobbing headlight to betray him. As it was, the battlefield was well enough illuminated by a score of crackling fires for him to find his way around the scattered corpses and debris.

It started coming back to him when he had traveled fifty yards or so: the freedom of two-wheeling, the technique of balancing himself and leaning into turns. The bike's rear tire lost traction once or twice in the sand, but he recovered quickly and continued on his way. When bullets whistled past him from the darkness, he ducked lower on the seat, his grip white knuckled on the handlebars, but there was only so much he could do to keep himself from being shot.

The trick, indeed, would be to leave the camp and roaring guns behind him, let his soldiers stand or fall on their abilities, while he made tracks for parts unknown. Once he had reached the nearest town, he could reach out to the surviving members of his company and find some shelter for himself.

The war could wait a month or two, however long it took for him to take stock of the damage, fill his ranks with new and willing soldiers, try to figure out if he was running from Marawi Bol or someone else.

The questions were on hold for now, as he accelerated toward the camp's perimeter, with darkness beckoning beyond. There would be time enough to punish all his enemies, but first he had to save himself.

Hassan Jubayl hung on and opened up the throttle, running with the night wind in his face.

THERE WAS A POINT in every battle where the living realized the tide had turned. It might be subtle, something in the air, or as obvious as armored cavalry attacking over open ground. For some, the change brought certainty of triumph, while for others it was redolent of death and loss.

The sense of change, of something *tipped*, hit Bolan twelve or thirteen minutes into the attack. That was a long time to be ducking, dodging, killing, and in spite of Bolan's physical condition, he was feeling it. The days of hot pursuit and combat that had gone before this moment weighed on Bolan as if he were carrying a field pack filled with bricks, but even his fatigue couldn't disguise the change.

A glance around the battlefield showed Bolan nothing special, and yet he knew.

Around him, others seemed to sense the shift, as well. Away to Bolan's left, three Palestinians broke off from firing at two of Yousef's men and turned to run. He dropped them in their tracks, a waist-high burst from right to left that piled them on the ground like broken toys.

During a heartbeat's hesitation in the general firing, Bolan heard a motorcycle engine, whining, revving, warped by the Doppler effect until it seemed to be approaching and retreating from him all at once.

He saw the bike, roughly sixty yards due east and making for the outer limits of the camp. It would have been ridiculous for him to claim that he could see the driver's face, but in an instant Bolan knew Hassan Jubayl was slipping through his fingers, breaking out and running for his life.

Elation at the thought of victory turned sour in an instant, giving way to bitterness. He snapped up his rifle in time to see the motorcyclist disappear behind the mess tent, lost to sight, the echo from his tailpipes fading rapidly with distance.

With Jubayl at large, it hardly mattered what became of his abandoned soldiers. He *was* the Spear of Allah; he had built his fighting cadre as a cult of personality, the soldiers as devoted to him personally as they were to killing Zionists and their supporters in the West.

Hassan Jubayl alive meant they wouldn't be finished, even if they swept the field and slaughtered every Palestinian in sight. The camp was large, well manned, but it didn't contain the whole of Jubayl's fighting force, and while he lived, there would be new recruits drawn to his cause like moths to a seductive, ultimately self-destructive flame.

The tide of battle changing, Bolan thought as he turned back to finish off the butcher's work. Another ten, twelve minutes ought to see it done.

And then he could begin the hunt again.

CHAPTER TWENTY

"So, this is good intelligence?" McCarter asked.

"The best we'll get," Bolan replied, thinking of Siraj al-Mahdi, wishing that he could have double-checked their latest information with the gutsy Sudanese before he split. It was too late for that now, and they had to go ahead as planned, base each move on the Intel they possessed, while standing ready to improvise if anything went wrong.

The bloody trail had brought them back to Khartoum. Their target was a private home this time, the residence of one Marawi Bol, a colonel in the junta who was assigned as the liaison between his government and several Palestinian guerrilla units training in Sudan. Officially the terrorists weren't even there, but off the record, they required a fair amount of coddling while they worked up nerve to sacrifice themselves for Palestine's sake. They needed arms and ammunition, money, physical protection from the world outside Sudan, plus any creature comforts they decided were appropriate to keep them all in fighting trim.

Liaison was a world away from personal involvement in the Arab cause, but rumor had it that Marawi

Bol was known to cross the line now and again. This time, according to the scuttlebutt, he was protecting one Hassan Jubayl, not in a safehouse or stockade, but in his private residence.

Two birds, one stone, Bolan thought as they motored through the suburbs of Khartoum in yet another rental car, McCarter at the wheel, with Gary Manning in the back. The big Canadian was busy double-checking weapons, magazines, grenades. There would be no time to examine the equipment once they had begun their final push, and Bolan trusted Manning to make sure each piece was functioning properly before one of them needed it to save his life.

Another night had fallen on Khartoum, and while the neighborhood inhabited by Colonel Bol stood squarely in the upper middle class, it still showed symptoms of neglect. The streetlights here were few and far between, and while police patrols swept through the area occasionally, watching out for beggars and the like, to help them on their way, the local crime rate had been rising ever since the civil war began.

"Up there," Bolan said, pointing to a fenced-in property ahead of them.

"I'm on it," McCarter replied.

Colonel Bol believed in personal security—that much was obvious—and with a special guest whose life was presently in danger, he would spare no effort to defend the place. Still, Bolan understood the limitations of his enemy and reckoned they could at least get inside to put the ball in play.

Security, around Khartoum, didn't include sophisticated gear like that found at the White House, or in modern corporate headquarters. There would be no closed-circuit television cameras or seismic sensors, infrared sensors or the like. There *would* be soldiers, maybe supplemented by Hassan Jubayl's guerrillas, but a drive-by told them that the colonel hadn't turned his home into a total fortress.

Bolan concluded the man believed they'd be afraid to risk another confrontation in the capital.

It went to show you just how wrong the army brass could be.

They found a place to leave the car a block away, and spent a moment strapping on their gear before they locked it up, enabling the explosive booby trap that would protect the vehicle in their absence. If anybody tampered with the car, he would be on his way to Hell, the echo of the blast a warning they could hardly miss. Of course, it would destroy the car, but theft or vandalism would be equally effective when it came to stranding them. This way, they at least had the satisfaction of knowing that the man or men who stranded them would never make a profit on the deal.

"All ready?" Bolan asked the others as he finished daubing war paint on his face and hands.

"I'm set," Manning replied.

"Ready as I'll ever be," McCarter said.

"Okay," the Executioner told them, "let's do it."

"SIT DOWN, for heaven's sake!"

Marawi Bol was swiftly losing patience with his

houseguest. Barely sixteen hours had passed since he
had received the urgent phone call from Hassan Jubayl, no more than twelve since he had brought the
Palestinian into his home, and even now, the colonel
felt his frayed nerves jangling every time he saw the
man or heard him speak.

There had been several options open to him when
Jubayl requested help. He could have told the Palestinian to screw himself, withdrawn protection from the
Spear of Allah altogether, but the risks inherent in that
course of action had dissuaded him from any rash decision. An alternative suggestion would have been to
place him into protective custody, arrange a safehouse
for him, maybe even stash him at an army base, for
all the good that might have done. Bol could have
recommended that the general staff transport Jubayl
and his surviving soldiers to another country, but the
trick would be in finding any nation to accept them
while the heat was on.

The ultimate solution, hiding the guerrilla leader at
his home, involved more risk to Bol, but there were
also benefits. He could control Jubayl's communication with his soldiers and the world at large, while
watching every move he made. If Bol could bring the
general staff around to his position that Jubayl was
more a liability than any asset to Sudan, the junta
might approve his liquidation—in which case, the
colonel simply had to take the pistol from his desk
and do the job himself.

It was a notion that he found increasingly appealing
as the night wore on.

Jubayl was frightened; that much would be obvious to anyone. No special training in psychology was needed to observe the fear in his eyes or note the way he chewed his lower lip while pacing endlessly around the room.

"I'm tired of sitting," Jubayl said. "I should be doing something."

"What exactly did you have in mind?"

That shut him up. The terrorist leader had nowhere else to go for help, and they both knew it. It would take prolonged negotiations, possibly a hefty bribe, to make some other country welcome him, with all the bad publicity he had received in recent weeks. The colonel had a sense of what it felt like, being trapped, but he could find no sympathy within himself for the man. After all the trouble that Jubayl had caused, demanding special treatment for his so-called soldiers, bringing so much bloodshed to the very nation that had sheltered him, embarrassing Marawi Bol no end, it seemed like simple justice that he should be squirming now.

Jubayl sat, but couldn't stop himself from fidgeting, his fingers drumming on the chair's stout arms, his left leg jumping as if he had been afflicted with a nervous tic.

"The soldiers are in place?" he asked at last.

"Since you arrived," the colonel said, unable to resist a smile. "As I informed you once already."

"I cannot take chances."

"Then I submit that you are out of business," Bol

replied. "A terrorist who won't take risks is beaten well before he starts."

"My men are freedom fighters," Jubayl said, "not terrorists."

"Of course. A mere slip of the tongue." Bol made no effort to disguise the mockery. "But surely it is all a matter of perspective, yes?"

"You suddenly have sympathy for Israel?" Jubayl asked.

"I think—"

The colonel lost his train of thought completely as a burst of automatic-weapons fire erupted from the grounds. He vaulted to his feet, still slower than the Palestinian, who rose and raced across the study to huddle in a corner farthest from the windows.

"They have found me!"

"If so, they will regret it," Bol assured him, thinking even as he spoke that it was possible one of his sentries had been spooked by shadows, nerves strung taut from the repeated warnings Bol had given to his men.

The thought had barely formed, however, when more weapons joined the chorus, rattling loudly in the night. It seemed impossible that one excited sentry could have touched off such a racket on his own.

The only way to find out anything, he knew, would be to go outside and find out what was happening himself. With only fleeting hesitation, Bol retrieved a semiautomatic pistol from his desk and started toward the door.

"You'll be safe here," he told his cringing guest.

"You're going out?" Jubayl seemed stunned by the idea.

"How else can I discover who my men are shooting at?" the colonel asked.

No answer was forthcoming, and he favored Jubayl with a sneer before he turned away. The door swung shut behind him with a sound of grim finality as Colonel Bol went out to meet the enemy.

MCCARTER BLAMED HIMSELF for touching off the firestorm prematurely. He had scaled the fence without a hitch and was proceeding toward his target from the north side of the house, when he almost collided with a soldier just emerging from some shrubbery, zipping up his fly.

The Sudanese was startled, gaping at him, opening his mouth to warn the other sentries even as his right hand started reaching for the AK-47 slung across his shoulder. McCarter stepped in close and hit him between the eyes with a butt stroke from his own rifle. The blow dropped the soldier on his backside, but he had a finger through the AK's trigger guard by that time, and the impact of his fall unleashed a burst that scorched the lawn and cut down several decorative ferns.

And there went any hope of getting to the house unnoticed, literally shot to hell.

With nothing left to lose, McCarter put a bullet through the soldier's forehead and left him stretched out on the ground. From both sides, near and far, he heard excited voices shouting in Arabic, the reinforcements rushing to assist their comrade or avenge him. Either way, it spelled disaster for McCarter if he stood and waited for them. In the circumstances, he decided it was better to attack.

And so he did, advancing on the house where he would find his quarry, moving in a rush, head down, the AK-47 thrust in front of him to meet all comers. Fifty feet beyond the point where he had killed the guard, McCarter met another pair of sentries, closing on a hard collision course. They didn't seem to know exactly what was happening, and he resolved their moment of confusion with another burst from his Kalashnikov, killed both men where they stood and dropped them sprawling on the bloodstained grass.

How many more troops were there on the grounds? He had no way of knowing, but the Briton was unhappy with the thought of several dozen riflemen all rushing toward him, throwing up a ring of death to box him in. If only there were a diversion…

Suddenly, as if in answer to his thoughts, McCarter heard another burst of auto fire erupting from the far side of the property, immediately followed by more shooting from the west. The sentries he could hear began to speak more excitedly, a fresh note of confusion creeping in, and several of the voices were receding now, in the direction of the posts they had abandoned to pursue McCarter.

Now, at least, he had a fighting chance. Floodlights blazed on around the house he was approaching, casting several guards in silhouette. Four men were spread out before him in a thin defensive line, with some twenty-five or thirty feet between them.

Unclipping a grenade, he yanked the pin and let the bomb fly from twenty paces, dropping prone as it touched down between the soldiers to the left of center. One of them glanced over at the lethal egg, appeared to recognize it, but his time ran out before he drew a breath to scream. The smoky thunderclap swept both men off their feet and left them squirming on the grass, their comrades gaping in amazement as McCarter sighted down the barrel of his AK, index finger taking up the trigger slack.

He dropped them both with short precision bursts that took them out with no time for return fire. They were down and out before he scrambled to his feet and moved on toward the house. The floodlights hurt his eyes at first, and made him feel like a performer stuck at center stage, without a band to back him up, but he kept going, ready for the bullet if and when it came.

In front of him was a smallish flagstone patio, with sliding doors of glass that would grant entry to the house. A light was visible inside, the draperies wide open, showing him no sign of any gunmen in the room beyond the glass. It might still be a trap, of course, but he would never know unless he tried, and it appeared to be the only way inside, from where he stood.

Rushing toward the wide doors, he gripped the handle, tugged it smartly and was almost startled when the door slid open on its metal runners. Stepping through into a room that smelled of strong tobacco, he caught movement from the corner of his eye, a man just entering the parlor from a door off to his right. McCarter ducked behind a sturdy couch as gunfire hammered at him, bullets swarming overhead like angry bees.

It seemed less like a trap than plain bad luck, but either one could kill him if he let his enemy seize the initiative. To save himself, McCarter knew that he would have to be aggressive, push it to the limit, risk it all.

He took a breath, expelled it from his lungs and came up firing, fighting for his life.

Jubayl had learned his lesson at Sannar. When he couldn't prevail against an enemy, the one solution was escape. Let younger men be martyrs for the cause, if they were so inclined. The leader was a vital, guiding force behind the movement, and wasn't as easily replaced as soldiers in the field.

Escape was one thing, though, when he designed the camp and knew each detail like the inside of his own eyelids. It was another thing entirely when he found himself on relatively unfamiliar ground, with no clear access to a vehicle. He was familiar with the layout of the house and grounds, in general terms, from monthly visits to Marawi Bol, but that was far from comforting. If he should leave the house right now, with soldiers firing on the grounds, he might be killed by accident.

The colonel would be brokenhearted over that, no doubt. Jubayl wouldn't have put it past him to arrange for such an incident deliberately, render the Spear of

Allah leaderless and thus divest himself of the responsibility. Such treachery was typical of men who used the Palestinian guerrillas for their own agendas, taking bows when soldiers of the Spear, Jihad or Hezbollah pulled off successful raids against the Zionists, denying any link to the beleaguered freedom fighters when they needed help. In the United Nations, pious hypocrites were pleased to take the podium and lie about their dealings with resistance movements, but they still took secret satisfaction anytime a Zionist was killed.

Jubayl had been relieved of weapons when he came to hide out with the colonel, but he had retained a derringer, unknown to those around him. It held two rounds only, but they were enough to help him get a better gun, spare ammunition and the keys to one of Colonel Bol's vehicles. It was a desperate ploy, and would demolish any hope he had of future dealings with the junta in Khartoum, but there was no point in maintaining an alliance that had failed. Once he was safely on his way, beyond the junta's reach, it wouldn't matter what they thought of him.

The terrorist leader removed the little handgun from its ankle holster, double-checked that it was loaded and proceeded to the door. A peek outside showed him no sentry in the corridor; Marawi Bol was trusting him to cower in the study while his enemies moved closer, fighting through to trap him in the house.

He stepped into the hall and shut the door behind him, standing with the derringer held down against his thigh, concealed as much as possible from any soldiers he might meet along the way. If it was one man Jubayl would seize the moment and disarm him, using lethal force if necessary to obtain the arms and information he required. From that point on, all his bridges would be burned, and he would have to make good his escape or wind up in a jail cell at the very least.

He steeled himself with grim determination, started moving down the hallway toward the dining room and kitchen. There would be an exit there, unless the floor plan of the house was totally bizarre. Outside, along the west side of the house, there was a carport large enough for several cars, at least four vehicles lined up and waiting for him, once he found the keys.

Behind him, from the general direction of the patio, a sudden burst of automatic gunfire rattled through the house. Unless he was mistaken, those shots came from *inside,* meaning that his enemies had breached the first line of security. If they had come that far, they could catch up with him in minutes, maybe less.

He panicked, broke into a run that took him through the formal dining room, into the kitchen, looking for an exit from the house. One of the colonel's soldiers stood before him, an AK-47 held in at port arms, staring at him, wide-eyed.

"You should not be here," the private said.

Jubayl whipped up the derringer and shot him once between the eyes. The soldier stood before him for another moment, crimson dribbling down his face, then he melted, crumpling to the kitchen floor. The Palestinian scooped up the rifle, stripped the soldier of the bandolier that held his extra magazines and stepped across his body, toward the exit.

And he paused there, one hand on the doorknob, frozen by the image of an ambush waiting on the other side. It was conceivable, one strike team roving through the house, another waiting to receive him when he fled.

His options were reduced to zero by the dead man on the floor, another burst of firing from the parlor, well behind him now, but close enough to make the sweat bead on his forehead.

Go!

He whipped the door aside and rushed into darkness, moving toward the cars. If he could find one with a key in the ignition, he would have a chance.

He focused on the positive and went to meet his fate.

THE FIRST WILD BURST of firing on the grounds had startled Gary Manning, but he knew what had to be done. One of his friends had met with opposition, and he couldn't let the whole defensive force descend on a fellow commando en masse, despite the fact that it would make his own approach much simpler. With a grimace, he had fired a short burst from his AK-47 into the air and kept on jogging toward the house, prepared for anything.

He met a pair of sentries doubling back from their initial break in the direction of the early shots. They saw him coming and tried to raise their weapons, but the big Canadian was there ahead of them, unloading with his AK from the hip, both soldiers jerking, stumbling, going down.

He left them there, proceeding toward the house, and met another rifleman before he covered thirty yards. This one was older, although not by much, and quicker off the mark. He opened fire as soon as he glimpsed Manning's clothes, his camo-painted face, but nerves sent his initial bullets high and wide. Before he could correct, a burst from the Canadian's Kalashnikov ripped through the soldier's chest and abdomen, explosive impact spinning him and dropping him against the smooth trunk of an olive tree.

The house was closer now, but Manning had to get there in one piece if he was going to achieve his goal of joining Bolan and McCarter, helping them track down Hassan Jubayl and any Sudanese who sheltered him. A few more yards, and he would have the house in sight, floodlights and all.

A group of men in uniform was clustered at the front door when he got there. One was barking orders, brandishing an autoloading pistol while he told them where to go. Light glinted from his collar tabs, and while Manning couldn't make out the insignia from where he stood, there was no doubt in his mind that he was looking at an officer.

Perhaps *the* officer?

He took a chance, unhooked a frag grenade and pulled the pin before he lobbed the bomb overhand, a high toss toward the porch. One of the soldiers turned in time to see it coming and barked a warning to his fellows, but it only set them running into one another.

The officer was better, quicker, but he wasn't quick enough. A couple of his soldiers blocked the front door to the house, and shoving them aside would only be a waste of precious time. Instead, he turned and threw himself across the low porch railing, into a tidy shoulder roll that took him into the nearby flower bed. When the grenade went off, its shrapnel ripped through flesh and khaki, cleared the porch of able-bodied men, but none of it came close to scoring on the prostrate officer.

Manning closed in and started mopping up. A couple of the soldiers on the porch were still alive and struggling to their feet, though scarred with shrapnel high and low. He dropped them both with mercy rounds, moving on to check the bodies the blast had pitched out toward the lawn, while part of his attention focused on the flower bed and its reclining occupant.

When he had closed the gap between them to a dozen feet or less, it was apparent that the officer was feigning death. There was no sign of blood, and barring cardiac arrest, Manning could see no other reason for the man to lie still where he was.

Unless, of course, he had a trick in mind, a not so subtle backup plan to save himself and maybe bag one of his adversaries in the bargain.

A short burst from the AK-47 churned up soil beside his head, and Manning saw the "dead" man resurrected in a flash. He lumbered to his feet, and there was no sign of the pistol as he spread his empty hands.

"Do you speak English?" Manning asked him.

"Yes."

"Where is Hassan Jubayl?"

"Inside," the officer replied. "I'll show you."

Right, when monkeys flew, Manning thought. But he said, "You lead the way."

The officer showed no emotion as he turned and climbed the porch steps, moving past the shrapnel-punctured bodies of his men. He hardly glanced at them, in fact, except for one who had slumped back against the wall in death, just to the right side of the door, a submachine gun in his lap.

Manning saw the move before his prisoner had finished scoping out the opportunity. He was prepared and waiting when the officer appeared to stumble, throwing out a hand as if to catch himself, the fingers stretching for that submachine gun in the dead man's lap.

It wasn't bad, all things considered, but he never had a chance. The AK-47 stuttered briefly, slammed a burst between the khaki-covered shoulder blades and draped the officer across the lifeless private's lap.

Manning would have to find Jubayl himself, if he was still inside, but he could do without an escort who had treachery in mind.

THE CARS WERE CRITICAL, in Bolan's mind. Whatever else went down, he still remembered standing in the ruins of Jubayl's compound and watching as his quarry fled, a trail of dust the only trace he left behind. The Palestinian had run before, and he would run again, if he was given any chance at all.

Which meant that Bolan had to watch the cars, or else disable them somehow before he started to check out the main house, one room at a time.

There was a sentry on the carport, but his mind was elsewhere, focused on the south side of the house, where an explosion and more gunfire spoke of trouble on the way. Behind him, Bolan took advantage of the loud diversion, closing with a Ka-bar fighting knife in hand and opening the soldier's throat with one deft slash. Instead of warning cries, a crimson torrent foamed out through the opening, and the Executioner's opposition crumpled at his feet.

He turned back toward the cars, was leaning through the driver's window on a gray Mercedes-Benz and looking for the hood release, when he heard a door slam. Bolan glanced up from his task and saw Jubayl, no more than twenty feet away and moving toward him at a rapid pace.

Dumb luck, he thought, but he wasn't about to look a gift horse in the mouth. He rose to his full height and aimed his weapon at the Palestinian before he spoke.

"That's far enough."

Jubayl stopped dead, eyes narrowing, lips twitching into an expression that could easily have been a smile or snarl.

"You are American," he said.

"It doesn't matter," Bolan replied. He was aware of fleeting time, but couldn't let the moment pass. "You and the Spear of Allah are an insult to the world."

"An insult to the Jews, perhaps." Jubayl was stalling, clutching his Kalashnikov, still pointed at the ground between his feet. "Are you a Jew?" he asked.

"Not even close."

"Yet you treat me as your enemy. Israel has drained your treasury, increased your deficit with endless foreign aid, and still they bite the hand that feeds them. Surely you are wise enough to see the truth."

"I see a man who's out of time," the Executioner replied. "You blew it, guy."

Jubayl stared back at him defiantly. "I'm not alone, you fool!" he snapped at Bolan. "There are thousands, *millions* more who feel as I do."

"I'll go look for them tomorrow," Bolan said. "Tonight it's your turn."

With a wordless cry of rage, Jubayl raised his Kalashnikov and tried to fire. A burst from Bolan's rifle got there first, however, ripping through his chest and pitching him back toward the open doorway he had passed through, where another silhouette was blotting out the light. The sights of Bolan's AK-47 found the new arrival's face and held there, while McCarter smiled.

"Let's not be hasty, son," the tough Briton said.

"The rest?" Bolan asked.

"It's all done in here. I wouldn't be surprised if there were still some soldiers on the grounds."

"Where's Manning?"

"Here." The voice came from behind him, making Bolan turn to face the big Canadian. "I tagged an officer back there before I heard you with the guest of honor. He appears to be the highest-ranking member of the team."

"The colonel?"

Manning shrugged. "I'm not up on the Sudanese insignia, but he was calling all the shots."

A glance at Bolan's watch told him eleven minutes had elapsed from the first sound of gunfire. Any reinforcements summoned by the neighbors should be arriving soon, and he didn't intend to be there when the cavalry arrived.

"I'd say we're done," he told the others. "Anybody feel the need to hang around?"

"Next time, perhaps," McCarter said. "I left a little something on the stove."

"In that case," Bolan stated, "let's hit the bricks."

The three of them were halfway to the fence, still unopposed, before the house went up behind them, bright flames leaping in the darkness, hungrily devouring the colonel's home. It was a beacon and a funeral pyre, all wrapped into one.

"I cannot thank you all enough for helping us," Manute Yousef said.

"It was the other way around, from where I stand," Bolan replied.

"Then perhaps we can agree that we have helped each other?"

"Fair enough."

The boat Yousef had summoned was already waiting for them, three miles out from shore. The motor-driven skiff he had provided from an unknown source would get them that far, and the boat—owned by a rebel, as he had explained—would drop them off at Jiddah, on the Saudi coast, with time to spare before sunrise. A military escort would be waiting for them there, a long drive to the airstrip and an even longer flight that would eventually land them back in the United States.

They didn't speak of fallen comrades. Bolan hadn't known the men who died on his behalf, and it would be an insult to their memories if he pretended otherwise.

"You come again sometime, and help us finish up

this business, maybe," Yousef said. The crooked smile told Bolan he was no more than half-serious.

"I couldn't promise that, but I know some people who might be in a position to assist, if you had any plans to relocate."

"This is our home," Yousef said. "A man does not desert his house when thieves break in. He fights."

"You've got a point."

"Until we meet again, my friends."

They shook hands all around, as close as any men could be who had been total strangers four days earlier, their lives colliding with the force of two express trains—and with similar results, for some of those involved.

And there was nothing left to say.

They climbed aboard the skiff, a couple of Yousef's soldiers pushed them off and they began to paddle, Bolan firing up the little outboard motor when they were a hundred yards from shore. He glanced back once, but there was nothing to be seen along the coastline in the dead of night.

"They have some guts, that lot," McCarter said. "I'll give them that."

"All those years," Manning observed. "It's a long time to be fighting for a cause when you've got nothing but the scars to show for it."

"Sometimes the scars are all that matter," Bolan said.

"It would be nice to have some hope, though, don't you think?" the Canadian asked.

"There's always hope," the Executioner replied, "as long as one of them is still alive."

"Still, it's a life I wouldn't choose," McCarter said.

The irony of that remark hit home a moment later, Bolan grinning at the former SAS commando from his cramped seat in the stern. McCarter shook his head and chuckled, with Manning joining in.

The skipper of the tramp that waited for them stood and listened, frowning at the sound of madmen laughing in the pitch black of a moonless night.

A violent struggle for survival in a post-holocaust world

JAMES AXLER

DEATH LANDS.

Watersleep

In the altered reality of the Deathlands, America's coastal waters haven't escaped the ravages of the nukecaust, but the awesome power of the oceans still rules there. It's a power that will let Ryan Cawdor, first among post-holocaust survivors, ride the crest of victory—or consign his woman to the raging depths.

James Axler

OUTLANDERS™

SAVAGE SUN

A reference to ancient mysterious powers
sends Kane, Brigid Baptiste and Grant to
the wild hinterlands of Ireland, whose stone
ruins may function as a gateway for the alien
Archons.

But the Emerald Isle's blend of ancient magic
and advanced technology, as wielded by a
powerful woman, brings them to the very brink
of oblivion.

Available December 1997,
wherever Gold Eagle books are sold.